A House
Named Brazil

Also by Audrey Schulman

The Cage

Swimming with Jonah

A House Named

Brazil

Audrey Schulman

For Barbara —
Oct 2000
I hope the book
makes you like family
tales even more.

WILLIAM MORROW

An Imprint of HarperCollins*Publishers*

Audrey

HarperCollins books may be purchased for educational, business, or sales promotional use. For information please write: Special Markets Department, HarperCollins Publishers Inc., 10 East 53rd Street, New York, NY 10022.

FIRST EDITION

Designed by Claire Vaccaro

Printed on acid-free paper

Library of Congress Cataloging-in-Publication Data

Schulman, Audrey, 1963–
A house named Brazil / Audrey Schulman.—1st ed.
p.   cm.
ISBN 0-380-97799-0
1. Frontier and pioneer life—Ontario—Fiction.
2. Women pioneers—Ontario—Fiction.
3. Mothers and daughters—Fiction.   I. Title.
PS3569.C5367 H68 2000
813'.54—dc21   99–058669

00   01   02   03   04   RRD   10   9   8   7   6   5   4   3   2   1

For Mom, who told me all about her Brazilian childhood full of tall tales, black magic, and women with glittering jewelry.

For Mama, who'd been born in Chile, raised her children in England, and died in Toronto. She told me she had been everywhere in the world and I believed her.

For Papa, who, each morning when he shuffled down to breakfast, cupped his coffee in his giant paws and thanked 5-year-old me for dancing with him in his dreams so divinely round and round the ballroom.

And of course, for Great Aunt Tina, who taught me patiently during all the summers of my childhood how to play every card game known to the Western world, and who, each time I asked her what was for dinner, answered in her gruff Chilean, "Caca con mojo pipi."

This is a work of fiction.

Acknowledgments

Thanks to: Scott Campbell, Tyler Clemments, Beth Castrodale, Elizabeth Graver, Karen Jersild, Pagan Kennedy, Lily King, Nicole Lamy, Tia Maggini, Maryanne O'Hara, Lisa Poteet, Bill Routhier, David Rowell, Lauren Slater, Ted Weesner Jr., Dan Zevin.

And of course Jennifer Hershey, my editor, and Richard Parks, my agent.

It often seems as if there were an impersonal Karma within a family, which is passed on from parents to children.

—C. G. Jung, *Memories, Dreams and Reflections*

A House
Named Brazil

Chapter 1

People don't like to believe it these days, but she was a saint, and that's not a figure of speech. I'm talking actual miracles, visitations, a papal research committee.

But while she lived no one suspected it because she had 14 children and had never married. So no one knew, not even her kids, until 7 months after she died.

It was the winter of 1887. You can read about it in history books. Even as far south as her Ontario farm, the ground froze as hard as metal. Blue ice covered everything, started to cover even your face if you exhaled outside more than 5 times. It was so cold that the snow— like they say happens in Antarctica—became dry and raspy as sand, tiny shards of glass. You couldn't sled on it or ski. You couldn't make snowmen. The snow would cut at your skin and scrape against your coat while you slogged through a drift.

It took more than a year for the ground to really thaw from that winter, for the air to really warm. The summer in between was shy and short-lived, mostly just a short gasp before the next, more normal winter. Nowadays people would have a scientific explanation for all this. They would have words to make sense of it, like "cold fronts" and "low-pressure systems." The weather would become smaller and more understandable with gimmicky TV maps and gesturing weathermen. The weathermen would know where the cold air was coming from and how long it was going to stay; they could reassure you with precise temperatures and the number of records broken.

But back then people didn't know. The weather just arrived and it stayed and it stayed, and sometime during the beginning of that year and a half of almost solid winter your great great grandmother died, leaving her 14 children all alone in an isolated farmhouse.

Her children didn't know what to do with her body. They couldn't bury their mother in the frozen ground, they couldn't keep her in the warm house, so they put her in the attic of the barn. She was there for more than 7 months before the paltry summer finally hit in the midst of July. Summer lasted for all of 8 tentative weeks, but for those 8 weeks the ice melted and the ground mostly thawed and some plants did grow while the children struggled hard to remember something of farming. In the midst of all the changes and the work, it was almost August before they finally remembered their mother up in the barn.

Of course, once they remembered, it took them another few days—no more than a week of that warm weather—before they got enough courage to climb up there, climbing together in a clump of childhood to the top of the ladder, peering so cautiously over the piles of hay.

They saw their mother had not changed at all. She still lay on the floor by the window. Her face still wore that same look of harsh patience, her body straight as a board. Her apron knotted firmly around her narrow hips, her bonnet still on.

The only difference was she now smelled so heavily of lilacs, lilacs so full and thick with life, that even the bees were fooled. There were so many bees, so many, after that long dead winter, that they covered the walls and floor and ceiling like a shimmering womb of wings.

Are you listening to me?

Chapter 2

APRIL 19, 1977—The first time my mother called me, I picked up the receiver about half an inch, then put it right back down. The few calls I got were always wrong numbers. I went back to reading. There was peace for 5 slow seconds. The kitten in my lap went back to purring.

The phone rang again.

The kitten bolted away, its claws scratching across the linoleum, its hindquarters fishtailing round the corner.

I turned to look at the phone, an old phone, black and dented with age. From the 50s, perhaps earlier, when phones were cast from metal with bells inside that had real clappers. It shook with the urgency of the sound.

I picked up the receiver, balanced its weight in my hand and placed it uncertainly against the side of my head. Somewhere on the other end of the line, a plate clinked, water was shut off. My mother's precise and unmistakable voice boomed out of my childhood and into my ear.

And it's not like she never called. She called, once every 6 months or year, whenever she thought of it. Abrupt, chatty, furious, like she'd never left. She would hang up within 5 minutes, sometimes 7. Me still clutching the phone with surprise, having barely said hello.

And at this point I guess I should say I had been living my life on the assumption that her absence was only temporary. From the moment I had discovered her and the Plymouth gone, I had decided to act as though she was not gone for good. She would be back, I told myself. She would return. She was not a quitter. Not from family. From other things, but not from family.

I told myself she had just gone on vacation.

For 4 and ½ years. For the majority of my adolescence.

Fran, my mother said. Listen.

Mourne Family Tree

Great Great Grandmother & **?**
b. 1855   d. 1887

Celia	Cessil	Samantha	Matthew	Mikey	Sid	Nat	**?**
b. '73	'74	'75	'77	'78	'79	'80	'81

Cliff	Alexis/	Rebecca	Beth	Marthe
b. '82	Elizabeth	'84	'85	'86
	'83			

Chapter 3

Your great great grandmother lasted 4 months in that ...

Wait, wait, I said.

My mom hated to be interrupted, especially during a family story. There was silence on the line for 3 long seconds.

What? she asked.

Well, ah, I fumbled. Don't you want to know how I'm doing? Catch up a little? You know, chitchat. Where have you been anyway?

She exhaled. Through the phone I heard metal clicking briskly against a bowl, something being beaten.

You're still on the farm, she said.

Well, I said. Well, yes.

Hmm, she said. She put the fork down, grunted lightly and an oven door squeaked. After a moment the flame of the oven popped on. The oven door closed.

Hey, it was summer last time you called, I said. I could have gotten married, had a sex change, become a trucker. My name could be Ted for all you know now. Ted the married trucker.

I had promised myself I would say this, I had been drafting

these lines since winter. I found myself making a gesture with my left hand, rolling it forward through the air to suggest all the other possible changes rolling in after those first ones, perhaps also to suggest truck wheels. My fingers were shaking slightly.

I heard sugar pouring into a metal bowl. The paper rustling, the sugar pouring like static. Sounded like a lot of sugar, more than half a bag. She was probably making chocolate macaroons. A big vat like she used to make, even when there was just the 2 of us. 200 macaroons. It took 36 eggs. Just the way her grandmother used to make them. The smell so sweet and hot, filling the whole house, the front yard and driveway. Arriving home, on days she cooked macaroons, I would pause outside for a moment inhaling egg-sweetened chocolate. As a child I always believed I wouldn't actually have to eat if I could breathe in enough of that air. Still, once the macaroons were done, both of us would eat. We would eat and eat until our stomachs were tight and our skin warm with sugar. Then, knowing we wouldn't want to look at another macaroon for weeks, we'd pack the rest away for our neighbors.

The neighbors always loved us. Well, I guess, more accurately, the neighbors loved my mom. Such a beautiful woman, they told me, such a hard life. Such a good cook. After she left, the neighbors didn't talk to me as much. Perhaps it had started even earlier, when I left for McManus, the boarding school Mom had sent me to. Maybe around then the neighbors got out of practice at inventing subjects to discuss with me. I seemed to be able to bring out a close-to-existential confusion in almost anyone, trailing sentences, lengthy pauses. It got worse with each awkward encounter.

These days, when, by mistake, both me and someone like Mrs. Green happened to appear down by the road at the same time, she would straighten in surprise. Resolutely then she would raise her hand in a hi from her lawn across the road, waiting there for a moment with her mouth open, her hand still up there, no idea what to say. I would obediently return her smile, return her wave, wait for her words. I'd seen her talk to the other neighbors, talk easily and at length. I'd seen her slap grouchy Mr. Berk on the back. But in that moment with me, her hand still raised, she would let out a nervous chuckle at nothing in particular. And at that chuckle I would feel pity sing through me. Pity for her, pity for me. Without my strong-willed social mom around anymore, I would wave again in greeting, in farewell, then head back up toward the house, me and Mrs. Green slipping gratefully apart.

Over the phone I heard the sound of metal scraping a bowl. I saw my mother for a moment beside the stove, 3 spoons clenched between different fingers, tossing all 3 spoonfuls onto the cookie sheets at the same time, fast as a machine. Thwap thwap thwap. I closed my eyes.

There were times during the second year of her absence— I guess I'd have to say my angriest year overall—when I believed I could actually have shot her, if I'd had a gun and she'd reappeared for a moment with those spoons, that batter. That smell.

Even in just thinking about shooting her, I'd known her eyes would have had to be closed. I'd known I would have had to almost touch the gun to the bridge of her nose. So she would feel the least amount of pain, of betrayal. No more than a slap.

So it would be for certain.

I tell you there are times when I've pictured that moment. That moment, and afterwards.

Well, have you? asked my mom.

Have I what?

Have you done any of those things? The sex change, the marriage?

I looked out the window. It was dark outside. All I could see was my own looming reflection. The skin beneath my eye was jumping.

Well, I said, No. But I . . . I did graduate high school. Third in the class. Got a job. Where you living now anyway?

In spite of how well my mother got on with everyone, she had always had difficulty with social conventions. I had never heard her inquire how another person was doing, never. She assumed they'd volunteer the information if it was important. She assumed if it was important she would find it interesting. If someone started talking about how they slept or ate, she simply walked away. Not rude, not angry. She just didn't have any interest, so she got up and left. Right in the middle of the other person's words.

Look hun, she said straight out. I'm not getting any younger. I've decided it's time for you to hear the family stories.

What? I asked.

It's time, she said a little louder, like my hearing was the problem, For you to hear the family stories.

But I already know them, Mom. You think I don't know them?

(The anger I felt then, for using that word, *Mom.* That word made me weaker.)

Hey, said my mom, All you know is a few adventures of a few relatives. You have no idea how they all fit together. It's time for you to hear the whole of them, from start to finish. Do you want to or not?

I closed my eyes. I could see her fingering the hang-up button. I thought the next time she called me might not be for a year, 2 years.

So, I said. My great great grandmother lived for 4 months.

Yes, said my mom. Yes, yes.

. . .

*Your great great grandmother lasted 4 months in that great cold,
during that strange frozen fall.*

*The temperature had gone below freezing the first week of Sep-
tember, didn't come back up. When October finally hit, she stepped out
on the porch and looked about at the world, at the forest and the
fields and inside her barn.*

*That fall there were no wild animals moving among the trees, no
deer, wolves or even mice. Everything was quiet. The birds had all
flown south a month earlier than normal, around the time the squir-
rels had built nests twice their usual size and disappeared into them,
plugging the holes shut with leaves and their own hair. The chickens
in the yard no longer pecked and scratched. About a week before they
had cocked their heads up at the grey and empty sky, sniffed that
strangely persistent northern wind, and then one by one draped themselves across the snowdrifts, wings spread and necks limp, small
humpbacked napkins willfully freezing to death. In the barn the bay
mare had stepped upon its own foal's head, then lay down to die
beside it.*

Hey, I interrupted, You describe that nice.

There was silence. Tick, went the clock behind me. Tick, tick.

Excuse me, said my mom with her voice so cold. Did you say
something?

Well, ahh . . . This just off the top of your head?

Mom said nothing.

Mom, it's much prettier than I remember, a lot more detail.
Did you write this all out?

Dear, she said, I don't know how your memory is, but these
stories were always pretty.

I heard her breathe, slow and deliberate. She exhaled.

*And your great great grandmother looked up at the sky. The
color was not the rich crisp blue of fall, the kind meant to go with*

bright fall leaves. It was the grey of sick skin, the grey of low-hanging clouds, the grey of real and extended cold. There was not a breath of wind. There was not a movement. In that ancient Canadian forest that extended almost without a break from one side of the continent to the other, there was not a sound. My great grandmother and her children seemed to be the only things moving upright in a world that was cold and empty as an old boot.

And you've got to understand, this was a time before there were that many of us humans on this continent. Before the inventions of the car, the push-button phone or TV. Before clear-cutting became popular, or concrete, photo ops or strip malls. The forest back then was immense. Migrations would darken the sky, deafen your ears with the cries. Geese, ducks, flocks of passenger pigeons. Trees grew thick as hair. You could run a basket blindly through the river and pull out fish. Life was so much more thickly anchored to this world. For every person you see now, for every house and car, imagine a deer, moose, beaver and mice.

But then, that strange fall, there was nothing. No sounds, no movement. Just a ringing silence and all that cold.

And your great great grandmother knew what was up. She didn't need a fortune-teller. She didn't need a weatherman. She said not a word. She wrapped her apron twice around her straight hips and set to work. She filled her house with everything she could carry, her larder with every edible and non-edible object she could find, her living room with every burnable and non-burnable object she and her children could drag in. She took in grass and logs, acorns and apples, the mare and the foal, chickens, twigs, rocks and soil. She worked day and night, her hands and her feet until they bled, her joints until they squeaked like an old rocking chair. She worked each day until her traitorous body simply clicked on over into a sleep, a sleep so deep and sudden she didn't feel her body crumpling, didn't feel the hard earth slap her chin.

And when she woke, she would pull herself back up and work again. She worked until she was done, until she had packed the house so full of weight and mass, of food and lumber, that the walls rounded out like a fat woman's sides and the children had to crawl about through burrows near the ceiling. She filled her house so full that not even a winter as cold and clever as 1887's could find its way through.

By then it was November. It had been below zero for 2 months, and your great great grandmother, her backbone and her gaze still straight—having provided for her children—did what the bay mare had done after it stepped on its own foal's head. She lay down one final time, stretched out in front of the living room fireplace. She did not eat, did not move. Lay there without speaking.

Perhaps she'd tired herself out. Maybe she believed there wasn't enough food for both her and her kids. Maybe after that fall, after 14 kids, she just wanted to be someplace else. Great Aunt Celia said that the times her mother's eyes were open, on nights when all her kids were gathered about her playing, her expression was as inward and dreamy as when she used to breast-feed the baby. After the first week her lids opened only with an effort when her kids called her, her eyes taking longer, each time, to focus. She spoke not a word.

Her children gradually adapted, lost interest. They were young, the eldest just 14. The younger ones braided her hair while she lay there, played dress-up with her, used soap and fireplace ashes as makeup. They only noticed for sure she was not breathing anymore sometime just before Christmas.

After long arguments about how to bury her, after one shovel dented outside on the frozen ground, the 2 eldest carried her up into the attic of the barn. Brushed out her hair, wiped her face clean, put her in her normal clothes. Made sure her dress and bonnet were as straight as they had always been in life. And left.

. . .

That spring was very quiet, no sound from the trees, no sound from the barn, no sound from the 3 closest neighbors' houses within the forest, the strangely quiet houses in which no one moved anymore and from which a smell like rancid beef ran out under the doors with each warm breeze. Everything quiet but for my great grandmother's house. It was noisy. It was filled with the noise of 13 of the original 14 children, 13 hungry active surviving children searching for another meal.

Chapter 4

The next night, the phone rang again. I looked at it, didn't answer it.

In the intervening 24 hours, I had decided it would be better this way. Kinder to both of us. The phone rang on, 5 rings, 6. I kept my hands clenched in my lap.

Last time she'd left me, 4 years and 8 months ago, I hadn't been able to eat for a week. I don't mean only a sandwich here or there. I mean I couldn't eat anything, not a cracker, not a grape. As if the fact of her departure had been an actual object wedged in my throat, dry and large, the consistency of a big dust ball. I could feel the human hair in it. I had no hunger, just thirst. Drank water, a lot of water. A week. I stayed on the ground floor in the living room, suddenly scared of all the creaks upstairs, the ones that had always been there.

After a week, when standing up to go to the bathroom, I fainted. I was growing rather quickly then, already bony. Needed my regular nutrition. Woke up draped across the arm of the couch like an extra blanket. Walked shakily to the kitchen, forced myself to take a bite of an apple, to start to chew. I opened the fridge, the freezer, to see if anything looked good.

And there in the normally near-empty freezer I found stacks and stacks of Tupperware containers. Inside each was a foodstuff cooked by my mom, neatly labeled, instructions about how to heat it and what other container of frozen food would best accompany it. Some of the instructions were unreadable for all the frost that had built up.

Weeks, I thought she had been secretively cooking, perhaps months. Filling the freezer bit by bit while I was in town or upstairs asleep.

Perhaps this was the origin of the hate—not that I hated her then, I loved her, wanted her back under any conditions—but the seed of that hatred was planted then, the seed that would grow. Growing from that image of all those frosted-over plastic containers stacked up so long they'd started to fuse into one lump.

The phone was still ringing. My mom didn't redial, didn't doubt what number she had reached, that I was there, listening, counting. The phone rang 20 times, 21. Implacable. Precise. The ring sounded like her. The precise even alternations of silence and noise was exactly the way my mother would have rung the phone if she'd had control over it, with push buttons for "Ring" and for "Silence."

Each of the food containers in the freezer had held its own recipe, rolled up neatly in a baggie, so I could learn how to cook the food on my own. A lot of the instructions were written with my particular weaknesses in mind. Now, Frannie dear, said the instructions, Don't get impatient here and turn the milk on high.

Tonight, when the phone had started ringing, I'd been eating dinner. Yes, by now I had taught myself to cook, but not her meals, not curries flavored with fenugreek seed or puff pastries built from layers of butter-brushed phyllo, not calamari for which Mom bought the squid fresh from the store to tug out the transparent bones herself, not Brazilian shrimp grilled with ginger, lemon and chili sauce. Instead I mastered narrow cross sections of hot dogs held between Nilla wafers. I mastered peanutbutter and onion sandwiches, and cooked-solid *slabs* of spaghetti (cut in half like slices of bread) with cream of mushroom soup ladled in between, straight from the can.

I savored each meal partly because I knew it tasted bad and had little nutritional value or culinary appeal. I allowed no garnishes, tried to eat out of the actual cooking pot if at all possible, and never set the table. This night, as the phone rang, I put a spoonful of macaroni flavored with ranch dressing in my mouth, chewed a little defensively. I pulled my head down between my shoulders, as if my mom might suddenly step out of the ringing phone to thwap the backside of my head.

Still the phone continued to ring. 33 rings, 34. For 4 years I had dreamed about this: her calling every night, her talking to me for more than 5 minutes. Although I sometimes pretended otherwise, she was the main reason I'd returned to this town, to this house, after graduating from McManus. I had thought if I moved somewhere else, the chances of her finding me, of her contacting me, would be less. Also, ever since I had been a child, change in my life had always happened all of a sudden, without me expecting it. All I desired now was for things to remain the same. After graduation I had come back here to curl up in my old house like in an old bed.

During that year right after Mom left, I tried not to leave the house at all when I was home on vacation. When I was at school I tried to spend as much time as possible in my dorm room. I wanted to be easily locatable when she came back, or if she called. Otherwise I pictured her arriving, looking around a bit—so quickly frustrated—then impulsively leaving again.

The few times classmates invited me to do something after classes, I told them I was expecting a phonecall. If they asked me to visit during vacation, I told them that my mother and I had plans. I hadn't exactly been popular before, but this was the start of my real isolation.

At home, during vacation, I made enough food each night to include the possibility of 2. I changed her bed on Sundays.

My mother had always been charismatic. I'd seen it. Strangers followed after her with their eyes, people phoned her after meeting her once, after listening to her talk for just 20 minutes. Men, women, it didn't matter. They asked her to do things, see a movie, pick blueberries, come over for dinner. Her voice was so certain, her gestures dramatic, her walk suggested she knew something. Her eyes wide and focused. People wanted to be around her.

I was not the only person she captivated. I was just her daughter. It was just she was all the family I had. Her face the upholstery of my memories.

After 2 years, on a Sunday during summer vacation, I dragged her mattress out into the yard and burned it. It took a full can of kerosene. I seared an outline right into the lawn, an outline of the mattress, an outline of the kerosene splashed in wide arcs all about. I was 16. Angry, sullen. Lovers' anger has nothing on the fury each of us can hold toward our mother. For her being too distant, for being too close, for being too stern, for spoiling us. For bringing each of us into existence to imprint on her face hovering above, her hands, her breast, to love her as the whole world, to love her so completely that all later loves would just be echoes.

Even then, as the flaming mattress burned low, I caught myself glancing over to the driveway at the sound of a car coming up the street.

Now, sitting here at the kitchen table, I was surprised somehow by the blare of each new ring of the phone. Tense during the silences, in fear the next ring wouldn't come.

Over the last 4 and ½ years, I'd received from my mom 9 phonecalls, 6 postcards and 56 checks, a check mailed on the first of each month by her Ottawa law firm. The checks generally arrived within 3 or 4 days, oversized plain blue business checks, written out in a stranger's hand, signed LEVY & SONS, INC. I believed the handwriting was of an American, for no other reason than that the person wrote out 5's with a curved line for the body and a separate line for the cross stroke at the top; the same way my mother made 5's.

I picked up the phone then. 47 rings.

I guess I wanted to hear in her voice that I had scared her, that I had shown her I had changed in her absence. That I had become an adult. I thought as soon as I heard the fear in her voice I could hang up.

Instead, the moment I picked up, her matter-of-fact voice was just there, almost mid-sentence, without surprise or gratitude, without explanation. I forgot how well she knew me.

She was my mother.

Your great great grandmother's eldest son was named Cessil Rilke Mourne. As an adult, he grew to be a strong man, not thin and efficient like today's athletes, but filled with the strength of a less cynical world. Like an old-time strongman, the kind who wore a tiger skin knotted neatly over . . .

Wait wait wait, I said, still angry she had known I would pick up.

The silence was as if no one else was on the line. Like I had dreamed her calling.

What happened with that winter, the winter of 1880-whatever-it-was? I asked.

Silence.

Mom, you there? I thought you were going to tell me all the family stories. You skipped a bit. What happened to the 13 surviving kids and all?

Silence.

And then my mother spoke, her voice so clear, harsh, so *put upon*. She declared, Dear, I will tell you the stories. I am telling them in the order that is best. Stop interrupting me.

She inhaled, thought about it for a minute. She added almost slyly, I might have a problem remembering things if I am interrupted.

I heard her exhale out her nose. I heard her purse her lips, smack them. I could picture her eyes slowly begin to focus beyond whatever wall she was staring at.

Yes, Cessil was tall and wide with a belly like a ship's, and this belly made him only more powerful, for it was hard with muscle and heavy like steel. He, unlike his mother, ate and ate well. In his baggy pants and suspenders, his stomach bulged out like the side of a furnace in front of him. Instead of holding his belly in, he moved to a country he believed would have even more room than Canada.

He went to work for the railroads in Brazil, back when they were being built. He started off delivering the paychecks to the men working way down the line, 50 miles of tropical jungle. Yes, he carried the money, gold, silver coins, ingots, pounds of riches each time he went, hiking through the jungle alone along a single pair of steel tracks.

Tracks that pointed the way back and forth through a steaming twisted mass of jungle. Those rails were the only straight and civilized things that this man born in British Canada could see (This man who had been raised with placid cows like slow-moving hills, with cold that cut like a razor through his lungs, with trees he could hug round with a single arm. This man raised on summers that were as well-mannered and retiring as girls from private schools). He walked through a tropical jungle that grew so quickly sometimes even the outlines of the rails were lost under creepers, branches and the bones of broken animals. He would have to feel his way with his toes like a blind man. Walking along between tree trunks looming as wide as barns, birds screaming, everything in shadow. Each time he went, walking alone through the jungle, the railroad went in a little farther and the sack was a little heavier with the pay for more men.

I don't know what he learned during that time, what he thought about. For most of his life my grandfather was a fairly quiet man. When I knew him as an old man, I knew he did not like loud music, that he always seemed to enjoy food. I know that at his death, after all those years of working for the railroad, he had never travelled by train. And I know the few times he got angry, he lost all control and his left eye wandered. That he once mentioned, near the end of his time with the railroad he had been attacked by 3 men. Not Indians, but 3 white bandoleros with steel weapons and guns. 3 men, 3 guns, machetes. Those steel and unerring rails and 4 bodies struggling on top. My grandfather killed all 3 with his bare hands and the weight of his ingots, and he walked on through the jungle to deliver the money, leaving 3 bodies and 2 of his own fingers behind.

Your great grandfather met your great grandmother in a bar when he came in from the jungle at the end of a trip. She was smoking a cigar, arguing politics, in the days when women were supposed to stand out-

side bars and wait. She stood leaning up against the counter with her small foot on the brass foot railing, a scotch in front of her. She was young, 22, 23. No taller than 4 foot 9, which was short even back then. A face flat with determination. Her straight voice gravelly already from smoking all those cigars since that first one she had smoked when she was 12, smoking it with a field hand out in the pasture, that first cigar around which she had stretched her mouth and puffed out a satisfying cloud as dark and smelly as the feeling she had found within herself. She had smoked cigars each day and every day since that first one she had put out on the field hand's face when he tried to pull up her skirt.

There was my grandmother, Anita, standing up at the bar, angry as always, a young woman so used to using the bony flat front of her finger to jab her point into the chest of whomever she was arguing with that in later years her finger jabs became the sign of affection to her children and grandchildren.

There she was talking politics and Cessil thought to himself in his slow and quiet way, Well now yes.

And they got married. It was the last year of the 19th century.

Carefully I listened during her story for paper rustling, for a page turning as she read what I believed she must have written down. I could hear nothing but her voice speaking so clearly.

Mom's matter-of-fact voice. On the phone it was just as precise and penetrating as I remembered. Sometimes she smacked her lips just before she spoke, to warn you she was about to speak, to warn you to shut up. It was not in any way a wet sound. More like the click of a large machine turning on, something mechanical and necessary. Even though she'd been raised in the American South, her consonants clipped off one at a time, crisply cut, only a few of the vowels were rolled out, enjoyed. Purely Canadian. Her voice was the kind you would expect to hear in emergency situations, over all the screaming, her voice explaining necessary movements one at a time and with the correct amount of rotation. Her voice would be clear, authoritative, demanding. Terrified.

On the old phone, even when the static rose to cover all else—a roar like a storm in my ear—my mother's words still cut through cleanly. It was as though all the noise were outside and she was inside with me, telling me what to do. Always.

The only difference in her voice was a certain new raspiness. She had always had a deep old woman's voice, for as long as I could remember. The kind which would ask you loudly just what you thought you were doing. But now there was an added hoarseness, like Lauren Bacall in her later years. I believe I am fair when I say this kind of voice had been one of Mom's aims.

My mother was 37 years old.

And my own voice, how can someone describe her own voice? The time everyone in the tenth grade was tape-recorded for Oration class, I had real difficulties recognizing my recording. The voice that I'd imagined inside my head had been so clear and thoughtful, strong and melodic. Listening to the recording, I had only a distant sense that this voice was familiar, the timing, the tone. Someone I had known a long time ago and then just peripherally.

After I turned 13, over the phone some people believed me a man, called me sir.

Back then I constantly worried whether what I was saying was factually correct or socially appropriate, even when I was simply asking a question. Perhaps because of this, I tended to pull my chin in a little when speaking, I tended to *suggest* words instead of clearly enunciating them. I moved my hands around a lot, vaguely outlining the nouns of my conversation, as though the listener might be able to follow my thoughts from these hand gestures alone.

I used these hand gestures even on the phone.

Mourne Family Tree

Great Great Grandmother & **?**
b. 1855   d. 1887

Celia b. '73	Cessil '74	Samantha '75	Matthew '77	Mikey '78	Sid '79	Nat '80	**?** '81

Cliff
b. '82

Alexis/
Elizabeth
'83

Rebecca
'84

Beth
'85

Marthe
'86

Cessil & Anita
m. 1899

Chapter 5

I had always meant to be the kind of person who could hang up on someone.

I had always meant to dress in brighter colors.

I had always meant to be one of those petite bland-looking women no one remembered all that clearly from highschool, even though she purposefully wore bright trendy clothes, even though she sometimes screamed at her boyfriend or a cashier in a fit of temper. The kind of short forgettable woman who could never get herself a beer because the bartender would overlook her small upheld face every time. The kind of woman who went on to university and then to a job chosen for its upward mobility, in finance or perhaps in sales.

Instead I worked at the Oldtyme Men's Wearhouse in Navan, where mostly I stood in the back of the store looking out the display window. A lot of my job there consisted of waiting to fetch shirts of uncommon sizes from the shelves along the far wall. I was 19, had graduated from highschool almost a year ago. My ambitions, such as they were, were rather limited.

The Wearhouse was one of those old-style clothing stores

you find only in the country, the smell of mothballs, the jangle of a bell at the door, shelves all the way to the top of the 12-foot ceilings. We specialized in unusual sizes. I retrieved the required pieces of clothing for each customer from the shelves. I used the rolling ladder even when I could probably have reached the clothing on my own. I liked the way the ladder moved so smoothly and silently in its track. I liked the solid feel of its safety railings in my hands. Things like that entertained me, made my day worthwhile. The store was dark and quiet and so often there were no customers at all. For at least an hour each day I could stand near the far wall and breathe in the smell of the place, looking outside at the people passing on the sidewalk, none of whom knew I was in here at all.

I had always thought the Wearhouse had been here forever, that the mall had grown up next to it. Last fall I found out it was only 3 years old. Started as an experiment by the people who own The Gap. I found this out by asking the manager about it the day I noticed—while climbing the ladder—that each rung had a small MADE IN TAIWAN stamp on its underside.

Your great great uncle, whose name was Egbert, worked as a thief. He was very successful at it, a famous thief, a pickpocket. By the time he was 30 in 1901, his alias was known to every policeman from Tampa to Toronto. The rumor of his presence sent whole cities into panic. He was systematic. He pickpocketed crowds. Upon reaching a new town, he headed directly for the baseball stadium or town fair or policeman's ball, and wandered through the center of whatever crowd it was, drinking lemonade. He pulled out his handkerchief a lot to sneeze into, put it back within his pocket. He got the lemonade from the lemonade cart Great Aunt Celia would be working on the edge of the crowd. In spite of what was normally a brisk business in lemonade, she would have trouble wheeling away the weight of the cart at the end of the day.

And then they would move on to a new town. All Egbert left behind was his trademark, a card left in the pockets of one of his victims. The card had printed on it in a large and fancy script, "Gratefully, Don Mario García de Lollosa." And the police would scour the hotels of the city looking for a dark-skinned man who asked for the best suite with an accent and probably paid in raw diamonds.

The secret to Egbert's success, the reason he never got caught, was his face. He did not look as though he should steal. He looked like someone who should get stolen from and be left to stand there gasping on the corner with a hand over his heart.

He was born with his father's face but his own original personality. He had a brittle nose, a weak chin and the astonished eyes of a simple mind. He had hands made thin with the love of danger. Once he had picked a victim he would sometimes walk in the opposite direction, sigh, and then back up to ask in a wheedling voice for directions to a nearby and obvious landmark. His eyes stayed nowhere for long. They jumped about with what appeared to be deep fear at the workings of the world. People, irritated simply by his voice, by the curve of his neck, worked to forget him before he had fully turned away. He could disappear in a crowd of 2.

He was said to be a nice man, a warm uncle. His father had worked in the government for 46 years, from 8 until 5 P.M. every day, until the work had stripped the flesh from his nose and cheeks, leaving only those large yellowing eyes and a mouth that repeated office hours. His father had not been allowed to take a day off for Egbert's birth. His mother had taken a single look at her baby's face and *fled from him, from the both of them, back to her family's place in Georgia.*

And at the age of 10, Egbert also left his father to run away with the circus. It was in the circus he learned his trade.

Your great aunt Babette had nice things to say of her uncle Egbert, whom she met only once. He was an older man by that time, somewhere in his fifties. He had flat grey hair that smelled like the oil her mother used to cook with, and his feet were large and pointed away from each other. He wore a bow tie. He put her to bed and sang her a song about a spider and a drainpipe in a high and toneless contralto. Patted her head with his skinny hand and kissed both braids right on the elastic. He tiptoed out the door with stork-toed exaggeration. She said she remembered noting that none of the adults (except his wife, Celia) ever seemed to look at him. Babette didn't understand why because he made her laugh.

He never had children of his own, although he and Celia loved each other with the kind of fierce comprehension that kept them from arguing throughout their entire transient life of hotels, suitcases and lemon squeezing. His wife, Celia, also felt her love tempered with a secret fear for Egbert's safety, a fear that lent her the strength to handle the lemonade cart (no matter what the weight) as though it were only a simple cart. A fear that helped her smile at policemen with a kindness she did not feel. A fear that made her carry underneath her skirt, on the outside of a specially-made garter belt, a large and dully-shining Colt .45 that she had bought with the lemonade money and that in the 24 years and 7 months she and Egbert were married, she always kept within 3 feet of her hand.

She had frequent dreams from which she awoke to blindly reach for her husband. The dreams would dissolve as smoothly as an aftertaste, so she was left with no image, no warning more specific than her throat clenched tight with the hot taste of terror.

. . .

Later on, when Egbert's fame had reached the point where little boys'
tin gun sets were called Don Mario, he turned himself in for amnesty
and stole only on the stage to the applause of finely-dressed men and
women. Cummerbunds and necklaces were his specialties, and he
and Celia began to dine at the homes of people whose plates and sil-
verware were worth more than all the goods they had stolen within
their entire careers. Their social activities began to be written up in
the society columns, and Egbert took to lisping slightly and gesturing
about with floppy wrists, believing (in spite of having met the rich)
that this was what the rich did. Celia spent so many hours having the
maid pull in her corset that she did not have time or room for the
dreams of before. She simply held her breath while the whale bones
stiffened up her back and chest into an iron-clad swelling silhouette.

Why're you telling me these stories now? I asked when her words
had stopped.

What?

Why're you telling me these stories now, at this time?

You're my daughter, dear. You need to hear these stories.

Oh please Mom, I said. You generally don't call me more
than twice a year, and now suddenly you have to call me daily to
make sure I know who my great great grandmother was?

She didn't answer.

I sighed. Where you living, Mom? I asked, trying to enunci-
ate as clearly as she did.

What?

Mom, I said. I've been listening to your stories like you asked.
Answer one question. Tell me one thing about your life. Where
are you living?

I held up one finger like she was there with me, like she could see me. One thing, I said.

Across the state, my mom said, From where I lived last year. I knew you'd still be there.

And what state is that? I asked, determined. Then I weakened and added, You knew what?

I knew you'd still be there. That I could count on you. I knew you wouldn't move to another town.

How can you say that? I said, I hate when you say things like that.

My voice sliding back into its mumble.

Oh, please, hun, rasped my mom, From the moment you were born you've been like my mother. Same eyes, same smile. You know that. You have no desire to be anywhere else but that house, never have. You'll stay in that town your whole life.

My mom's been proclaiming things like this since I was a child. From early on she'd always cut my hair to look like my grandmother's. A 40s bob cut waved across the top. I was 3 years old. My mother would brush it out that way each morning. I remember the bristles of the hairbrush tracing and retracing the way my hair should fall across my skull, while my mother told me more about my grandmother's character, about my character, about what would happen during my life.

In the beginning I had had such simple feelings toward this. I loved it. It used to be my favorite time of day. I listened to my mom. I snuggled into her lap, her arms around me the whole time. I felt happy. I had her attention, or at least the top of my head did.

As I got older, 8 and 9 and 10, as I got more independent, she didn't spend as much time with me. She spent more of her time staring at the driveway, still watching for my dad, even though I, at least, had realized long ago he wouldn't be coming home. She spent her time cooking, or picking at a suspicious mole on her skin, or noting down the attributes of a new pain in her gut that came only in the afternoons. When I was a child, each time she paid attention to me, I believed it was the beginning of a new phase in our relationship, that now she'd be more attentive.

When I was 3 and she had brushed my hair, I smiled down at the floor, silly with happiness. I nodded at all her predictions, didn't care what she told me I would do with my life. I just sat there in her touch. Perhaps I listened harder than I thought. I did assume she knew so much. I remember her hands moving around my face, their smell of hot peppers and yeast. I remember listening to the catches in her breath as she struggled with the curlers.

My mom needed, needed so many things. As a child I could feel that clearly. I could feel her weaknesses, her fears. I knew how important it was that I help. You should understand she was not used to 2-way communication, to questions, to answers. She was used to—she grew up on—a kitchen staff, orders, precise timing, a single team ambition. With love, she was used to someone like my father. As a 3-year-old I had known so well how she had to have her love delivered, what packaging was necessary for her to recognize it. I sat still in her lap while she brushed my hair. I listened quietly to her summary of my character, tried to smile the way she told me my grandmother had smiled, to hold my head the way my grandmother had held hers. I molded myself for my mother. I delivered time after time. I'm sure even now some of my mannerisms are affected by this training. My head tends to tilt to the left, I show emotions mostly through the clenching of my nostrils. I cradle my own hands, the back of one in the palm of the other, holding them as if no one else would think to.

Mom, I said into the phone, so slyly, so cruelly. I don't know, I said. Do you really think I'm that much like your mother? I'm not so sure we even look related.

And my mother hung up the phone. Just like that. Click.

Mourne Family Tree

Great Great Grandmother & **?**
b. 1855   d. 1887

Celia
b. '73

Cessil
'74

Samantha
'75

Matthew
'77

Mikey
'78

Sid
'79

Nat
'80

?
'81

Cliff
b. '82

Alexis/
Elizabeth
'83

Rebecca
'84

Beth
'85

Marthe
'86

Celia & Egbert
m. 1894

Cessil & Anita
m. 1899

Chapter 6

And she didn't call back the next night.

That wasn't so bad. That didn't bother me. I'd gotten along without her for years. I didn't need her, not her or her stories.

Now things could get back to normal.

Chapter 7

Now that 20 odd years have passed since these phone conversations with my mom took place, I can now admit to you that I did, in fact, look a bit like my grandmother, in the softness of our eyes if not the exact shape. In the way we swallowed a bit of our chins. Perhaps it is easier to see such things in photographs that are no longer current, no longer so personal. It is true, according to the pictures of her, our hair was a similar light honey color. Although hers was wavy and mine lankly straight, emphasizing the overly long line of my face.

Of course, it's not like we were twins. There must be 20 million people across the world who share that color of hair, something like those eyes, our chins. It's not *that* unfair a thing to say. That we didn't look related.

When you close your eyes and I say the word Male, probably an illustration from highschool biology flashes before your eyes. A man standing nude, arms held a little out from his sides, legs a little apart. Caucasian, stocky, broad-shouldered, firm jaw. A man not overly muscled and not Chinese-thin. Not bearded, not old, not Jesus, not a child. Not Buddha, not crippled, not bald, not obese. Probably (in spite of the vast world of possibilities out there that can be implied when I say the word Male) for most people an image would pop up similar enough to be different police sketches of the same man. 5'11", 170 pounds, dark hair.

And I would have to say, you should work at the Oldtyme Men's Wearhouse. It would do you good. You'd be surprised how many different shapes appear in a store that has a reputation for having the clothing to fit those shapes, for treating everyone equally. At the Men's Wearhouse, the unusual clothing sizes weren't just for those men who were exceptionally tall or short, not just extremely fat or thin. There are a lot of other differences out there, things harder to imagine. Very short arms or wide necks on an otherwise normally-shaped body, rib cages that continue all the way down to where someone else's hips would be, huge thighs. I know those men couldn't all be from Navan. I think some of them must have travelled from as far away as Hull just to shop at our store.

And their faces were just as noteworthy as their bodies. The variety of expressions alone when they asked for their sizes. Shyness, fear, anger. Frustration.

The only time we staff were allowed to honestly stare at the customers as much as we wanted was through the display window, when they walked back to their cars with their purchases. We stayed in our stations even then, our heads still pointed forward the same as before. Only our eyes moving, following. So many types of walks.

Each day I thought—each day I marveled—at how utterly utterly diverse the human race was.

Each day I thought, *Freaks!*

The times a customer's family came along (which was more

often than you might think with most adult men), I carefully noted the similarities. Mostly, a family wasn't consistent in their height or the color of their hair, not the length of their arms or width of their mouths. I didn't know why my mom was so interested in these details. Shared blood seemed revealed to me more often, more powerfully, in how they laughed, in the hang of their hands and the sway of their walks, the way they all said Mahvellous. The whole family's shoulders squared out, as proud as wings.

I never did meet my grandmother. And my mother didn't look like me at all.

And, with your eyes closed, if I say, Female, to you, probably something completely different flashes in front of you. Of course it is possible it's a medical illustration, some sort of normally-built solid woman with breasts that are just breasts; she stands there with her arms slightly out, facing you, level straight-on stare. The kind of stare a woman doesn't normally give, especially when naked.

More likely, though, when I say Female, you think of a neon sign, hips gyrating. Or a young woman with long black hair walking in a field, looking back at you over her shoulder. You can't help but imagine this, even if you're a woman. Even if you've no interest in following this woman through the field. Perhaps, instead your image is of a truck's mud-guard reflector with a woman's silhouette; one third of her body mass is breast, she is seated with her side to you, not even allowed to return your stare, those exaggerated breasts and a slim knee raised in simulated desire.

Whatever you think of, whatever it is, it isn't likely to look like me.

. . .

Back in 1977, when my mom was calling me each night to tell me the family stories, I loved going to work. If I could have, I would've worked every day of the week. Every day. Unfortunately, the store closed on Mondays and the manager, Frank, didn't like any employee accumulating overtime. I was assigned the morning hours Tuesday through Sunday, some afternoons. I stood against the back wall for so long my knees locked up, my back hurt. I didn't care. I looked out the window. I saw more people in an hour than I saw all week long from the front porch at home; I saw them up close walking through the mall parking lot. They each looked so different from each other, and I don't mean just my customers. Every person going by looked so different. The way they held their mouths, how they used their eyes, the kind of pocketbooks they chose as stylish. I watched them all. Watched the cars driving by. I thought anything could happen out there, anything.

I hungered for that Anything to happen to someone out there in the parking lot, for that Anything to happen to one of the cars or people on the street, happen so I could watch from somewhere nearby.

Recently—I guess for a few months before Mom had started calling—I had been feeling a bit restless.

That morning a package arrived from Mom in the mail. She must have sent it even before she started calling. She had always been so confident, thought she knew what everyone would do and how they would react, long before they actually did so.

Although there was no return address on the package, the postmark said Needles, California. I looked it up in the atlas in the living room. Needles was almost 3,000 miles away. On the edge of the Mojave Desert. A population of 1,100, at least back in 1958, when the atlas was printed. The air dry, I imagined, the people old. The heat remorseless. I tried to see my mother there. Leaning forward into people's faces, telling them what foods to eat, how to cook, what errands to run. Her matter-of-fact mandates. Her total-body gestures learned from her South American grandmother, Anita. When she shrugged, her whole body shrugged. Her face shrugged, she curved her back, her toes curled, even her knees slightly bent out, pushed by the fullness of her shrug. I tried to imagine her there, in the U.S., on the edge of a Californian desert, around old people. Shrugging, laughing, ordering, berating, telling stories in her raspy voice. I tried to see people's reactions.

I felt victorious looking at the postmark, tracing the inked letters with my finger. I'd always thought I'd just have to wait long enough to find out where she was. Now I knew she wanted to call me nightly, send me packages. If she could just get over me saying I didn't look like my grandmother, if she just called me again, then I might have her. She would come home to me soon. I would have won. I pictured her walking up the driveway, the Plymouth parked below, her defensive glance up at me, her expressive hands hidden away in her pockets. If that happened, I knew finally the tables would have turned and I would be the one in power.

I opened the package slowly. It was packed carefully. Newspaper, cardboard, more newspaper, tissue. Inside was a picture of a man, a glass slide, taken in the years between daguerreotypes and kodachromes, a publicity shot. A faded piece of paper glued along the bottom said:

Don Mario García de Lollosa,
Necromancer of Your Belongings

Heavy glass sheets covered the delicate lines and colors of his life. The details were hard to make out until I held the picture up to the light. Then it exploded into sharp color. He stood before a red velvet curtain, one hand upheld with the palm outward in a gesture both ceremonial and obscure, like some forgotten deity. The photo had originally been sepia-colored, but other colors had been painted in at a later date. The curtains apple red. His eyes cobalt blue. His cheeks blushed like a young girl's, the same color as the curtains. Although I knew his hair had actually been flat and went grey early in his life, in this photo it was painted raven black and the curls rose high above his skull (escaping the etched outlines of his real hair).

I must say it surprised me a little to see the picture. It wasn't that I thought he didn't exist or that he hadn't been a thief at all; it was more that I thought my mom might have tried molding his story a bit the way she had tried molding my life. Editing him in the way she had tried to edit me. I thought maybe he'd only stolen for a few weeks and that, rather than being a pickpocket, he had perhaps dabbled in the white-collar crime of an accountant.

In the picture, my great great uncle was wearing one of those circus costumes I associated with acrobats, a leotard with rhinestones about the belt and neck. It was as though he was about to do something strenuous and physical. He had a middle-aged pot and his shoulders hunched forward. He was standing still—one might say stiffly—one hand up. His head held above his shoulders like an egg, he was trying to smile.

I imagined he probably didn't like cameras that much, didn't like publicity shots. They might have reminded him too much of another type of shooting.

. . .

My mom called the third night, precisely at 6 P.M. as she had on the nights before. She didn't even say hello. Just started in on her story.

As I listened, I saw the scene of her waiting for me to answer the phone. I saw that scene as sharply etched as in the flash of a photo. Her compact determined body standing there, her mouth opened impatiently, her head high, waiting for me. Waiting.

For the whole first minute of her talking, I grinned wide as a house. I hooked a pillow off the couch with my foot. Lay back on the kitchen table with it. Made myself comfortable.

By the seventh month of that extreme winter of 1887, Cessil hated his older sister, Celia, with a boundless and inhuman passion. This was before he moved to Brazil, back when he was younger, when he still lived at home on the farm with his 13 siblings and his dead mother's body in the barn's attic.

Oh good, I said, Back to the kids. Back to that winter.

Celia and Cessil were my great grandmother's 2 eldest children. Cessil hated Celia because she had grown. They used to be best friends. For the whole first part of that winter it was like they were playing house, they were the parents for the rest. They ruled absolutely and each got more power from the other. They were the ones who carried their mother's body, light and crumpled as if she were already long dead, stiff as leather, brittle as paper, so cold she burned their hands whenever they touched her bare skin. They carried her across the yard to the barn and up the ladder in a mixed and struggling pile of bodies so that which was dead and that which was child were pressed flesh to flesh and became indistinguishable. And when they placed her down on the hay (although she was light in weight, not that different from a twisted pile of blankets or straw, and although they let her go gently, with both hands), the hay rustled like a breath. The wood beneath her creaked and sagged down. Nails pinged out at both ends of the boards like bullets.

Both children stepped back and it was over. Their mother's body lay still.

Celia and Cessil were close enough to adulthood to understand that this winter of grey soggy skies, squeaking snow and no adults would end at some point. They were old enough to have nightmares that it would not.

And in the spring of 1888, which didn't arrive until July, it was Mikey-the-crybaby who reminded Cessil to return to the barn to bury their mother. Celia no longer lived at the house.

In the beginning, Celia and Cessil ruled their siblings with a combination of children's spontaneous kindness and violence. They shared the power, ruled as a pair. They capitalized on each other's ideas and judgments and called one another "Oh Great Being of Light." They held great respect for each other's individual talents.

Celia had been born with a quiet smile, delicate facial features and the ability to—deliberately and with will—beat every child in her family and from the neighboring farms into the ground.

Cessil, on the other hand, never picked fights, but if he was made mad, he lost all control. His voice choked wild in his throat, sounds rolled out segmented and guttural, and his left eye began to wander. His whole small body gathered itself as a donkey's legs did just before it kicked, and then his fists and feet and head lashed out again and again. The children stood back in fear and respect. His face got so small and tight it was like he was all gone and just his fighting remained. And this was long before he was a large man. This was back when he was only a skinny boy with an older sister a full foot taller. Still, he scared even her sometimes.

Even in the beginning, when the 2 ruled well together, something had changed within the family without their mother around. Sometimes in the confusion the children began to play a little rough. There was no one to stop them. They began to have larger than normal scrapes and bruises. Once Rebecca, the 5-year-old, got slashed on purpose by Nat with a nail sticking out of a toy; her hand sprayed out blood like the kitchen pump, and Celia and Cessil had to kneel on her wrist until it slowed down. A few weeks later, all of them emotionally exiled Matthew, exiled him for not much more than being too skinny, for walking with a sort of jolt forward in his hips like a giraffe, for the way his lips had the tendency to be wet. Not one of the children spoke to him during the rest of the winter if they could help it. No one slept in his bed, no one shared food with him, and after a few weeks he began to chew on his lips and pick at his fingers until both were ragged. And after the second month without a mother or any other adult, Mikey-the-crybaby stopped crying and started having conversations with himself in 2 different voices, one of which was clearly female.

Thus for 2 months the 14 children played together in that lonely Canadian farmhouse with no one to tell them what chores to do, how many vegetables to eat, or when to play nice.

Until in the midst of this cold, something quite strange happened. In the middle of the coldest and longest Canadian winter on record, Celia became warm, hot, fetid. Celia's body began to heat up and bump out in different places. In the space of 3 months, Celia, in the frozen land of children, became a woman, an opulent woman, a woman with long black powerful hair and a body so cooking with the chemicals of the dramatic change inside her that she typically wandered about their burrows in drawers and undershirts that swelled out in ways new to all of them, for their mother had never been more than a thin board of a woman.

The rest of the children wore layers, many layers, wool and cot-

ton and flannel, so many layers of their own and their mother's clothing that they bent awkwardly at joints that seemed all wrong. So many layers they had worn for so long that winter, not even taking them off for bed, that all of them had forgotten what their own children's limbs looked like, the curves and colors and grace. They could remember only matted wool and flannel ratty with dirt. And there was Celia standing among them, warm enough to steam, the air wafting white mist and vibrant smells off of her long limbs and body, her skin bared and silky human among all their bulky dirty wool.

The children were fascinated by Celia's body. They had never known any woman to look like this, and they all wanted to stand close to it, to look at it, to touch it. They wanted to touch the skin and long arms, to nestle in against the outline of those breasts, to sit in the warmth of that feverish lap.

The thing was, Celia suddenly looked like a mom. Maybe not their skinny mom in particular, but a mom all the same. She looked like an adult. Or close enough for them.

So she became the sole ruler. Just like that. She did not fight for it, Cessil did not lose. She just became. She ruled with the opulence of her body and her hair and the familiarity of her face, and not even Cessil could do anything about it, for she was a woman and he was only a boy. Her rule rested on worship, because she was in just as much awe of her new flesh as they were. Perhaps more so, for she had always been a tomboy, a tough kid, the eldest child doing the chores on a farm with a family of 13 younger ones. She had never really noticed her body except in its ability to get tasks done. Now she made the other children feed her new body, admire it, bow down to it.

Of her old body, only her face remained. A face that had yet to receive the growth spurt of the rest of her body. It was still the same, the face of the Celia they knew. Her face looked down on this worship and this body with an expression of stunned satisfaction.

And Cessil, instinctively, hated the new her, hated just to look at the whiteness of her flesh, at that which used to be his sister, a child, his equal, a human, his friend. Some children take to the end of childhood with glee, others don't. For some, adolescence strikes them as a betrayal, all their assumptions so fundamentally changed. Even to glimpse Celia's growing flesh out of the corner of his eye made him want to spit and pound his small and chubby hands against his sides. Hands still of a child, pounding with the feelings of a true adult against a body which hadn't yet grown. A body smaller than his older sister's by 20 pounds, a body still filled with the pale roundness of babies. And Cessil's brain and veins pulsed with visions of strong men, real men, men in tiger's skins with bald heads and ripe melons for muscles. Strong men who could hold his older sister by her pale and shapely ankle, suspending her far above the ground with one hand, her soft body squealing and wiggling with fear.

He vowed that if the winter did ever come to an end, he would travel to a continent that had never seen his sister's largeness. He wanted to live in a place that was innocent of what her flesh promised was inevitable no matter how much a child might wish otherwise. He vowed, if he ever got the chance, to kill his traitorous sister, Celia.

And as time went on, the children wanted more. They wanted to sleep in the bed with Celia and bathe with her and help her get dressed. They wanted to touch each of the places where the changes had occurred, not just on the outside of the clothing, but inside, underneath. They each wanted her to be only theirs, forever and always, and they began to fight about who got to sit closest, in their struggles rolling about like ferrets. Celia got hit sometimes in the excitement. And still the excitement only grew, for with each day that passed she was becoming more voluptuous. And in that farmhouse, in the midst of a winter that had lasted as long as their children's memory, there was not one other new thing to see.

Yet still, at the top of that body that they were all so interested in was the face of their sister, the one who had beaten each of them up so many times. Her expression was beginning to change when they touched her. She began to make her body back away from them and it only made them want to touch her more, touch her harder, grab and hold on.

The fight started one day in early May, while the winter outside was still hunkered down and waiting, while the snow still had more than a month to go before beginning to melt. The fight started with no warning. Alexis, one of the fighting twins, had been next in line to sit in Celia's lap and Mikey cut in front. Alexis went for his eyes. Celia tried to pull the 2 of them apart and suddenly all the children were in it and Celia was at the bottom. No one knew how she got there, but not one of them let her get back up. That body so pale and warm, squirming beneath them all, without threat, soft and white. She was the strongest child, but she could not fight all of them, not their combined weight. She was their oldest sister and she was sprawled underneath them, helpless and twisting.

It was a quiet fight, not childlike at all. No threats, no pleas, no protests. The desire to touch can be changed so quickly to the desire to hit. They were in earnest. Cessil was in the center, slamming his fists and feet into her again and again, his left eye wandering free like it was watching something completely different. There was breathing, harsh and determined, and sounds like someone clapping. There were two distinct cracks. After a while, a certain stillness was felt beneath them. They paused, backed away, one by one. She lay motionless, on the floor. Her body twisted on her back with a hip and breast raised up. The expression on her face was of minor concentration, as though she were about to sneeze. Her eyes half open.

They snuck away, quiet and scared, to their rooms.

And the next morning, when they came out to examine—and maybe to play with what remained—the body was gone.

There was a quiet period afterward.

I doubled the pillow over and turned onto my side, lay back down again. I thought about those 14 children, about Celia and her growth. Over the phone there was the clink of ice against glass, my mom swallowing long and slow, the working of her throat. I heard her exhale afterward.

God, she said with her raspy precision, I get so thirsty, so thirsty these days.

Hell, I exhaled, I've never heard that story before. We got murderers in the family?

I'll tell you more tomorrow, said my mom.

Oh, come on. Just answer that. They killed her, eh? Broke her neck?

Tomorrow, said my mom.

I was irritated. I don't mind saying so. I wanted to exercise the new power I felt I had over her. I took a new tack.

Mom, I said, I got the picture of Egbert.

I tried to keep the smugness from my voice as I picked up the photo. I tried to say lightly, So you're a Californian now?

There was a pause.

And then, while I held Egbert's picture in my hand, holding it up to the kitchen light, while I looked into his face, my mother spoke. Her flat precise voice said, You do remember how he died, don't you?

She waited for me to respond, waited a second, 2 seconds. Then her voice continued, softly, so clearly.

. . .

A House Named Brazil

It was a warm fall night. In a crowd on the street after one of his performances, people clustered tightly waiting for his autograph, 2 days after the end of World War I. The Americans were victorious, insane with it. Whole cities drunk, ugly, looking for an enemy, a German, a person from Turkey, anyone in a fez. Violence hung poised in the air.

All it took was a single loud voice. A single loud voice yelling, Thief. And the crowd tore Great Uncle Egbert apart limb from limb so even little children were smeared with the evidence. It took only 4 and 1/2 minutes while his wife huffed and puffed through the crowd like a train, with her back so straight, her hands under her dress, her corset so tight, quite unable to reach her gun's handle.

Dying that way, my mom added, Must have been quite painful, such a surprise.

And when my mother finished talking, she hung up the phone. Just like that.

You can see why my childhood was difficult. Well, not my childhood. That was easy. She was the parent and I obeyed. At an early age, it is a good thing to have a determined parent. My first few years were our honeymoon period. Near the end of my childhood was when we began to have difficulties, once I got to be 8 and 9, once I got to be 10 and older. She was less enchanted. While I was supposed to be finding my own voice and activities, she continued to tell me what they were.

I remember one afternoon, an afternoon when she told me I didn't want to go swimming. She told me I wanted to take a nap instead. She told me I was overtired as it was. I stood there in my tie-dyed swimsuit and lime-green flip-flops, staring at her. I was 12 years old. She was not asking me what I wanted to do, she was not ordering me to do something. She was telling me what was in my heart of hearts. I was filled with a deep-down near-immortal sense of unfairness. A sense of unfairness only exaggerated by how tired my limbs were.

I went swimming anyway and got a huge headache from the heat and the long walk. The next day I came down with the flu. I shivered in my bed, turning off to the side occasionally to vomit into a bucket.

I must say the reason I was most furious at my mom—furious to the very depths of my soul—was for being right.

My mother was beautiful. It gave her a distinct power, part of her compelling charm. I realize you might not like her from what I've been telling you about her, but you probably know better than to judge a person from her own child's description. I'm pretty sure if you'd met my mom, you would have liked her, wanted to spend time with her.

Think of her stories. Her stories are the best description of her there is. Imagine the kind of person who would tell them, her personality, the way she'd lean forward, the fullness of her smile. You would have fallen under her spell. Even into her late thirties she was one of those women you might imagine walking away from you through a field, looking back over her shoulder. Except, instead of walking, she would probably be running, sprinting, in fact. Her head would be down, legs pumping, while she beckoned you on with her entire arm. The only thing slowing her down was her laugh. When she laughed she gave herself over to it so completely that afterward she sometimes had to stroke the front of her neck for a while to get herself to breathe normally again, patting her neck and sternum, making little *shh shh* noises. Like you would comfort a child you loved.

On the street, people turned to look at her. She had thick

brown hair and green eyes, and there was a ring of orange around her pupils that lent her eyes an extra sharpness, as if she were always shocked or in love or angry, and her eyes bright with it. Her body had the compact muscular perfection of a person who had spent her childhood swimming and running and fighting, who had never had a problem with health, who was naturally adept at tennis and dancing and hockey, whose body had always done just what she wanted it to do. The kind of body that later on in life would probably have tended toward a plumpness that she'd experience as a great betrayal, but at least for her youth and early middle age she glowed from how fiercely she was alive.

She was a young mother. She'd given birth to me at the age of 18. That wasn't that unusual back then, in 1958. People got married so young. I started my big growth spurt at 11, grew taller than her that next year. Like I said, she was compact, not what you would exactly call tall. I labored stooped and slow-moving alongside her graceful bounce, and from a distance most people thought her younger than me.

Her hands were her dance, her love, her communication. Partly the South American influence, partly something more. As she talked, she made gestures like people do who work with their hands: carpenters or handymen, as cooks do also, the ones who, like her, used to work the dough each day, pounding and turning, searching for the motion with the minimum of effort, the maximum result, twisting and punching down. Living through her fingers. Always she moved her hands while she talked, in an imitation or a command, showing her emotion, every gesture slow and methodical as though the air were yet another medium to work with, to push into place and consistency, to turn and knead in the correct order of events so the dough rose just right.

And if you grabbed her hands, held them still, her voice would stop as quickly as if you'd grabbed her vocal cords.

She used to tell family stories when I was younger, to the neighbors, to her visitors. It's not like I didn't know my great grandmother's name, my great great uncle's career. But, like so many of us who know little bits here and there of our families, I did not know much more than that. Sometimes, perhaps, I even got the stories confused, thought it was my grandfather who was the pickpocket, thought Anita was the one with the gun. My mother had never taken the time to tell all the stories, not all together like this.

And when I think back to childhood, snippets of stories heard over my shoulder while I drew with crayons or galloped my plastic horses all around the porch, I still believe the stories were not as pretty back then as the ones my mom was telling me now. Perhaps the stories only felt prettier because now I could appreciate them more as an adult. Or perhaps instead, they'd actually gotten prettier, because she'd edited them, polished them. Maybe they got prettier with every family generation, every storyteller's contribution.

Back during my childhood, during the stories, people sat there staring at my mother, listening, leaning forward, their mouths slightly open and their breath so shallow, like they were no longer even in their bodies while they listened to her, while they watched her. I watched them, I watched my mom. She looked out at the night, focused somewhere far out there, moving her hands to the stories: climbing up a ladder, popping palms out flat with surprise, folding them rigid across her chest. Her hands were graceful. She moved them like she was actually looking out at the events happening and her hands and her words were doing all they could to describe what she was seeing for the people sitting near her.

Once she had finished, everyone would blink, shift around, refocus, my mom included. Some people were quiet then, sitting on the porch, looking out at the night like my mother did. Others acted as though they were embarrassed, like someone might be making fun of them. They would begin to question some of the facts, some of the premises.

And if they started that, the questioning, my mother would scrub her face with the heels of her hands, scrub good and hard, then just let her hands fall to her sides. She would sit there, afterward, not a tall woman, when you looked at her close she was surprisingly narrow through the shoulders. She would sit there after the stories, a woman barely medium-sized, looking very small.

She was only big when she was angry or when she was in the midst of telling a story. Both times she got much bigger than me, even once I was actually taller than her; she got bigger than anyone else nearby. Telling stories, she kept her head forward and her mouth tight around the words, hands rolling and twisting and describing; and when she wasn't glancing with her orange-ringed eyes right into each listener's soul to check that each of us was paying absolute attention, she was looking over our shoulders, down the road, over our heads, as though some other, more interesting people might be arriving at any moment.

Chapter 8

My boss didn't like me. Had wanted to fire me from the day he'd taken over from Oliver, the manager before him. Oliver was the one who'd hired me. He'd quit last summer to relocate to a Vancouver nudist colony. When he'd quit, he'd told all of us who worked at the store that he was sad to go, but he couldn't stand the daily irony of being a confirmed nudist working in a clothing store. I must say I'd always appreciated Oliver, even before I knew that last part. He was one of those rare people who smiled with his ears. If he heard something he considered funny, his mouth wouldn't move at all, not one more tooth would show, but his ears and a little bit of his forehead would move up and back until he was quite obviously grinning.

It wasn't that Oliver never noticed I was different, or pretended he didn't notice, he just never seemed to give it much thought. His eyes didn't wander more or less toward me, his conversation addressed me equally.

He left for Vancouver 4 months ago, in December.

Frank, my new boss, didn't like my posture, didn't like the way I wore my uniform, didn't like having a woman in a man's clothing store, especially a woman like me. There was one other woman who worked in the store, Roberta, but she was attractive and confident and had a way of leaning forward into each customer's words, a way that made each customer feel like he was saying something rather clever.

I did what I could to keep out of Frank's way. To be on the careful side I took twice as long as the others to fold all the shirts at the end of my shift. I folded exactly, running my fingers over each crease. I double-checked every calculation before cashing out.

Perhaps Oliver's departure marked the start of my restlessness, when I started staring out the display window at every person passing by. Or perhaps that was merely when I began to notice the restlessness. I had graduated from high school almost a year before. Back at school I hadn't had any close friends, but there were people I had studied with, had eaten meals with. There were people always around, people my age. Since Oliver had left the Wearhouse, I didn't talk much with anyone. At home there was just me and my cats. I read, I assembled puzzles, I talked to my cats. Of course I also had chores to do: clean the dishes, feed the peacocks.

I could probably have gotten another job in town, at the library or in the mall. Recently I'd started thinking more about that, about looking elsewhere. I imagined being a waitress at Pizza Hut or shelving books at Daltons, but I was so used to avoiding change. Change, in my experience, had always been something that had happened to me, without warning, without wishing. Also I liked the Men's Wearhouse, the smell of it, the routine. It was my first job, and seemed a miracle to me. I liked answering the problem of each new customer and then watching the way he walked back to his car fingering the edges of his bag. I liked imagining each customer's happiness trying on all those perfectly-fitting shirts.

I liked their physical peculiarities.

Whenever I thought seriously about a new job—where I wouldn't know immediately where things were and what the proper paperwork was, where I'd be the new person inspected by all the rest—I felt miserable.

Sometimes when a new customer walked in, I'd glance up at the man moving in his gait through the door. I would think with great satisfaction: *circus material.*

Last night I dreamed about that last major fight with Mom before she left. I guess the dream is understandable, what with her calling and all. Still, before this I had been so proud that almost a full year had passed since any of the old dreams.

Back then, maybe a month before she left, our arguments had been getting pretty bad. She had sent me off to boarding school, to McManus, the previous year in hopes of decreasing them. Still we fought—a lot worse actually, each time I returned. We had to pack so much fury into just a few weeks, like others pack in affection during a brief reunion.

She had begun informing me, not just what I wanted to do, but also what she required me to do. When I was back at home from school she didn't let me walk into town alone anymore, even during the day. I had to go to sleep by 9. Her rules, the restrictions, got more strict with each vacation. It was as if I was becoming younger rather than older, as if I had turned 7 rather than 14. All over again she told me how to brush my teeth, she wanted to be there in the bathroom to critique. Down from the gums, she said, from the gums.

It seemed like that whole last summer together before she left, she always had a hand upon me, no longer in affection. Her hand had weight, pushed against me, holding me back, holding me down. Stopping me from growing, from getting older or taller.

What's strange is that I didn't want all that much to grow up. Perhaps because of the examples of my parents, adulthood had never seemed to me to be such a perfect or desirable state. Unfortunately, I had no choice. I was growing—my adult face forming, my voice deepening, my height. Each time my mom came to pick me up at McManus, each time she saw me again after a while apart, her chin kicked back into her neck with surprise. With every inch of my growth, my mother sought to control me more.

So I dreamed about that last clothing fight on the driveway. In the dream she wanted me to change out of what I was wearing, to put on one of my old T-shirts and a pair of pants from the year before. Even if I'd been willing to bend to her wishes, the clothes she remembered me wearing last summer just didn't fit anymore. The pants ended above my ankles, the shirts showed a slice of my midriff. I dreamed she was yelling at me again, screaming at me to get re-dressed. We stood halfway down the driveway; I was on my way into town to get an ice cream. I was going to go alone. I was going to defy her, defy her the only way I was able to, which was stubbornly, furiously silent. I dreamed the scene so exactly, our positions, our clothing. I was wearing the new brown cords I'd gotten at school with the money left over from buying school books, I was wearing an old button-down shirt of Dad's I'd found under a bed. She was leaning forward, her face 6 inches from mine, eyes squinting, mouth open wide. She was yelling at me to listen. She told me she was my mother.

I dreamed Mom's hands were on me again, on either side of my ribs, close to my breasts, always close to my breasts to show me that there were no breasts there yet, that my body was still a child's, still a child with a mother, still hers. As though with her hands she wanted to press harder, press hard enough to wad me up into her pocket and keep me there. I kept my eyes down, my shoulders hunched. I did not push her hands away, but I did not go back to get my old clothing either. I did not tell her she could come along with me into town. I just stood there, wearing my new clothing. Silent, stubborn. Growing.

Yes, the fights had been getting worse and worse, or at least her voice had been getting louder and my silence had been getting firmer, until finally during this last fight—this was in reality, not just in the dream—in the midst of this last fight on the front lawn, the strangest thing happened. In the middle of her screaming (her neck red and veined, her lips wet, her whole head rocking forward with each of her words), she turned away from me to look sharply down the driveway, like it had called her name.

And the fight stopped having meaning for her. Her mouth closed. Just like that. Click.

I couldn't help myself. I assumed my father had come back, was running up the driveway toward us right now. I jerked around to see, my hands out.

But there was only the parked car sitting there, the Plymouth, green and gleaming on its new tires.

Stupidly enough, I just didn't understand.

She left a little more than a month later. During August. The heavy heat of a tired-out summer lying down everywhere.

For 3 years after my mother left, I had dreamed about that last fight. The clothing/driveway fight, the moment of the car, the moment of the click. The fight would appear in the midst of another dream, a normal dream. The fight would be like a dream-commercial. The normal dream would be rolling along, perhaps about finding a secret passageway in the back of the kitchen closet, or about making a speech in front of school without any pants on. Perhaps I would be stepping into the secret passageway, just the first step in, and already there would be fish darting all about through the air. Or I would be standing up there at the podium just beginning to sense the fresh air all around my legs, when the normal dream would pause for the fight-commercial.

Abruptly, no matter what was happening in the previous dream, I would be back there in that moment—that moment when she abruptly looked over at the car—all the details would be so real, the colors, our positions, our clothes. The fast intake of my breath.

It was played exactly the way it had been.

Tonight the dream was no different, except in my thoughts. I stood there watching my mother turn to the car, her eyes intent, her profile to me. In that bright sunlight, I saw for the first time that my mother's face looked a bit like the person I'd been picturing as Celia, the same bone structure.

In July after that long cold winter of 1887, there was a sudden spring. It was in the third week of that moist heat that Mikey-the-crybaby remembered their mother's body.

Cessil stalled successfully for almost a week before he, as their new leader, was finally forced up the ladder of the barn by the united strength of the other children.

Cessil carried a burlap bag into which they had all decided he was supposed to put what remained. He distinctly heard his heart stop beating when his hand touched the ladder's first rung. His heart had been pounding out a rather loud and fast beat before, so the silence after was noticeable. He climbed slowly with the lonely hiss of his own breath in his ears, the rasp of the bag against his clothes. This was the only moment during his whole long life in which he allowed himself to miss his older sister, her determination and strength, the mass of her shoulder beside his. He missed her all the more fiercely as he neared his destination and began to hear, over the rasp of his own breath, the mindless buzzing of some horrible power.

When Celia's body had disappeared, an unspoken pact had emerged among the remaining children. The pact was that they would pretend that the incident had never happened, that their oldest sister had never happened. In their new mythology Cessil had always been the eldest. The children did not meet to discuss it, they never talked about it. It was like all the games they played; they acted as though it were true, they spoke as though it were true, and soon they could feel it was true. The room in which the incident had occurred remained as empty of people as it had been ever since that morning when they had all come silently and en masse to the door.

There was no blood, there was no body. There was no hint that anything had ever happened.

And from that day on nothing had. The room was erased from their minds, as Celia's bedroom was from their paths. They even, in a way, erased each other, for after that day they tended to look less directly at each other. They spent a lot of their time sleeping, and when they got up they brushed their teeth and hair, washed behind their ears. They went off to separate rooms to play quietly, each by themselves, and their backs were stiff and their heads pulled forward as they waited for the blow. So they spent the final month of the coldest winter on record in the middle of that great Canadian forest. And now Mikey not only talked to himself, he picked up the habit of rock-

ing in the corner with his back against the wall, his hands tugging at his clothes.

As my grandfather, at the age of 12, was climbing toward where he had left the body of his mother, as he was missing his older sister, he began to experience the first of the headaches. These afflictions would later on start to push him out of control, like a pole through the brain, whenever he approached the body of an adult woman, alive or dead.

The rest of the children stood below in the warm familiar hay of the barn they all knew, and the sounds of their questions came up to him like distorted swirls of smoke. As he approached the top of the ladder he began to smell something very sweet. The sounds of humming life became louder and louder. Then his eyes rose over the hay, and a foot in front of his nose was an unfocused mound of something that was not dead at all but fuzzy and shimmering with insect life and his heart beat again and again and his hands let go of their holds so fast he fell all the way down the ladder and rolled away across the hay, scrambling and then running without saying a word, without even whimpering, running away from the children as though from death herself, running through the woods and beyond, straight on to Nova Scotia, to the sea, where he signed up to be a cabin boy on a whaler out for a 3-year cruise.

Of course the children were so curious and scared that they all had to run up the ladder immediately, all in a pack, hands and feet intertwined, pushes at the back and shoves at the front and all the faces fighting to rise over the hay to see the bees swarming now up into the air in a drowsy slow-moving cloud above their mother, their mother lying there narrow and determined, cleaned even of dust from the constant shivering of the bees' wings. Their mother lying there, exactly as they remembered her.

The remaining children did not bury their mother either. The next eldest child, Samantha, was a thin and entirely chinless girl who so wanted other people's approval that she never showed them her profile but always stood face forward, forehead tilted slightly down, like a bull. The line from the bottom of her lips receded backwards to the top of her collarbone without a bump or a shadow, and her eyes were ferocious with self-righteousness and shame.

After her older brother ran away, she fetched the town priest and the town priest fetched others to see the miraculously non-deteriorating mother with her swarming bees. Eventually the children built a small shrine and some beehives in the barn around the body and charged admission at the gate to friends and strangers alike to whom they also sold packed lunches, holy honey and lemon cookies.

In later years, as the sheen and color of their mother's hair and cheeks began to fade like curtains, they blocked off the windows of the barn, put in a museum-quality lighting and ventilation system and painted the body with a thin coat of wax like an apple. They polished her weekly, tended to the beehives and made enough money to send the last 6 children through highschool without those children having to have outside jobs.

And so they all lived there, for more than 30 years, without their 2 eldest siblings or a live mother, or even any interruptions in day-to-day life aside from marriages and births and 2 miscarriages. Then in 1918 Cessil returned to Canada as part of the American naval force, bringing 2 buddies over to what he assumed would be his deserted ancestral home. They were planning to get drunk in the field and talk about women and their commanding officer, but when they stepped up toward the door, to see the inside, the 3 adult faces of Cessil's youngest sisters peered out around the door and one of their children shot Cessil 6 times in the head with his finger and with an exploding noise that came from deep within his chest.

It had been while Cessil was still a boy, fleeing straight toward the coast, that he first began to notice the disgust he had for the female form. Each time he stood near one, the arches of his nose would begin to flutter and the right side of his mouth would rise. He would feel nauseated and be unable to eat, would sweat and talk very little. For instead of smelling the mild sweetness of perfume or the musky heat of a human female body, Cessil smelled the stench of rotting flesh, of fish meat split open with heat and shimmering with mumbling death. He smelled sickness and disease, and his young unfinished face became twisted, changing from that of a simple country boy to a young city man of secret troubles—unhappy, mysterious and sad.

And women looked on the boy with favor. Women wanted him, young though he was. They clustered around him like people cluster at the edge of a cliff, drawn—although they might maintain other-wise—partly by the possibility of a fall. Women stepped in close, watching him through sultry, determined eyes, as though his twisted face were a direct challenge to try to make him happy, to try to learn his secret thoughts, to try to make him blush with love. This effect was heightened over the 2 years it took for Cessil to get to the sea, walking all the way to Nova Scotia to find one of the last whaling boats to sign on to. During this time he began to fill out, to widen from a confused and running boy to a broad and ripe man of muscles and weight, of grace and confidence, of clear and cold eyes. He grew into the kind of man found only in history books and in working-class pubs, drunk and murderous and slouching on the stool with his elbows on the bar, as stunning as the unexpected sprawled weight of a leopard.

He became the kind of strongman he had so wished to be when he was a child. Women looked at that big growing body with his twisted face on top and they swayed forward to touch him, like columns of sleepwalkers.

Cessil, hiding his hands in his pockets, head turned away, backed up, holding his breath.

So it should seem natural that Cessil was overjoyed to get on that ship filled with pure men, men's men. Men who lived on their own in their own world, on board a ship without a single woman, without a woman's voice or touch or written scented word for 2 and 3 years at a time. Men at last living away from women's demanding touch and color schemes.

Cessil remembered the confidence he felt in the expedition when he first saw the captain at the wheel, the widespread legs, the upright torso, the snug sailor clothing which described so exactly the lack of womanly curves. The sheathed muscles of his back at the wheel, the muscles rolling with the ship's movement, the angles and rhythms of his ribs. Cessil remembered, from those years aboard the ship, the smell created by all the men, canvas and creaking wood. A smell not exactly foul but like a family kitchen on a farm, honest and hardworking, homey. He remembered the rhythm of working with them all, raising the sail, heave ho and 5 bodies pulling down, falling down with all their weight and strength into each other's lean-hipped laps.

And somewhere during the third year of no women at all, Cessil felt the rising of a warm confusion within his body. He was 19. He began, as much as he could on a constrained ship, to avoid the company of his friends. He began to think himself a pervert because in the lonely farmhouse of children in Ontario, he had never heard of such possibilities as those his body began to dream of.

So Cessil left the ship at the next stop, Rio de Janeiro, Brazil. He

*found the most isolated job he could, the railroad job, and he walked
into the jungle. He stayed away from all men, all women. He walked
alone with his own thoughts, his movements slow and careful and
lonely. By this time his muscles and belly had bulged so far outward
that upon sighting him, women felt more feminine, and so did men.
The women actually half-stepping forward without a thought, a
hand raised, fingers cupped toward his face. The men, standing rigid,
also wishing to reach right up but instead to slap him for the insult he
had made to them by his very existence.*

*Yet Cessil was still so young, only 20 or 21, and the reactions he
got from both men and women confused and hurt him. He retreated
back to the jungle after each encounter, resettling the knapsack filled
with gold and silver between his shoulders with a sigh, and then turning and pacing out the miles.*

*The third time Cessil went into Rio to pick up more gold, he was told
to report to a new man, and this man was a man even larger than
himself. He was a man whose muscles and fat rounded out to weight
inappreciable. Floors groaned beneath him, fine china and small
objects exploded at his touch. Reinforced chairs kneeled down beneath
him like old horses. Cessil took one look at the man's wide features of
a shaved bear and his heart beat quicker, a delicate blush rising to his
skin. At the first question the new man directed to him, Cessil felt such
a high and uncontrolled giggle bubbling up in his wide chest that he
had to block it from his lips by slapping the new man twice in the face
with the back of his hand and challenging him to a contest of arm-
wrestling. This was the popular and manly sport at the moment, and
the new man blinked twice at Cessil before his head sank forward in
acceptance, with the gravity of a boulder starting to roll.*

*The first table on which they placed their elbows blew apart into
so many pieces all that remained was a fine dust. The second table*

they tried was mahogany and it split down the center with a sigh. Finally they went outside and laid their weight on a solid granite block in the yard, used as a workbench by the blacksmith. Even the granite groaned and settled 3 inches farther into the ground, so no one was able to move it until, 50 years later, it was blown out of the yard and across the street with a stick of dynamite.

When the new man gently clamped his hand around Cessil's, Cessil felt every muscle in his arm and chest snap taut like a sail. The new man barely flexed and Cessil felt every bone in his arm twist and turn within their hinges. The new man smiled as he began to pull in earnest and Cessil felt a power and a strength such as he had never felt before, even upon the wide lap of the open sea. He sweated with the pain and love within his heart. But he fought as he had never fought before, his strength coming from the very face of the man he was competing with. Cessil's struggle was slowly and painfully marked out with the passage of the sun and the sweat puddling wet and traitorous beneath both of them.

For 5 full hours the battle continued, Cessil steadily losing ground while his palm beat a strange tattoo of love and self-loathing against this new man's flesh. Then, finally, the new man's wife stepped out into the yard against the setting sun, so her curved and womanly shadow fell across their clasped hands. Her voice was as rich and wide as Mother Earth's as she told her man that dinner was ready. The heat from her body filled the air even at 10 feet with the warmth of softly baking bread. When she turned away, her hair rolled along the sweep of her back like the black tail of some magnificent mare.

Cessil pulled the man's hand down. He pulled it down so fast he broke the man's knuckles against the back of the granite. Then, while the bigger man was at the doctor's getting his hand set and bound, Cessil ate the man's dinner, drank his wine and seduced his wife, making love to her so attentively that she sighed and begged him to take her away with him into the jungle. But, instead, he left her in the bed in the early morning in order to return to the jungle, left her for the bigger man to find sleeping, still nude and fragrant.

From then on, each night that Cessil was in civilization, he seduced tall and curving women with long black hair. And with each thrust he gave them, cruel and strong and triumphant, they looked up at his twisted face and thought he was a sensitive soul, a hurting boy only they could help.

After the seduction, the act of sex itself was always deadly quiet, for the women felt that if they let out a single moan they would scream without pause or meaning. They bore each thrust in cheek-bitten silence, gazing up at the veins on his neck bulging wider and darker and wider and darker, and as the start of a titanic wave of knowledge such as they had never known or would know again uncurled up their spine, they cried out in their minds with the length and breadth of his strength and told themselves again and again that this was a love that was true.

Cessil never murmured, never even whispered a word, for he was too busy holding his breath against the stench in the room.

And thus it was after 5 years of the jungle and the city, after 5 years of leaving a trail of moaning voluptuous women, their legs still freshly parted, after 5 years of trying to avoid all men, my grandfather first laid eyes on my grandmother, Anita, in a bar in Rio de Janeiro. He realized immediately that the main odor he smelled was the stench of her cigar, that he had no headache, that he wanted to kiss her nose.

Yes, the main feeling he had upon laying eyes on this rail-thin short stamping mouth of a woman, was relief of the most primal kind.

Well, he said, Now yes.

. . .

Some 20 years later, standing as an adult in the doorway of the farm of his childhood—while the son of one of his younger sisters shot him in the head 6 times with his finger, Cessil pissed in his pants with a relief that so completely voided his body of fear and hate and rivalry toward the siblings still living in the farmhouse that as soon as he returned to Fort Lauderdale, where he and his wife had settled, he began to build the start of a rambling mansion-house he named Brazil, a house big enough to fit all the remaining siblings and their families in relative comfort.

Shortly thereafter, the entire extended family moved from Ottawa to Fort Lauderdale to be with their newly-returned brother through their middle and older ages. For they had each discovered in their maturity a great respect and need for the closeness and understanding found only with their blood relations and in the shared experience of having grown up together.

And of all the many many words that the 13 brothers and sisters joyfully uttered within their new house during the next 5 years, clasping each other's hands and looking deeply into each other's eyes, the name of their oldest sister was not one of them.

I sat up on the kitchen table, hugging the pillow to my belly as I thought about this story.

Did Cessil have any previous experience on whalers? I asked.

What? asked my mom.

Did he have any experience on whalers, or on sailing ships of any kind?

Oh no, of course not. He was brought up on a farm.

How'd he get the job, then?

I don't know, said my mom impatiently. Why are you asking

about this? He talked his way in. He was young. He was healthy and strong.

Well, how'd he know he wanted the job, then, that he wouldn't be miserable in it, or not be able to pick up the skills? How'd he know he wasn't one of those people who vomit a lot on a boat, can't get over seasickness?

He didn't.

What?

He didn't know that.

Well, couldn't he have tried a shorter voyage first to see if he had problems? Maybe a week's cruise out to Newfoundland?

Sweetie, sweetie, sweetie, snorted my mom. That's not the way things worked then. Caution wasn't discovered until the 1950s.

Oh, I said and thought about that for a while.

Well, he must have been scared, I added, He must have felt quite lonely.

My mom didn't bother to reply.

Then I added, Hey, while I'm at it, didn't you say you were going to tell me tonight whether or not Celia was murdered?

Darling, my mom said, I lied.

What?

A storyteller has got to keep her audience interested however she can, she announced.

I could hear her smiling then, smiling down the phone line all the way from California. Grinning, really. She always smiled with such honest all-out enjoyment, without needing to watch other people's reactions to her joke. Her green-orange eyes crinkled, so bright and small. It made other people smile simply from the strength of her enjoyment, even if they hadn't gotten the joke.

Wait, does that mean she was murdered? I asked, allowing

my voice to show my irritation. Isn't the thief's wife called Celia? Is it the same Celia?

Maybe, she said, Maybe. I'll tell you tomorrow.

And of course she hung up.

I know that might seem like a bit much to you. You might think no one person could possibly hang up on another this much. Not on her own daughter.

Well, I can only say, even from my few observations at the age of 19, becoming a mother physically doesn't automatically remake a person into our Disney ideal of motherhood, not any more than being born a daughter or son makes us any good at those roles. I can only say that, no matter how many kinds of people (Disney mothers and others) you can imagine in the world, there are always more. My theory is that you don't hear stories about these other folks because everyone is so busy editing, pretending they themselves are normal: normal moms, normal children, normal friends. All you hear, day to day, from each person, are the good-to-tell stories. Mostly we do this editing so well we forget we're even doing it, that others are doing it, that strange stuff still exists out there. Until something happens to you that isn't so normal, that isn't what it's supposed to be. Then, because of the editing, you end up feeling so different from everyone else, alien. You feel so much more alone.

I can only assure you, from my experience in the 20 years since my mom told me these stories (since those nights when she hung up on me every once in a while), that there are people out there who have literally done—without feeling self-conscious at all—every single thing you have ever imagined. As well as so many many things you haven't.

Chapter 9

First thing, without even saying hi, Mom asked, So, you grown much taller?

I was flustered for a moment, then answered simply, for there's not much point in trying to hide it. Yes, I said.

She didn't ask how much. She just said, Oh.

It's probably my fault, she added, For eating so many bananas when I was pregnant with you.

I did not bother to question her medical reasoning here. She believed so many theories left over from the last century, I guess from all those years spent learning the stories of the past. She tended to believe in the healing properties of babies' teeth beneath the pillow or roosters' feet wrapped in lace.

When she mentioned this belief about bananas though, I imagined myself curled within her, like a banana in a tight C-shape, so close the 2 of us were one. I imagined us so close that when she ate those bananas it was unclear whether she was eating for her hunger or for mine; it was unclear when she inhaled if it was for her veins or for mine. I imagined the hug of her innards pulled so tight around me that in response, not knowing any better, I kicked at her.

Don't, said my mother, Blame yourself about your height.

I was not sure how to respond to her statement. In the hiss of the phone line I could hear metal tapping metal. The tapping sound wasn't at her end or at mine. It was just some stray static caused along the way. I wanted that static silenced out of respect. This was my time with my mother. I had lost out on so much of it.

OK, she said, I guess I'll tell you more about Great Aunt Celia and her figure. Celia grew to be a big woman too.

Aha, I cried triumphant, So she was *not* murdered.

The night after the children's attack on Celia, the snow twirled down thickly and slowly. That winter even the tops of many of the trees had been lost beneath the drifts, so Celia escaped from the house alone into a world that in places looked as bare and new as an egg. Painfully and slowly throughout the night, one hand to her broken rib, limping slightly on her broken toe, she walked. She paced out the distance, from the house where she had lived her whole young life, to the town and the world beyond where she would live out the rest until she died. The only sounds in the frozen world were those of the snow squeaking beneath her weight and the slight hiss of the steam that rose from her belly, breasts and brow.

As she walked, she battled a deep and silent chill that did not come wholely from the subzero temperature of the night, or from the wind which sucked at her face and hands. This chill was deeper than any mere temperature difference. It was a chill that started in her heart and in her broken toe and rib and joined forces together at the midpoint between her hipbones. The chill was such that even the oven-baking heat of her womb began to wane. For the first time since adolescence had started heating up Celia's young body, she felt the tiniest bit cool and noticed the hungry squeak of the young snow beneath her feet.

It was then, as she was looking down at the pure innocence of the new snow, that she realized without the slightest shirking of the issue that her sisters and brothers had, all 13 of them, tried so earnestly to kill her that they had mistaken her unconsciousness for death. This was the point at which the second and stronger wave of cold exploded into her body, entering through the aperture between her legs to freeze her womb so solid that as an adult she never was able to have children with her husband, or even to enjoy sex as more than a distant sort of sparkle.

It was in the brightness of the cold from her pelvis that her hands rose to her ribs to hug tight the warmth left in her body. The stab of her broken rib into her side was enough to push her to a knowledge not normally given to such a young and untraveled child. The simultaneous stabs of pain from her side and below from between her legs prodded her mind into the clear and simple knowledge that she would never suffer under the normal inefficiencies of guilt or wishfulness. She recognized this knowledge as her body's sacred promise, a promise that she would do exactly what she wanted to do with her life and would savor every moment of it.

Her feet did not pause once in their journey and in the first town she reached, her knock on the tavern keeper's door was as strong and resolute as the beat of her heart in her chest.

Celia settled down 3 towns away from the house where her siblings still lived. She worked as a waitress while she thought about what it was she had been promised. The promise became more evident each day, for by the time she was 15 her chest had developed so much she had to assume the habit of keeping both hands on the small of her back or on her hips to offset some of the weight, and her face was so luminous that even little children sucked in their breath. But in the whole of the town where she lived, not a man would touch her, because—along with her beauty—her spirit and muscles had developed since the time when she was simply the bully of children, for waitressing is no easy job. Her new muscles were how, as a 15-year-old, she had beaten with one fist the first man who had tried for her.

She had not fought him because she thought that was what she was supposed to do. She had not fought him because he was 20 years older and drunk. She fought him because he simply grabbed a handful of her body without any warning or permission as she passed his table. Her reaction was immediate and strong. In front of the entire restaurant, she twisted her upper body away from him—so for an instant he probably assumed she was pulling away in fear—and then she swiveled back out of her wind-up into a straight-armed backhanded swing with her whole body behind it. She hit him so hard his head shot backwards like a puck and the rest of his body tumbled leisurely after it to hit the floor heavy and limp. Celia and another waitress dragged him out to the sobering cold of the snow and thought no more of it.

But, from then on the townsmen thought about nothing else. They thought it unnatural. They thought it terrifying. The scene became more frightening and vivid in their minds and in their talk. Before the end of the second month it was accepted as common fact that Celia and the other waitress had not dragged the man outside at all. No, instead that was where the punch had landed him, clear through the door and down the front steps. From that day on, the men in town did not dare do anything but sit around in the restaurant where Celia worked, and watch her body forlornly. Not a man among them ever

*again raised a hand to touch her, especially not as the years passed
and the legend of her fighting exploits grew with her figure, grew to
the point where most believed that she had actually been a pro fighter
who toured with the circus for a while, that she had beaten in a fair
brawl the entire Kingston Huskies hockey team. The legend and
myths building each year without any man flirting with her, much
less touching her. Instead the town's men seemed content to own her
through talk and to caress her with their stares as she flowered before
their eyes into a 20-year-old whose beauty made even old women
touch their cheeks and remember.*

*In frustration one day, she actually pushed one of the younger
men in town into the backroom of the restaurant and stripped herself,
slowly and with ceremony, in front of him until he was presented with
such luscious curvature of flesh that every ounce of his body became
as limp and useless as a wet rag and he cried.*

*Thus, Celia was forced to apply for a mail-order husband. She
required this husband be from the States, as she thought they might
build them better down there. In 1894, she left on the day of her
twenty-first birthday, leaving by boat on the Ottawa River, a boat
bound for New York City, and was seen off by all the men in town,
who went down to the harbor to look at her, but nothing more.*

*Great Aunt Celia commonly referred to the men of that town as
"lily-livered wimps."*

*Now, Celia wanted to make very sure that in this marriage she
was not going to get a husband like the men she had known in her
town, so she specified to the mail-order company that the man she
married must be either a captain or above in the army, a robber
baron, or a successful criminal. She was informed that her new fiancé
was of the latter category, so the dress she bought to meet him had a
pattern made of stripes.*

*This was a truly beautiful dress, the kind you just don't see any-
more. It was made during an era when people took all the care in the*

world because they hadn't been told there was anything shameful about spending the time to do something well. It was made with details and with love, made back during a time before assembly lines and efficiency studies. Made during a time when you could lock a whole family into a factory for 14 hours straight, pay them with 3 pounds of potatoes and they would be grateful to you.

Yes, this was a well-made dress. It was a dress made all the more beautiful by Celia. You had only to see it on her to know that this shape, this fabric, this material had all been created with the ideal of her in mind. It was a dress and she was the kind of human that seen together in the correct light could justify most of civilization. It was a blue dress with yellow stripes that she loved on first sight, and it had cost so much she had to sell all of her other clothing, furniture and her entire black column of hair, all 37 measured inches of it, shaved off at the scalp, so that she took only a small purse, a cheap wig and that dress into her new life.

She stayed naked and bald-headed inside the cabin for nearly the whole trip down to New York, the dress hanging wrinkle-free in the closet. Only 3 times did she put it and the wig on to go up on deck to stock up on food and fresh air, and she never sat down while she did so. When the boat landed, she combed out the wig as best as she could, put it and the dress on and went outside in front of her cabin to lean over the railing, scanning the crowd below, in which stood, somewhere, the man so soon to be her husband.

Her fiancé, of course, was your Great Great Uncle Egbert, the man who made famous the alias of Don Mario García de Lollosa. And just as Celia had specified, he was a successful criminal, but he was a criminal who had never used violence, who had no dealings with organized crime, who had never even held a pair of scissors in a threatening manner. He was a transient, unthreatening, natural pickpocket, and as such had always had a hard time meeting women.

A House Named Brazil

He had never stayed in any town long enough to do more than exchange pleasantries with a woman in the grocery store or at the baseball game. My great uncle's face was not a face one would naturally think of flirting with, not even when he was a young man. It was a face of which—at the most—one asked in a neighborly fashion if the pork chops didn't look a little bit on the mealy side today.

And so, in desperation, one spring day, he had filled out the form of a marriage broker. He had filled it out thoughtfully and truthfully even to the matter of his career, for he thought his wife surely had the right to know. For 3 years he had waited then, with no response, not even a possibility, until one Friday in July of the year 1894, he was informed by mail that on Tuesday afternoon at 3, his fiancée would be standing on the top deck of the boat called Saint Bernadette *wearing a dress of blue and yellow, and she would need his help getting through customs.*

For the next 4 days, Egbert could not hold food down, could not shave, could not even steal. He merely sat in his hotel room, trying on different colognes, wondering what sort of a desperate hag would agree to marry a criminal.

But Tuesday afternoon at exactly 3, Egbert found himself standing on the pier, by the boat, near the gangplank, letting his gaze wander slowly up the boat's side, past the portholes, past the lifeboats, over the 2 lower decks, where waiters dressed in red, white and blue were carrying glistening glasses of champagne from cabin to cabin and yelling into each open doorway, Welcome welcome welcome. Egbert's gaze continued to rise slowly, cautiously, with fear to the top deck, where the blue and yellow silhouette of a woman was leaning out over the railing just like the prows of olden boats.

He stared up at this image for 4 full seconds before her face and figure finally registered within his mind, and his heart skipped beating so that he thought he would never get a chance to touch this wonderful woman, but would instead crumple onto the pier like the scaly fish clubbed and dumped there each night. Thus, even before his heart could start beating again he was dodging through the crowd, leaping over one small child; he was sprinting up the swaying wood of the gangplank and sliding around the corner to the stairs; he was rising up the stairs without even knowing if it were his feet that were moving him or the power of his heart, he was watching his vision tunnel down the deck, to see waiter after waiter float aside, champagne and glass sprinkling up and around him in fountains of light, and then to see her, her face, her body, approaching so quickly, looming so large and real that he was there by her side and grabbing hold of her hand, her flesh, even before he had fully stopped, skidding slightly. He stood on the deck by her side and he could hear his heart was definitely beating again, beating too quickly now, and there was a high buzzing sound within his ears. This woman turned to look at him with so much grace. Her hand was smoother than an infant's, warm and wide and soft, but with the muscles beneath filled with an underlying power, a barely hidden strength that he knew could take anything and everything life dished out.

So he picked her up without even introducing himself, staggered with her into what he hoped was her cabin and slammed the door.

Great Aunt Celia was stunned that here was a man actually touching her. She was literally stunned motionless, so she crumpled into his arms and did not hit him for a moment, and it was a moment long enough for Egbert, still charging desperately full speed, to throw her down upon the bed and himself beside her, his eyesight bored narrow and true on the next destination, the fine buttons of her dress swelling out and over the weight that they concealed.

And Celia still did not hit him even though she was now recovering quite a bit. She found herself rather taken with his enthusiasm after so many frustrating years in her town, because at 21 she was also still a virgin. Then, as he started the process of unbuttoning her dress, she forgot even the idea of hitting him, for she saw in his urgency, he did not rip that beautiful dress of hers apart or yank at it in impatience. The stranger with the sallow and thin but adoring face cuddled his body in as close as he could get to her, and opened each one of the buttons quickly and tenderly and very gracefully, with hands which she could tell already were exceedingly clever. When he reached her corset, although his fingers had begun to shake so hard they did not work completely, he still did not rip or tear anything in his frustration.

Celia even began to forget her previous image of a real man as she watched this not-so-large man pause in his industrious work on the ties of her corset to reach a gentle hand up to her cheek and then down between her legs, to touch through the corset and the slips and bloomers the place where he was trying so hard to go.

When he finally turned around from hanging up the dress and corset and slips and bloomers in the closet, he saw her naked in her entirety for the first time from a distance great enough to get the full effect. His legs slid out from under him like water. Then it was Celia who picked him up without a word, put him back on the bed and took off his clothing piece by piece.

And that Tuesday afternoon on the Saint Bernadette, my great aunt, Celia Jeanette Mourne, helped Egbert Oliver Scullaley bring out within her that tiny sparkle that was all she was capable of and which she definitely liked and wanted more of. And Great Uncle Egbert was so satisfied by the whole episode that when Celia's wig fell off, he just assumed in the excitement, her very skin was loosening its hold on the world.

By the time they both stepped out of the cabin and looked around, they were long out of the port of New York City and on their way to Charleston, and neither really cared. When they got off the boat in South Carolina in 1894, both knew that only death could separate the match they had made.

. . .

There was a breathing space after Mom's story. She drank water again, the long draw and then the swallow. Susan, the 6-toed kitten, was sleeping on the pantry shelf above the radiator, between the teacups. Susan made tiny guttural snores through her nose, exactly like an old man who weighed only 2 pounds.

For the phone conversations I had brought a blanket down to the kitchen. I lay on my side across the kitchen table on my pillow and blanket, working on a puzzle of a pizza slice that was made up of 2,000 separate puzzle pieces of mingled tomato sauce and melted cheese. Somehow, working on puzzles has always helped me concentrate. I don't believe I am the only person who has ever felt that way.

Over the phone, I heard the rasp and snap of a match, and then my mom inhaling hard several times on something, the little pop of her breath.

Mmm, she said and exhaled slow.

Mom, I said so surprised, You're smoking cigars these days?

She didn't bother to respond. Puffed instead more contentedly.

Don't you know those things are bad for you? I asked. They give you mouth cancer and stuff.

She snorted in amusement. Puffed once, then snorted again.

So, I said, Celia just got on a boat bound for a different country to marry a man she'd never met?

Ahuh, agreed my mother.

She didn't even have a photo of him?

Nope.

Just knew he was a criminal?

Yep.

I paused for a moment.

Couldn't she instead, I asked, Have dated someone from a town or 2 away? Someone who hadn't heard the rumors about her? If nothing else it would have saved her some ferry fees.

Mom didn't bother to respond. I don't think she was angry; instead there was just a silence between us, almost like there used to be during the long summer nights on the farm those final weeks when Mom lived here, after she stopped fighting with me, after that final driveway fight. Back then, for hours each night, it seemed there would be no sound but the occasional *bzup* of the electric bug zapper. Sometimes then I could even believe the silence was peaceful, could almost think that I had wanted this silence, sought it out.

With that silence again between us, I actually began to believe for the first time that my mom would keep calling and calling, phoning from closer and closer until one day she drove up, parked her Plymouth in the driveway and I could finally talk to her face to face. Then, I thought, then my anger could finally show.

Mom, I asked cautiously. How do you know some of this stuff?

Some of what stuff?

Well, all that at the end of your story. The sex stuff.

There was a pause.

Honey, said my mom, Don't ever call me a liar.

Her voice rising. The change in tone so fast.

I didn't dare to say a thing.

We were both silent, breathing there, waiting. I did not question her anymore. I tried to breathe agreeably, obediently, tried not to let her hear my fear. As you've probably guessed by now, my mother really knew how to fight, didn't mind it. She could yell and slap her chest and shake her fists all around. 10 minutes later she would hug you hard and complete. And from the moment the first harsh words were spoken, her cheeks would be as rosy as if from exercise or love.

Me, on the other hand, I would stand there, trying to hunch over even more, so as not to intimidate the person arguing with me, while I worried at the same time about my soft spots, my stretched-thin bony places. I blinked at another's loud voice or harsh statements, wanted to cover my face, my knees, the bones of my spine. Saying not a thing. I understood so viscerally the tenuous impermanence of relationships. I knew with the certainty of experience that things I said or did could make the other person go away forever.

And after an argument, I held a grudge for years.

On the phone now, my mother seemed to accept this silence as my version of an apology. She sighed out her nose.

Honey, it was your great great aunt Celia herself who told me this from the wheelchair she was confined to. She told it to me straight out, never needed any coaxing or even questioning. I was quite young then, no more than 7. Still, she told me all of it.

My mom snorted lightly, her breath amplified by the receiver. Celia loved it, she said. At the risqué parts a wide smile spread on her lips. To picture her you got to know her dentures glowed unnaturally from all the Efferdent she soaked them in, double-strength because she believed in neatness, both visual as well as bacteriological. She would sometimes forget those dentures in the glass for days, while she lived off coffee and grapes, the gummed grapes leaking into her whiskers. When she did wear her dentures, her stories had a slight lisp to them, perhaps from the dentures' fit or maybe from the speed of her words. I would look up at her—back then, even in her wheelchair she was taller than me—her words spilling out over where her hands rested on the shelf of her drooping breasts. I was just a little kid

then, when she first started telling me the stories. I didn't understand a lot of them. But I remembered them. Perhaps because I
didn't understand. I filed them away to figure out later. They
seemed so important to her.

Honey, my mother said matter-of-factly in her flat almost-
man's voice, Don't you ever ever call me a liar again.

Chapter 10

When I came in from the storeroom this morning at work, Frank, my boss, stopped me. He had been employed at the store for all 3 years of its existence and had taken it perhaps too much to heart, working his way up from stock boy, talking without irony about the company's aspirations and personality. Also, perhaps because of the store policy of not staring at customers, he seemed to have difficulty looking anyone in the eye anymore. Instead his eyes moved all around, up to the ceiling and over to the window, across the other person's brow, like he was following the ambling pattern of a fly. I believe he did this much more with me than with the others.

He asked if I had slept well last night. Suspicious, I said I'd slept well enough. I tried to imagine what I had done wrong. He was smiling too much. I realized for the first time his body looked a bit like Cessil's must have looked, at least in the belly and the width of his shoulders. Only Frank didn't have enough muscle on the rest of his body. I imagined Frank's neck size would be about a 17, whereas I bet Cessil had probably been about an 18 and a ½. That was my professional opinion.

That's good you slept so well, he said. I'm glad nothing bothered you, nothing niggled at you or kept you awake. His eyes moved from the front door to close to my right ear, then roved back away again.

Because yesterday, he said, You forgot to record your sales. There was $187 more in the till than anyone could explain. It threw the next 2 shifts off. Everyone had to recheck their numbers.

I looked at him, startled. I wondered what I had been doing yesterday to be so forgetful, to be less than careful. Of course I had been thinking about Mom's phonecalls. I had been going through my normal routine, but I had been thinking about Celia. I had been imagining her living in the present instead. I had been trying to figure out how she might live her life today, what kind of car she'd drive, what breakfast cereal she'd eat, what adventures she'd find in today's world.

Of course I told Frank I was sorry. I told him that 3 or 4 times.

I told him I wouldn't let it happen again. And right then, for just a moment, he looked me straight in the eye and we both knew I wouldn't let it happen again because if I did, he would fire me.

Once Cessil had run away to the sea, Samantha, the third child, didn't immediately bring the village priest back to have him take a look at her mother's body. This was because Samantha had been born not only entirely chinless, but also without what the rest of the world would call imagination or insight. She was devoid of anything beyond the stingy practical intelligence she exhibited so proudly each day, an intelligence about on par with that of a brainy duck. Thus she was exhilarated when at the age of 12, she was given the responsibility of raising 11 younger children.

This was partly because Samantha had always thought her mother and older siblings had been too lenient in their parenting.

Children, she believed, should be made to understand from an early age just how harsh the world was so as to avoid later disappointment. Samantha herself had been deeply disappointed in the nature of the world during the course of the past winter. She had gotten her first period on a night colder than hopelessness, and with the light of the candle she could see in the bathroom mirror that as a new woman she still had no chin. Beset by a mournfulness that would ebb in and out of her soul throughout her life, she dyed the children's clothes a respectful black and told them to walk slowly at all times.

For the first few mornings after Cessil ran away, she gave each child a checklist of self-castigating chores and penances. Matthew, for example, had to carry a bucketful of sand everywhere he went while he considered the weight of his sins.

The children, already orphaned 3 times in one year, felt that family was family. They did all she requested, and even helped her think up new punishments when her lack of imagination impeded her. In their spare time the children did what they could for a farm rapidly falling apart.

Thus they were surprised when the first week passed and Samantha's demands for meaningless chores became less frequent. In their places were inserted new and more practical instructions delivered in a style reminiscent of the way their mother had ruled the house. Once again they were told to brush their hair and take care of the garden. The day little Elizabeth had a cold, her chore was to stay inside and care for the fire. Because every one of the children knew that Samantha, in her normal state, would be incapable of such generosity, they began to fret for the sanity of her, their fourth caretaker. They arranged to take turns watching discreetly over her, clutching the only tools they could think of, the dinner bell and a 30-foot length of old horse rope.

During the week that the children watched Samantha, she was seen to spend an awful lot of time up in the loft of the barn, where their mother's body still lay undisturbed (because none of them was certain if they should bury a body that did not deteriorate). At first they assumed Samantha was praying to their mother, but it was 4-year-old Rebecca who figured out she was kneeling simply to observe the body. The strength of the concentration Samantha poured onto the corpse of their mother scared little Rebecca so much she had to sleep in the same bed as Sid, snuggled up against his side and waking him several times each night to make him check for scary things under the bed and in the closet.

Samantha's lists of things to do began to incorporate their mother's pet names for her children. At the same time, the children began to notice that Samantha was not sleeping through a lot of the night. Sid said she must be staying up and reading, that's why they could see the light under her door. But Elizabeth, one of the fighting twins, said No, you can hear her voice. Alexis, the other twin, said You ninny, she's reading out loud. And the children sat about her door until delightfully late each night calling each other names and debating the problems of caring for their newest caretaker while in the next room Samantha's voice could be heard murmuring on and on with long and thoughtful pauses.

And in the mornings Samantha looked more and more tired. She took to napping fitfully in strange places and positions. She took to falling asleep while talking or writing out the chore list, the list punctuated with spidery puddles of ink showing the points during which she had momentarily napped. Once she nestled her chin sleepily down onto her pancakes and began to snore. Another morning she flopped off the outhouse seat so quickly she got a nasty splinter in her right buttock. Still, her light was left on late at night and her voice murmured on and on under the door into the morning hours. The light continued to stay on every night until the day she fell out of the second-story window against which she had been leaning while taking a short rest on her way up the stairs. She fell through the air, still slack with sleep up till the moment she hit the thick sumac bushes.

Even before Samantha hit the bushes, little Rebecca was in the window swinging the bell up and down as hard as she could and the children were leaping in from everywhere, holding ropes and saucepans, dinner forks and a shovel, bandages and the baby Marthe, arriving all before the bell had rung 3 times. There they were each halted by the sight of a single leg emerging from the sumac. They breathed slowly and let their arms fall down limp by their sides, a line of 10 children in front of a bony leg sticking up out of a bush, the sock rumpled up about the ankle, no shoe, and above them all, in the window, the eleventh child ringing the bell on and on for fear of admitting the newfound silence. The clear bell sang high into the air until it was stopped by Samantha's distinct voice asking them to please lower the racket, her head hurt.

The next morning at 6, Samantha started down the road to the priest's house, her head down like a charging ram, 4 separate bandages across her face where the bushes had scratched her. And it was in the sacredness of a priest's kitchen that she asked for the first time when exactly a person was considered dead. For instance, would a person's body be considered dead if it had been seen not to move during the day for more than 7 months, not even to sneeze when a feather was carefully drawn under its nose, and yet each night it was witnessed by a reliable person to be standing in a completely separate building, in the house instead of the barn, in the reliable person's bedroom, seen to be standing by itself facing the window, breathing quite distinctly, audibly as the tide, never turning around, never facing away from the darkened view only it could perceive, never showing its face, its expression, instead waiting there with a back thin and upright as a board in order to lecture to the reliable person in a quiet human voice, a voice as patient as it had had in life, about how to raise a family of 11 children?

That very afternoon, the priest and 5 elders of the town walked up the driveway to the farm of your great great grandmother, the first of so many pilgrims to the house where 12 children under the age of 13 lived without a known father or a live mother but with only a miraculously non-deteriorating body for a caretaker, a mysterious unchanging body that began to draw a steady and fruitful income for these children and later on for the children of these children as they stood by the gate, taking in tickets and answering questions about how the canonization procedures were going now. All the children ruled over by Samantha, loyal Samantha, who each night turned into her room with a step less and less like a charging bull and more and more like a world-weary mule, Samantha carrying a single candle and a notebook into which she copied all the commandments (numbered and in duplicate) of her dead mother, whom she reported visited her each night wearing the same dress she wore in death in the barn, and with her work bonnet and apron tied neatly on as though death perhaps was a messy place that needed some real attention. Each morning Samantha posted a copy from the notebook for the children to read and sent the other copy straight on to what, within a few years, became the Papal committee. She had to do all this each night before she could finally sleep upon the living room couch, waking up only to make sure that everyone did wash behind their ears.

I remembered that once, when I was 7, my mom told me she'd been very horny at my age. Don't ask me why I was thinking about this now. Maybe it's just because Samantha would have really disapproved.

Mom said when she was 7, she'd had a crush on a man, and spent a while each day masturbating. She said even at the time she hadn't felt ashamed of this. She said that the world didn't believe little girls could or should feel sexual, but she knew they did. She told me this while she was kneading bread dough, pounding it down, twisting it and then pounding down again. Her arms floury up to the elbows. She stopped then for a moment to lean down toward me, her eyes at that age still above mine, and she stared into my face while she said she didn't want me to feel weird if I was also going through this. Her eyes motionless and focused on me.

Like I've said, Mom had power over people, people listened to her: Mrs. Holt, the grocery delivery boys sweating with adolescence and adoration whenever they got near her, the bingo ladies, and both Mrs. and Mr. Green. I saw the way they listened to her, the way they looked at her. The excuses they came up with in order to check in on her after work, to do favors for her. They shook their heads when discussing her, even in front of me. Perhaps especially in front of me. Your mother, they said to me many times, She's special. They loved discussing her. Take care of her, they said. I could tell when they went home they still thought about her, the way you think about someone you don't know all that well, someone whose sad story isn't your own, someone whose life you imagine with a sort of sensuous horror, a fascinated hunger.

After she left, ran away from home in her thirties, these neighbors came over 2 or 3 times when I was home on vacation from McManus. They said they were just checking up on me, making sure I was all right by myself, that I didn't need anything staying in the house without my mother, but quickly enough their questions moved on to what had happened, why she'd left and where she'd gone to. When she'd be back or if they could visit. I told them I didn't know where she was or when she might be back. I don't think they believed me.

Regardless, at this point they would switch the subject to reminiscences, to talking over details and memories of her, as if they were at her wake. They wanted to describe the way she walked and her so-white teeth, those crazy stories she told and her coconut *beijinhos*. It was as if they wanted to canonize her. They wanted to seal her in a glass coffin and leave her laid out in my living room. I would get stiller and stiffer with every word they said, every remembered detail, with their half-smiles and their hungry glances all around. Using my silence, my lack of hospitality, my palpable anger puddling there about their feet, I pushed them out, once, twice, 3 times. I pushed them out in an obvious enough way that after a while they didn't try so hard to come over. I pushed them out in a clear enough way that probably they didn't think it was such a strange thing anymore that my mother had abandoned me.

Anyway, that day my mom talked to me about masturbation, I didn't care that I didn't even know what the word meant or that I wouldn't be interested in it until so much later, later than most of the other girls, not until I was 16 or so and still breastless. I didn't care that once I figured out what she had been talking about, I would feel shame for not wanting to start sooner, as she had, as the girls in school had. I have always wanted so much to appear normal, to be average, to wear normal clothing and do normal things, to blend in so far as to be invisible.

When she first told me that all little girls needed masturbation, that I could do it, that it was ok—when she first asked me if I'd done it yet, I knew what she needed from me.

I nodded. I said yes.

Celia a few years after her wedding.

Canonization Committee, 1913.

Egbert just about to steal.

Chapter 11

I am tall. You will have guessed that by now. I haven't told you outright how tall yet because I've been enjoying what sort of image you might have of me, a bit taller than my mom certainly, but probably no more than 5'10", athletic; maybe even your vision includes a boyfriend I've been keeping secret. I imagine the way you've pictured me: honey-blond hair, weak chin, soft eyes, a boyish walk. I try to get that image clearly in focus.

I was 6'2" last time I measured myself. That was back when I was 15 years old. I don't know how much I might have grown since then.

Don't forget this was back in the 70s; the average height for a woman was 5'3". Each time I met a person back then, a potential friend or employer, each time I met a man, I noted with such clarity the person's surprise, then the way the face closed down.

(And in a way I must say I could understand. For a woman, yes, I was tall. Still, I'd like to add that no matter how often it happened, how often I saw another's surprise, it shocked me a little each time, that I should be judged so quickly, summarized.

That from just that one piece of information about me, my height—maybe also from how I stooped embarrassed under the great ambition of my body—from those meager details, all the people I met jerked their heads back, narrowed their gaze, looked as if they'd already gotten the gist, felt they understood, knew all they needed to, could tell others the pertinent facts of my life.)

Of course after they'd looked at me like that, when I did talk to them, my voice already had reserve in it, distance. If that's all they wanted to know about me, that's all they would know. I gave them nothing. Not even my smile.

Since my mother left, I'd been known in town as Stork just as much as by my proper name, Fran. I understood. It was because of my stoop-necked height, my folded arms. It was because of the way I stood there so still, staring.

The last time I measured myself was the winter after my mother left. Each new number had made me depressed for so long afterward: 6 foot, 6 foot 1, 6 foot 2. With each new inch I would stoop more. Sulk. My back hurt from the weight of my knowledge.

Without the measuring, at least I could stay 6'2" in my mind. In my mind at the top of my body.

My family doctor started all the official worry when I went in for my annual checkup at 13. I was already enrolled at McManus, it was spring vacation. I remember the moment so clearly. Really I was nothing more than a kid, still played with dolls, still had a child's face and hands—no breasts or hips, no weight, just height. The last year had been a doozie. I was very uncertain on my new long legs—a mass of skinned knees and barked shins. My feet so far below were always catching on thresholds and curbs. I was always falling over, a crumpling puzzle of knees and elbows, of stick-thin limbs and flailing hands.

So I walked into the doctor's office, concentrating on the walking, imagining the nap I would take later on. During the worst of my growth my whole body ached all the time, ached for sleep, ached to be laid down. I used to be able to fall asleep in a chair with my head only beginning to roll back from the upright position, the simple fact of breathing taking so much energy in this new oversized machine.

I want you to understand something. When you are growing that fast, adolescence is put off as something less than urgent, can be put off almost indefinitely. Until I was 17 and somewhere over 6 feet, my breasts hadn't grown a bit, my nipples hadn't even softened. My hips stayed narrow like a boy's. Even my face stayed unchanged up there, like a child's face on top of a ladder. I could see people wondering what age I was, this apparent 10-year-old who had been stretched. From the moment I first heard about Celia and her body's fast changes, I knew how she must have felt. I wanted to be able to talk to her. I thought we could have become friends.

So at the doctor's office, I remember stepping in so cautiously over the threshold, then looking up to see that the length of my new legs had taken me in too close to the doctor. He was standing just 2 feet away. I was taller than him now. I am rather good at judging heights (sort of uncanny at it, have been ever since I started really growing. I could guess people's heights sometimes more accurately than they could themselves, what with their wishful thinking. In a way people's self-estimates made me realize just about everyone is like me, a little unhappy with their height, in one direction or another). I'd say he was 5 foot 6 and ¾. Perhaps he was sensitive, felt manhood started at 5'7", wished each night fervently for that extra quarter of an inch. My eyes jumped to the small bald spot on the very top of his skull that I had not been able to see during last year's visit.

His lips tightened, and at this moment I believe I came to be defined as abnormal.

Within a week I was meeting with the experts. Perhaps if my family doctor had been a bit taller, if he hadn't started the whole official process, I would never have thought myself anything more than rather tall. Because of appointments with the experts I missed a lot of my afternoon soccer class that spring. My teammates already made fun of me for my concatenated canter down the field, my propensity to stumble and collapse if charged, so I didn't tell them or the teacher anything more than that I had appointments with a doctor. Let the word "doctor" build around me like the smell of tragedy. I had to work with what mystique I could get.

Toxins, the experts said, might have caused it. They did 3 CAT scans inside of a year. My head placed inside a metal donut. Keep still, they said again and again, Keep very still. Something inside the donut rolled small and fast, around and around my head. It whirred and clicked busily. They were looking for a possible tumor. There was talk of exploratory surgery. If I grew faster than an inch a month, if I grew over 6'4".

Sometime in there, around the worst of their talk, I just stopped going to them. It's not like I meant to. By this time I was 14. It was the fall. My mom had already left and the days passed differently without her. Even at school I felt all alone, the calendar less demanding. I saw the span of my life stretched out in front of me as elongated as my height. McManus and the experts' offices were all on the outskirts of Ottawa, within 25 kilometers of home. Each time I went into their offices, I had to make up a reason why my mother wasn't with me: P.T.A. meetings, interviewing tutors for me, a second honeymoon in Barbados with my dad. That fall, each time I returned to school I had to forge her signature on their documents. I got very good at it, practiced a lot. I have always been patient, repetition seems a comfort, tasks become something to concentrate on. After a while I couldn't tell myself which signatures on old checks were hers and which ones were mine. Still, I kept waiting for one of the adults to start pointing at me, pointing and yelling, comprehending my ruse.

So, at some point during winter vacation I missed an appointment, thinking it was on a Thursday when it was on a Wednesday. I realized my mistake Thursday morning. I didn't call immediately to reschedule.

It was amazing how quickly the doctors gave up trying to get me back to see them. They were supposed to be worried about my life, that I would die, my bones stretched out so far and thin they would shatter spontaneously with my weight. They were supposed to be worried about a tumor growing, pressing on the basic functions of my brain, against the site for breathing, or for my heart beating. 2 phonecalls and one postcard, these were all the experts' attempts at contacting me. Nothing more. I know. I waited by the phone. I checked the mail. I watched for a car to drive by. Instead all remained quiet, as quiet as it had been for months, as quiet as it had been since my mother left. Perhaps they thought I had moved to another province. I made excuses for them, created busy schedules, illnesses in their families. Now I think they must not have been able to imagine anything other than that I was going to another doctor. They could not imagine that I would just choose to stop the miracle of modern medicine.

Since then I haven't been back to the experts. Since then I haven't measured myself. 6 foot 2. I think by the time my mom started calling, I was probably taller than that. By then, to walk through the doorways of the old farmhouse I had to stoop slightly.

I was always alone in the house, except for the cats. They followed me from room to room. I fed them individually each night, in separate rooms. I closed them off one by one, one cat, one room, one bowl of food. I patted each one while it ate. I knew each cat alone in a room would eat slowly then, not eat more than it needed, not get indigestion. They would not compete for food or attention. They wouldn't have to wonder if I loved them. It did not take so much time from me, not very much energy. The books all said it was the best thing to do. I didn't know why more people didn't do it. I had the time.

I'd like to suggest that Samantha was lying. She was lying cleverly, this otherwise dull and literal child/woman who was only then realizing the enormity of the task before her.

Think of it. She was up against impossible odds. Either all her siblings and she would be dragged off to orphanages and foster families across the province, or they would starve to death on the farm the next winter because of their inexperience as farmers. For 2 weeks Samantha contemplated these alternatives, not sleeping well, not eating well, debating with herself until late at night. Each morning when she came out of her room, the children—her younger siblings—turned their hopeful faces toward her, looking for guidance. Looking at her to be both mother and father. And each day she spent more time in the barn, examining the only parent she had ever known, a body who refused to act like a normal dead body, a body who Samantha could only fervently wish was not really dead, who was perhaps in what Samantha had heard described once as a coma. Wasn't it possible her mother might arise one day, with no warning, to guide the family again, to tell them what to do? Samantha's list of chores for the family reflected such a desire, as she unconsciously began imitating her mother's speech patterns and nicknames.

And Samantha, perhaps, did not even lie. She went to sleep the night after she fell into the sumac bushes. She was exhausted. She was hurt and had bandages about her face and arms. She finally fell asleep after a week of endless worries, and to her tired confused flat mind came a slice of imagination, a dream, a vision, and in her delirium and inexperience with non-literal things she assumed it was reality. She assumed it was the spirit of her mother speaking directly to her. It was possible she continued to believe so, given the reinforcement of the priest and town elders the next afternoon, and the belief grew inside her, until each night as she bent her head down to pray, some portion of her mind began to speak to the other in the flat and factual voice of the mother she knew so well. Her internalized mother gently lifting the responsibility from her shoulders and telling her how to rule.

Mind you, I'm just exploring one option.

You're just saying that, I said, 'Cause you're pissed off at the Pope, 'cause you're disappointed in God.

There was a pause. Mom puffed thoughtfully on her cigar.

Sweetie, she said, When did you learn to be blunt?

I waited then. Began to get still, to shrink slightly into myself.

How old are you now? she asked, with her voice still considering anger.

19, I offered, my voice cautious.

Really, she said, honestly surprised. She laughed, 19, goodness. Her voice all light. She thought about it for a moment. Damn, she said, You're almost my age.

Well well well, she said, About the disappointment. I guess you're partly right. I used to have such hopes. Really, I guess I'd have to agree.

. . .

As a child my mother was raised a believing and dutiful Protestant. She had gone to church, she had prayed to God. She had known God was listening especially to her, watching her carefully. Even though she wasn't Catholic, she had thought of the Pope as a favorite older brother she just hadn't met yet. She had dreams in which the Virgin Mary fumbled open her bedroom door, holding out my mother's favorite breakfast cereal and still sobbing over the loss of her son.

Then my mother's mother, at the age of 29, died of an 8-pound tumor in her uterus. She had thought the tumor was a child. Now my mother hated everything religious in general, and the Pope in particular, with all the personal fervency that comes from childhood betrayal.

This afternoon, before my mom's phonecall, Roberta, the other woman who worked at the Wearhouse, had laughed at something a customer said, laughing close to him and surprised, as if she didn't normally laugh out loud like this.

Actually, she laughed this way several times a day, with each customer. Her eyes were warm and brown and seemed very genuine, yet sometimes I thought there was a lot that was secret behind them. Some part of her thinking about a whole different subject.

This afternoon she had laughed at the customer's joke so hard her whole face became longer, her brows moved up in surprise, her mouth stretched down. I wondered to myself if Celia laughs like that. Or laughed. Celia, I reminded myself, had been dead a long time. Still, I couldn't help imagining her alive. I thought she should have freckles like Roberta. Not big stagy freckles that you could see from across a room. No, just those faint speckles on the bridge of her nose and maybe her upper eyelids, small imperfections in her skin that made you look even closer.

Watching Roberta laugh, I took a step nearer to her and to her customer, tilted my head a bit to hear better, smiling. I had been standing about 5 feet away. They both jerked a little, toward me, surprised at the movement. Perhaps they had forgotten someone else was there. Noticed just the height and color of something tall to their right. Thought wood post, thought pillar or lamp.

My smile froze at their expressions. I caught a glimpse of myself in the mirror above them, long stooped neck, narrow face, lank hair. You'd think I would be used to my own reflection, I'd had years to adjust. Instead, seeing a mirror unexpectedly could make my head jerk with surprise.

I stepped back, turned away toward the display window. Worked at re-attaining invisibility.

My back hurts a lot, my knees. I take aspirin constantly.

Sometimes, in just the smallest of my steps, the most casual turn of my shoulders—to pick up a bag, to open a cupboard—something in my body creaks, a tendon, a joint, something makes a crackling sound. This happens to me sometimes even now in my late 30s. Back then, when I was 19 and still growing, it happened all the time. Then, as now, I would feel things shift, there would be a pop, maybe 2, like a badly-rigged ship sailing full on into a storm. Even now, each time, after a noise like that, I freeze. I wait for the escalating mechanical failure, the crumpling of my legs, the jolt of agony rolling up my back, the fall. I wait for my body to finally be true to the gravity it has been defying for so long.

This is what ultimately happens to most exceptionally tall

people, so the doctors told me, so my reading confirmed. They don't live long, their joints collapse, their organs, their hearts finally stutter from trying to pump too much too far uphill. Like badly-bred dogs, they get hip dysplasia and have circulation problems; they lie around panting on pain relievers, their eyes half-closed, focused inward. Robert Wadlow, the tallest man ever, lived only to 22. The tallest woman, Zeng Jinlian, had scoliosis of the spine so she could not sit up straight. I picture her lying back in bed, only her eyes moving free of pain. Her whole adult life she was no taller than the pillows propped up beneath her head. Measured horizontally, from foot to head, she was 8'1" when she died, tired out from growth.

I waited for this. I wait for it still. I knew my heart was designed for the average 5'3" woman, as were my knees, my spine. Honestly I wasn't, I didn't think, taller than 6'4". I didn't believe so. I didn't believe I was into the freak realm as the doctors defined it, although I wasn't sure. I wasn't brave enough to measure myself, to find out. Without the knowledge I was happier.

Without the knowledge however, I still lived like a freak.

I hoped that by living shallowly, barely, by living on the farm I had once been short in, my body would last longer, would remember how to move and function as a normal person's, would function as my body used to so perfectly when I was a child, short and compact as a cabbage, a little round bear with my sturdy limbs. So long ago. I hoped if I stayed here near the furniture that my body knew so well, doing the same chores, in the same house, things would go ok for me. Like keeping fragile crystal in the box it was bought in: you can't really use it but it's less likely to get broken.

I kept working at the store I had started working in. I did the same actions over and over again, every day, so there were no surprises.

. . .

Well, said my mom, Good night dear. Maybe tomorrow you can tell me a few more things about myself. I could surely use some wisdom these days.

I paused for a moment, looking down at the floor.

Good night, I said, Mom.

Chapter 12

Last year, traces of PCBs and other toxins were found contaminating the drinking water in this area. We were advised to buy drinking water, to not take long showers. Some parents even bathed their children in bottled water.

Some experts believed the poisons came from the American Dow Chemical plant, a recent spill directly into the lake or one of its tributaries. Others said the contamination came from the old tannery that had been closed since the 20s, a mixture of the tannery acids and the third-party corporate dumping that had occurred since then. It is true the land by the old tannery used to be littered with rusted-through metal barrels lying about on their sides. The scientists said if the toxins did come from the tannery land, they could have appeared any time in the last 20 years, soaking for decades through stone and soil toward the ground water. The water in my house came through old pipes. Turn on the pipes and there was a loud thumping, a sense of something subterranean. After a pause the water poured out silent and silvery as a Quebec stream. It had always tasted coppery, metallic, had the slightest smell of mold and rocks. Nothing like the city's over-purified water.

My whole neighborhood might have grown up on PCBs, been weaned on the chemical, cooked in it, bathed in it, made Kool-Aid with it, used it in children's tea parties. We could all be used to the taste, even prefer it, believing toxins to be the taste of purity, of fresh country water.

PCBs could be the reason I am tall. A small tumor on the pituitary gland and suddenly the body doesn't know when to stop, doesn't know how to say no.

Of course, the water might have nothing to do with my height. The doctors never did locate a tumor. The water might have been clean throughout my childhood, only recently become polluted. Most often we have no idea of the forces and interactions of our own plots. We can only look at the points when we finally noticed things had changed; we can only fill in backwards with motivations, events and clear unwavering decisions.

In the last few years the old tannery has been fixed up, made into a museum for school kids. I went once on my day off. I thought I'd visit the possible source for my height. The museum wasn't big: just 3 echoing rooms, poster-size photos hung up next to engraved placards describing over-simplified relationships in short sentences. Photos of fur traders, Indians and lieutenant governors standing stiffly in front of towering stacks of furs. In the background, rows of sinewy pale cadavers stretched out along the ground like they were still crawling away, only their paws left furry.

There were pictures of large vats of dingy liquids and men with handlebar mustaches stirring with wooden paddles and leather aprons. The men looked broad-chested and burly, eyes that stared out of time with a glittering intensity. They leaned in over the chemicals, seemingly quite healthy.

Of course, it could be that genetics accounted for my height. The doctors had asked me during my first visit to them—clipboards and pens at the ready—how tall my relatives were.

I told them, quite honestly, that the only family members I'd ever met were my mother and father, and both of them had been, quite clearly, on the short side.

And before you start doubting this next part, said my mother, I will tell you that I learned it in 2 ways. First, from asking questions of Anita. She wasn't chatty, always busy cooking for her store, but she would answer direct questions, on any subject in the world. Saw no need for privacy. Was too busy for it.

She was, declared my mother, The kind of obstinate person who—given a second chance to live life over—wouldn't change anything, not even her marriage. There was nothing I ever heard her admit she regretted.

The rest I found out through Cessil's diaries, Mom said. They were left in his room after his death. Still right on the shelf above his bed, dusty and waiting. 4 books in all, leather covers, the paper inside real thin like the stuff Bibles are printed on. The first book had been warped from the sea or fording a river, or maybe from falling in a bathtub. They were all bound together with a ribbon tied in a bow. The books covered his time on the sea and in Brazil and that first year of marriage to Anita. After that the entries got more intermittent. Maybe he got busy with family. Maybe he got out of practice.

There was a note, said my mom, Attached in his handwriting. You know, the kind of loopy lots-of-time penmanship everyone seemed to have back then. Written with the kind of pen that came well before Bic ballpoints, the kind of pen you stuck in an inkwell and filled with ink by pulling up on the little handle.

The note said these books were the property of Cessil Rilke Mourne and should not be read while the sky still clung to the earth.

I've xeroxed some of the key passages, my mom said. I'll try to remember to send them on up to you.

Cessil had always imagined that a marriage needed some place civilized to grow, so after the wedding he moved Anita from Rio de Janeiro to Fort Lauderdale.

There was no more explanation of the event than that.

At the time Fort Lauderdale was nothing more than a trading post for the mixed-race offspring of the Seminole Indians and runaway slaves who had hidden out in the bayou. The East Coast railroad had arrived only 4 years earlier. There were still free land packages for anyone who could be persuaded to settle there. No canals, no malls or air conditioning, no cars, no motorboats. No drunken sophomore classes flying down from Minnesota for spring break. Only the dark night, the swamp and its smells, the sound of mosquitoes rising toward you, an alligator coughing and the sound of something big out there settling deeper into the mud. There were bayou panthers then, what are called swamp screamers, hundreds of them crying late at night in the dark, sad and lost as babies. Less than a century ago.

If Cessil had been trying to make his fortune, there were few towns in the U.S. that would grow as quickly and dramatically over the next 30 years as Fort Lauderdale.

If instead he was really trying for civilization, for culture, for a staid and scholastic place to raise a family, there wasn't much in the U.S. that was worse.

Within Fort Lauderdale, Anita moved Cessil right into a house in the center of the trading. She required the bustle, the noise of the area, the continuous and varied voices floating up to their window. There was always bargaining, different pitches, accents and languages, people singing their wares out loud and hearty. Even at 10 at night she knew she could look out the window and see one last determined Indian and white trying to work out a trade over a basket of 2-day-old fish and what the white euphemistically called "lightly-used" blankets. At these times Anita would fiercely suck in lungfuls of the humid air of the market, the flavors of fresh bread, roasting lamb, urine and rotting cabbage. Deep in her blood she could feel this place would grow and grow quickly. Anita was born for this district and she knew it.

In her sweeping ecstacy, she even truly believed she loved her sleeping husband, such a new and big lump in her bed, the quiet and intensely handsome man who had appeared at the right time in her life, knowing hard enough for both of them that he loved her. He whom arguments and fast Portuguese boggled so that he tucked his head down at her first loud sentence and he simply started nodding, nodding emphatically and confused at whatever it was she was saying. Her will winning every time.

Quickly she negotiated her own shop to sell Brazilian pastries, candies and breads, and before the first week was through she had learned enough English and Seminole to insist hers was the best. She never let even a cocado be bought without an argument, and only allowed Cessil to be alone in the store when she was working out an important business deal or in labor with one of the babies.

The few times Cessil was left in charge of the store, he ate so much of the merchandise that frequently there was nothing left for the customers to buy. He stood in the back of the store with his hands in a tray of beijinhos as he looked out at the people passing. He ate mechanically. He found, now that he was here, he did not like all these people or the bayou. He missed the Brazilian jungle and hated Anita's customers because they scared him. He nervously waited for them to enter and look at him, the simple shocked intensity in their *eyes as they first saw him. This look they gave him was enough to make him push his hands into his pockets and his head forward into a nod that continued like a tic, no matter what was said. He would keep his eyes away from the women's stares and even more from the men's. He would hold his breath, forget to bargain at all. And when no one else was in the store and he was mercifully alone, the tension of the waiting filled him and he opened and closed his jaws methodically about the candies as he thought about the way a jaguar's yowl echoed in the dripping Amazon after a rain.*

Cessil still worked for the railroads, but now it was behind a desk in the railroad's southernmost Florida office. He shuffled thin sheets of paper about, which always got caught in his fingers or fluttered away. He'd chase the paper across the office, a large man feeling ridiculous. When his boss asked him his opinion, all the words in his possession would fly from his being and he would look at his hands with their 2 missing fingers and think about the way he had negotiated in the jungle. Each year he watched younger men get promoted above him, and after the second year running the store, his wife told him to keep his salary to play with, she would take care of the rest.

And after that second year, he began to take up with women on the side. Not such amazing women anymore, for he was no longer the man he used to be. His belly was no longer hard and compact like a potbellied stove. Keep in mind, people aged more quickly back then. People died younger. The age of 20 was a time of responsibility, of marriage and commitments. 30 was middle-aged, kids in school, worries about health. Cessil was 28. Since the start of the store and the end of hiking through the jungle, his belly had begun to alter its composition, softening, swelling up with sugar and milk and Anita's peanut cakes, so his belly was now wide and jelly-like and swayed when he walked. It surged down his chest and over his belt and spilled outward toward the floor, farther each day, so by the end of the second year he had to have his wife button up his pants and the bottom part of his shirt in the morning, and unbutton them again at night. His face, his strong twisted face, was getting buried and diluted under pounds of flesh, so his eyes looked out from under cliffs of white dough. By the end of the second year in Florida, he had changed so much that aside from his eyes—his imprisoned handsome eyes that tracked each movement of a customer's hands and mouth with the same speed and wariness that had kept him alive in the jungle—he no longer appeared to be the same man at all. He was relieved, for with each new pound he gained, more people left him alone.

Every morning he woke up from dreams of the rich sensuality of the jungle to his wife poking her finger into the flesh of his chest, using her pokes as a determined alarm clock. His diminutive wife with no bust or hips to speak of, a cigar always clenched in one fist, and a voice that clipped out words like a cookie cutter. His wife with the light fleshy scent of a true woman.

So he took up with women whom he had to pay. He went regularly to each of the 3 Seminole prostitutes in town, searching for the feeling of power he had gotten from those other women in Brazil. And with the prostitutes also, he held his breath for so long, he could feel his heart swell within his chest until it had pasted itself up against his ribs and begun to sweep them in and out with its rhythm like fear.

Anita barely noticed that her husband's weight had just about doubled. She was busy with the discovery of the high of money and of bargaining, and her heart was blind to all else. For the few minutes each day she was not working within her store—cleaning, cooking, selling, bargaining, and insulting—she stomped around town looking for rich and powerful people. Whenever she found one, she'd poke the person in the chest like a friend, and give advice in the short broken English that rolled off her tongue with the subtlety of rocks. And because Fort Lauderdale, indeed all of Florida, was growing so quickly in the midst of its land rush, it seemed as though each day there was a new powerful person in town to accost.

She stopped Jerrard Ives while he was walking to his mahogany-inlaid touring sulky. She looked him over and told him kindly, Florida not England. Make yourself sick you keep wearing all that sweaty tweed.

She told María Lopez in the week after María's annual charity dinner, feeding a meal to the poor is good; spend less on wine for all the journalists, you serve more food.

She advised Mayor Richards, You get elected easy, your daughter Tracy stop taking things from every store in town.

The townspeople loved this advice and her cigar so much that many of her walks through town became small impromptu parades.

Within 4 years of her arrival, she was the best-known character in the county, within 8 years the best-loved personality in the state. Once women got the vote in 1919, the only thing that stopped her from running for public office was her store, which by then had become so successful in the midst of the Florida land boom that the exact number of her staff was a mystery to everyone but herself.

Anita became pregnant the first year they were in Fort Lauderdale. Cessil and Anita both looked forward to their child's birth as the start of what they assumed marriage was all about. Anita started suggesting names for the child months beforehand and Cessil nodded, simply nodded at whatever she said.

The child was born at the Pompano General, the closest real hospital to Fort Lauderdale. The child was a boy and his mouth was already open on the way out. As he was pulled away from his mother, he shoved a red and pruney fist into his face at all the goop there, at all the lights cutting at his eyes, at all the abruptly noisy life around him. There was the unmistakable expression of rage twisting his tiny

old man face while he opened his mouth wide in a magnificent series
of shrieks that overwhelmed every sound in the room, that interrupted even the nurse who was way down the hall at the front desk,
for she thought the sound was a newly arriving ambulance. Shrieks
that came out even before he had breathed in, powered purely from
the will within his lungs.

This first son continued to live in just that manner. When he
wished for something, he wished for it with all his strength and being,
with more power than seemed possible. When he fought, when he ate,
when he loved and later on, when he spoke, he did so as strongly and
as effectively as he could, and life for him was an unrolling ball of
adventures, each trailing string woven of ultimate goods and evils.

Both Anita and Cessil took one look at him and loved him down
to his furiously kicking toes, for his spirit could bring out an equal
amount of love or hate within others, and his life in the dullest of circumstances was destined to be an adventure of unstoppable terror
and beauty.

Anita named him Semper.

The second baby came when Anita's shop was busier. It was a day
before Easter, a holiday the Seminoles celebrated solely for its sweets,
and even Anita could not keep the coconut pears, little-boys'-feet and
maiden's-drool in stock. She was running back and forth with the rest
of the staff, from the kitchen taking candies out, to the counter where
she was dickering with the crowd of customers for the price. In the
same moment she had gotten the highest price ever paid in all of
Florida for any tray of sweets and 3 more pans' worth were burning
on the stove, in the same moment that the hot flame of money and success was just placed within her hands, she felt the first birth pang. It
was a small pinching cramp that worked its way up her back like a
paralysis. It filled her soul with an irritation, a cheapness at the waste

of good food and money. It brought her lips together as though she had bit into a lemon.

This was the expression imprinted on the face of their new child, also a son. His birth was slow and miserly, and the bundle, when it finally emerged, came ass first. Thus the size of his genitals was the first thing anyone saw of the boy, and the genitals were the only thing not miserly about him. The doctor and nurses were struck just look-ing at that wattle of flesh between his pale peddling legs and missed the way his eyes opened, looking about, clearly surprised. Then his thin mouth sucked his first lungful of air in and began a tentative watery wail that the front desk nurse down the hall didn't hear at all until the baby was wheeled by in his bassinet just 3 feet away. Some-how, though, his cry lingered for so long after he had gone around the corner, she crossed herself twice for the sense of slow and icy fore-boding that tickled up her back.

This, their second son, they named Victor.

The manner of the 2 sons' births never left them the whole of their lives. Semper was not pretty, especially when compared to his younger brother. Even at the age of 8, Semper's face had to be called craggy, with only those bright blue eyes to save him. Big eyes, colored with the moodiness of the ocean. And he did horribly at school also, failing the first grade for 3 years in a row because he had been born with such an innate understanding of the brevity of life that he found it almost impossible to sit still or stand with both his feet beneath him. He would not listen to you unless you somehow really caught his attention and then he would go so still, listening, looking at you so hard it was like love or rage or a brain hemorrhage. His first-grade teacher hated him with all the considerable hatred a grade-school teacher is sometimes capable of. She had many good reasons: he was a disturbance to the other children, different, frequently disobedient.

She told him he was "bad" and "stupid" in private and used words like "incorrigible" around his parents. She raised the possibility of retardation.

In the midst of all this, of adults speaking slower when they addressed him, of his parents hugging him inexplicably at strange times, of his teacher smiling at him with victory in her eyes, Semper began his lifelong fascination with family, partly brought about by a first-grade assignment to draw a family tree. Of course, he got to do this project each time he went through the first grade, and by the third time through he had traced his family as far as his mother's second cousin who had once been struck by ball lightning and forever after that did not dare to stand fully upright out in the open. Semper had learned the name and dates and accomplishments of every person in the family his parents could remember. He learned about Anita's grandfather, second mate on the boat that had discovered the Southern Shetland Islands, just north of Antarctica, the boat which then turned around and left those barren rocky islands just as it had found them. He learned about Anita's great aunt who had helped to sew the wedding dress of Princess Amelia of Brazil, Anita's great aunt working specifically on the lushly embroidered pieces that were never seen by the public. He learned about Anita's deceased siblings, 2 who died of the measles, 2 of polio and one of something Anita called a very bad headache.

Unfortunately, of course, Semper could learn nothing about his father's family aside from the names and ages of Cessil's 12 younger siblings. Cessil would make no guesses about the identity of his father. He knew nothing about his mother's family or her exact age or where she had lived before the farm. This frustrated Semper completely, for he could already recite all the names and ages of the 9 aunts and uncles (both living and dead) of his mother with one breath. It was at this young age that the understanding began to burn within Semper's heart that a person's family was what one sprang from, was all that grounded one in this world, gave one identity and loyalty and a reason for living. He understood that family was the one thing at which one could ever really fail.

And after the third year, when his teacher finally released him reluctantly on to second grade (which she taught also), he obediently flunked that too, for he knew by now what was expected of him. Afterward, in spite of all his parents' attempts to prevent it—for Cessil and Anita thought that to ensure a decent career back then one should complete at least fifth grade—Semper dropped out of school for the rest of his life.

He spent his time off from work at his mother's store wandering around the neighborhood, talking to strangers and acting like the honorary grownup he figured he was. Then at the age of 12 he discovered the Spanish Mafia, which was starting to infiltrate Fort Lauderdale from Miami. For the Mafia, one needed no type of . diploma even from grade school, and the Mafia, like Semper, had a highly-developed respect for family. Semper decided he had found his calling. At that time the Spanish underworld was intent, ambitious and lively. It would get even more so during Prohibition, when the town would be nicknamed Fort Liquordale. Members of the Mafia would become some of the most wanted criminals in the state and also a significant percentage of the police force. The Mafia would become the unofficial insurance company, a slightly fickle bank and the only reliable garbage collection service all rolled up in one. It would own every restaurant, all the gambling casinos and racetracks, and 2 out of 3 of the state's major grocery store chains. As all that, the Mafia would soon hold quite a sway. Already they were beginning to feel the promise in the area.

Unfortunately, instead of trying to work his way up the ladder of the hierarchy beginning to establish itself—for Semper had never been the kind of kid who joined other people's games—he set about becoming an entrepreneur. The people in the area who knew what

Semper was getting involved in assumed it would be 2 weeks, on the outside, before he turned up on a major thoroughfare in several pieces with a warning for others pinned to whatever was left of his shirt. However, it was instead a full year before the Mafia could believe it was really this 13-year-old boy with an old man's face who was working their territory. And it was another month after that before Semper's meatloaf exploded one night during dinner. Meatloaf had been Anita's favorite meal to cook (up until this night), for she thought it was the most quintessentially American dish, a dish that showed clearly what a smooth transition she had made to living in North America. She made the loaf with annatto and malagueta peppers and served it with a side of ahí sauce. This meatloaf she had cooked in the store downstairs with all the customers coming in and out, just as she had cooked every family meal for 14 years; the whole family eating standing up around the counter, passing newly purchased loaves of bread to the customers over their salad and fei-joada, *handing back the change. Any one of about 40 people could have booby-trapped the meat as it lay on the counter cooling.*

From that day on Anita wouldn't make meatloaf anymore, wouldn't leave her family's food in front of even house guests, wouldn't trust any of her customers to do more than slip her their money across the counter.

The meatloaf exploded during the very start of the meal, blowing up half of Anita's working kitchen and store, as well as the current batch of cookies, so that the partially-cooked dough was blown sizzling into the rafters intermixed with the meatloaf. Afterward, the kitchen always retained that peculiar smell of meat and chocolate, which was particularly strong on humid days (which as you can guess in Fort Lauderdale was well over 70% of the year).

Luckily none of the family or customers were hurt, for they had all stepped into the street to see the 2 hissing swamp sloths that Antonio, the third son, had dragged over by their hind legs. Way back then there were a fair number of sloths in town, swinging their way slow as octogenarians from the branches of the trees to the gutters of the houses, hanging from their long-clawed toes, regarding people through their dining room windows with an expression of such disinterest that looking back into their upside-down humanoid faces was like returning the stare of an ancestor long dead. The 50-pound sloths, as calm and disdainful as if their vertices were correct and it was humans who were mistaken, tended to pull the gutters off the buildings with their weight, their expression changing not one bit as they fell with an extended screech of ripping metal into a pile of copper piping and bloody fur.

So these 2 sloths had just fallen from the house on the corner, in the midst of what they had been up to and, to their utter mortification as well as evidently a bit of pain, were not able to disengage their hind parts. In the spirit of Christian generosity, as well as scientific enterprise, all 5 boys were debating whether to yank the front legs of one sloth and the hind legs of the other, or to simply try to lever them off each other by slipping something in between the animals at the critical junction, like say a crowbar. They were all arguing this out, the boys and the rest of the family, as well as some of the more helpful store customers, when back in the kitchen the meatloaf exploded.

There was a bright and soundless flash that ballooned out, glittering into the night with glass and fire, billowing out into their vision, taking up the street and the dark and everything any of them had ever seen or heard or imagined, swirling it all together into light and heat. Distantly, after all this, rolled the sound so late and unimportant now it was like someone else very far away screaming.

And then it was gone, just like that, silence, darkness. Some smoke left, a little shrapnel of plates and silverware tinkling down onto the ground. Anita, the boys, Cessil, the customers were left standing there, hands limp by their sides, staring upwards, missing it. Even the sloths rolled their slow eyes up toward all the commotion. Every-

one gazing upwards except for Carlos, the fourth son, who'd been hit during the explosion in the back of the head by a loaf of Anita's pumpernickel. He had been hit so hard he was flat out unconscious on the sidewalk—unable to, once he awoke, remember anything from the entire year of second grade.

Thus, Semper, at the age of 13, moved out of the house that very night and into what quickly became an all-out war with the Mafia. There was not a small number of deaths on both sides, but Semper could always tell his mother honestly he had never witnessed a murder. He could say this partly because, like all successful managers, he quickly learned to delegate, and, partly, because the few times it was necessary for things to be otherwise, he had the involuntary and uncontrollable reflex to gunfire of closing his eyes.

So, except for once a year, no one in the family saw Semper again for over a decade after the kitchen explosion. On that annual visit he'd come to the family at night, appearing in the dark, moving from bedroom to bedroom, pronouncing each name (even the children who were born after he left, because away from the family he used his network to stay informed). He gave every person a single sentence of advice about the private intricacies of their lives, often addressing situations that they thought no one else knew about. He kissed them each on their mouths—both males and females—and handed them a bar of solid gold, while 3 men followed behind him, their guns sweeping all about, following their coldly-attentive looks.

It was Semper who with his single sentence of yearly advice arranged the blind dates that resulted in marriages for 4 out of 7 of his brothers, blind dates with loquacious strong-willed women who got nervous at too much silence, women who married the whole family and its noisy house as much as any one particular brother.

It was Semper who informed his mother, Anita, about the buy-out option for her competitor, Goodie Cookies, and who handed her the necessary cash to complete the transaction.

A House Named Brazil

It was Semper who declared his father should go to the doctor because he probably had gout.

And when Semper was 29, at the end of Prohibition, he returned home for good in the first car the family had ever seen up close, a Dusenberg. He was rich and fat, wearing white camel-hair suits all day long even in the heat of Florida, and the entirety of his life contained only 2 topics of conversation and their corollaries. The first topic was how a family has to look after its own, so they should all come to him with their problems no matter how complex or personal. The second thing Semper liked to talk about was the fact that he had learned his grandmother's life was being investigated as a prerequisite to canonization; the Pope himself had drafted a memo on the state of the procedures. Semper felt that because of this saint in the family, everything he did or had done was, in the bigger scheme of things, ok.

Victor, on the other hand, turned out to be a good student, a great student. He was popular and good-looking, resembling Cessil when he was younger, only Victor was slim, less bulky in the body and the lips, his streamlined build perfectly reflecting changing world tastes at the end of an age of seemingly-endless discoveries of new untouched land masses, at the end of monarchies and grand excesses. Victor grew up into an age of increasingly accurate maps and timetables, public knowledge of political leaders' lesser moments; the fascism of time-management studies and the profit margin. The age of life insurance and vinyl-siding salesmen. Victor ate less than his father, he made sure to exercise daily and he wore a watch from his tenth birthday on.

In grade school Victor had skipped 2 grades and his teachers loved him. He was the uncontested swimming champion for a year in junior high, until, in the spring, the bump in his bathing suit began to descend into a lump and then a bulge. The girls in the highschool sud-

denly began to attend the swimming classes held out by the lake, standing there giggling and blushing and staring outright. In high-school he was president of his class 2 years running.

Yes, Victor was everything he should be, and each night at dinner he told of his accomplishments in a modest and factual manner, his parents turning their bland open eyes on his face and saying repeat-edly, Yes yes, we are proud. And each evening before bed, in the years while Semper still lived at home, his mother cut off Victor's announce-ments in order to brush out the long dark locks of her eldest son, her hand on Semper's forehead gentle with love.

(The next day at school Victor would work even harder to be the sort of student any mother would love.)

There were so many possible reasons for the difference in how the first 2 sons were treated by their parents. There was the manner of their births, and Semper was the firstborn. Semper wasn't pretty or classroom-smart, and a mother's love is frequently given to the needi-est. There was the way Victor looked so much like his father as a youth, which might have made each of his parents uncomfortable in different ways. There was the tightness of Victor's lips, and something more than that, something more basic that was odd about Victor's face. No one could quite put words to it, but perhaps it was his reac-tions to the world over time. It was something noticed only by those who knew him for years; all of the relatives commented on it when they were asked about him later. They said his face seemed just the slightest bit distant even when he was looking right at you, like he was focusing on the dilation of your pupil instead of your eyes, on the surface of your skin instead of your expression. They said he was beautiful in a marble kind of way. They said his reactions were the tiniest bit slowed down, as though what came naturally to others—assumptions of what was right to do in a situation and what was wrong—for him had to be thought out.

Who knows if they were saying this only in retrospect?

. . .

Pictures of Victor arrived the next day. When the postman dropped off the package, he weighed it first within his hand, looking up at the farm. I didn't usually get much mail. Before Mom started calling I would get one or 2 bills a month, the check from her lawyers and that was about it. I sometimes didn't check the mailbox for a week, maybe more.

This postman was relatively new, lived over in Navan, hadn't grown up on stories of this place and my mother. The farm wasn't much to look at by this point. The fields were not planted anymore. The house was grey and deserted-looking, the ivy gone wild on the south wall and roof, the front porch edging farther each week into the frost-heaves crater, the back of the porch broken off entirely from the house. On the whole landscape of the farm, the peacocks were the only things still moving. There were 4 of them left. They got to their feet at the first sight of the mailman, their shimmering heads rising to their full height, then weaving from side to side. Their wide eyes did not blink. The dominant male, Cessie, snaked his head slowly forward, low to the ground, opened his beak and cried, Wah wah, just like a cat in heat or a baby fussing. Their tails rose with the forbidding rattle of quills.

The mailman put the package in the mailbox gingerly and retreated, his face turned over his shoulder to keep the peacocks in sight.

This time the postmark on the package said Bangor, Maine. She was moving closer, less than 1,000 miles away now.

I was startled that I'd been right, that she was getting closer, actually coming home to me. I pictured her in Maine now, in a down vest and long johns, the kind with the button flap on the backside. She was stirring chicken noodle soup, putting the spoon down occasionally to blow warm air into her cupped hands. The fire in the potbellied stove popped and settled. Out the window could be seen her beat-up Plymouth lit up in the cold spring light of Maine. She would be here soon. A week, I thought, maybe 2. I pictured how I would stand while she stepped out of the car, while she walked slowly up the driveway. I thought I might just stand silently near the front door, my arms folded across my chest, my chin up, staring her down. Or maybe I would try being seated in the living room, visible through the window, not even interested, my eyes turned off in some other direction entirely.

Feeling the victory of the moment, I looked Victor's pictures over slowly, savoring them while sitting on the back porch, the porch that was still mostly horizontal. Victor in family gatherings, Victor in the Princeton yearbook, Victor at the Columbia School of Chemistry. As a grown man during his wedding party at home just before he left for Europe on his honeymoon, he was standing in front of the group that made up my family. It was a beautiful Florida morning. One could see the promise in that morning even in the ancient black-and-white crinkled photograph. There were 2 herons rowing laboriously across the upper right-hand corner, wingtips raised to a blinding white.

Victor was facing the camera, raising a champagne flute to his lips, his features so perfectly balanced. I stared at the 40-year-old picture. He was handsome. Even by today's high standards of health, advertising and airbrushing, his face and body were definitely handsome. He looked a fair amount like the man you had fuzzily imagined during childhood as Prince Charming, your imagination perhaps not filling in all the details of a real human who farted and blushed and got zits. Your imagination giving the face instead only that idealized forehead, those *uber*-cheekbones. His face was grinning a many-toothed smile.

I looked at his lips, concentrated on them. So much had been said about them. It was hard to tell in such a small photo. Perhaps his lips, even in this wide-open smile, on what was one of the happiest days of his life, were a little tight, a little narrow, one could say cheap. Especially given the perfection of the rest of his face. I pictured the young women meeting him at socials, the introductions of him as the swimming champion, a Princeton senior, first-year chemistry grad student. They look, seeing a beautiful face, a hard chest and belly. He fit his clothes well, one of those people whom clothes took shape on. He was smart, well-spoken. It was obvious from all he managed to do with his life that he could speak convincingly.

He was educated, American, familiar, but the women eye his hair, his hair curly and thick and so dark, whispering dangerously, sexually, of Brazil.

I pictured the women who loved him, the men who trusted him, the few who felt cold in his presence. I wondered if he joked, what his laugh was like. I used a magnifying glass and got lost within the flat black-and-white shapes that recreated his 3-dimensional face. I wandered among them, mentally subtracting an edge from this one, adding a softer line to that one, trying to change things. They and a few other colorless bits of celluloid and paper were all that remained of the 5 foot 11, 165-pound man who was my great uncle and who catapulted himself to a brief and violent fame across the western world for crimes committed against humanity.

Fighting twins, 1899.

Anita's photo for her certificate of naturalization.

Semper (far left) and some of his business associates.

Mourne Family Tree

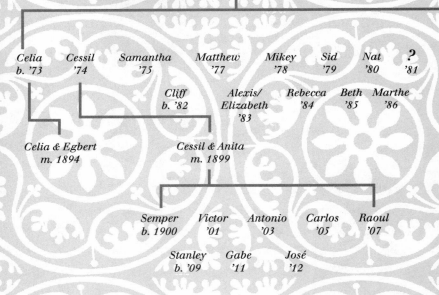

Great Great Grandmother & **?**
b. 1855   d. 1887

Celia   Cessil   Samantha   Matthew   Mikey   Sid   Nat   **?**
b. '73   '74   '75   '77   '78   '79   '80   '81

                          Cliff   Alexis/   Rebecca   Beth   Marthe
                          b. '82   Elizabeth   '84   '85   '86
                                          '83

Celia & Egbert   Cessil & Anita
m. 1894   m. 1899

              Semper   Victor   Antonio   Carlos   Raoul
              b. 1900   '01   '03   '05   '07

              Stanley   Gabe   José
              b. '09   '11   '12

Chapter 13

I didn't have a boyfriend. You have probably guessed that. Though of course it is true, until sometime before my eighteenth birthday, I had never really wanted one. I mean, at McManus sometimes I had said I wanted one, but that was just because all the girls were saying they wanted one and I always wanted so much to be one of the girls, indistinguishable.

Maybe, in the last year or so, since I reached 18, my growth had finally slowed, allowing me energy for other things. Perhaps it was only adolescence arriving when it got around to it. Not everyone goes by the same clock.

Over the last year I had found myself going to the grocery store more than I needed to, every 2 or 3 days, talking to Mrs. Holt while her son, Ned, packed my bags. He'd been in my grade at McManus, was 5 feet 10 inches tall. Well, almost 5'10". Actually, I'd put him at 5'9" and ½, and as I said, I can make pretty accurate guesses about height. The hair on the top of his head formed tight curls. Shiny curls. I realized the day after looking at Victor's photos, Ned's hair was a little like Victor's. The rest of Ned's features seemed evenly-shaped, except for his nose, which might have been a bit strong. I'm not really sure. I tried never to look at him straight on. I made him up of glimpses from the blurred periphery.

Let me be clear about this. I did not imagine he would start talking to me, that we would ever laugh together, hold hands. I did not dream one day he would crane up his head and I would lean down so we could kiss. The most I ever realistically dared hope is that when someone else mentioned my name, he might stop them from saying anything bad. He might say, Hey, she's ok, she buys groceries at my mom's place.

I just needed someone to think about, to wonder about. The ability to wonder is a muscle that needs to be exercised or it dies, just like any other muscle. I exercised this muscle religiously even though I knew I didn't have a chance with Ned. Perhaps that made the exercise all the more strenuous, effective.

He wasn't as noisy as most of the other boys in town. I thought that might mean he was gentle. Once I'd seen him at the age of 15 playing jacks all by himself out behind the library, hunched in concentration over the girls' game.

This morning a new package from Mom arrived. The postmark read Wichita, Kansas.

I realized with a shock that it had been sent the same day as Victor's photos, the ones which had come from Maine. I ran to get the envelope for the photos, laid the 2 packages side by side, looked from one postmark to the other. I remembered again my mother's vast facility for stubbornness, for duplicity. For some reason I did not feel a lot of surprise.

Yes, it might take more than a week or 2 to get her back to the farm, to me. Still, I thought, she was calling me nightly. I would reel her in. I had always been patient, had learned the skill very young.

This was something I was willing to spend some time on.

In this new package were Cessil's binoculars, the ones he had used on the whaling ship and in Brazil. I did some calculations. They were at least 80 years old, more than 4 times my age. These binoculars had travelled to the southern hemisphere, landed in many ports, maybe Oslo, Tahiti, New York. I had never been more than 50 miles from this farm where I had been born.

The binoculars' case smelled sweet with leather and old wood. The case was the brown of a dog's gleaming eyes, and the curve of its side had the feel of a thin woman's hip, smooth and functional. I drew the top strap open, and the leather did not crack. Many of the things on this farm were old, but somehow these binoculars seemed older. They seemed more than just secondhand, from another time. Mysteriously placed here whole and untouched.

In the letter that came with the binoculars, my mother told me not to clean or oil the case. She said she had done so once and for a few weeks it had smelled of soap and lemons, of kitchen tiles and bathrooms. It took a long time for Cessil's binoculars, with all they know and had seen, to return.

Looking at that letter, I realized I'd forgotten her penmanship, crooked and halting, leaning alternately to the left and to the right. For such a confident woman, I thought, her handwriting could break your heart.

Honey, continued the letter, I'm giving you these binoculars as an early inheritance. Something to have after I'm gone. Something with which to remember your family and me, something to remind you of the stories.

My mother had always been obsessed with death. With *her*

death. Perhaps it was her own mother dying so young, still in her twenties. Mom believed it was a sin to get really old, incapable, your sleeping habits and bowel movements becoming major topics of discussion. As my mom neared her late twenties, I remember her so well, noting down on the calendar the slightest headache, plucking at moles on her skin and pushing against any loose teeth. Each time she brushed her hair she would clean the brush afterward to see how much had fallen out. Still, I was sure she would never die young, her body was much too well made for that. Even when she got up to get the thermometer, it was with a muscular grace and jounce. But I also noticed that when she believed herself sick—when she tried to read the thermometer, when she was concentrated like that, examining the signs— these were the only times her face was really relaxed, her mouth falling open, slack as a child's.

Like my mother, her family had also believed she would die young. My mother always said, when she died, they would descend upon her house like vultures, reclaiming everything she had taken with her when she left for her honeymoon so many years before. She and her family all thought a lot about her death, imagined the funeral, picked out what they would wear. I knew they called her every Christmas just to check on her health. They never inquired about me. They tried not to acknowledge my existence, had a hard enough time with the fact that *she* was still alive. They had been so sure that, away from the family she loved so much, she would die in fairly short order. She had believed it too, believing it like in the fairy tales where the princess dies from a broken heart. Still, my mother's strong well-made body persisted, inhaling, exhaling, heart beating on, getting hungry, cooking, eating.

The inside lining of the binoculars case was pretty much worn away. I thought my great grandfather must have forded a few streams with the water sloshing about inside, tugging and eddying, the case taking weeks to dry in the humidity of the jungle. The lining only remained along the edges, small tattered bits of white silk printed with a beige fleur-de-lis pattern. Perhaps these were the original colors.

When I drew out the binoculars themselves, I could see at the bottom of the case a single feathery leaf, transparent as a piece of peeled skin, affixed to the bare wood. From Brazil, Florida, Ottawa? I could not identify the kind of plant just from the leaf's transparent skeleton. My hands felt large and clumsy. I held the case as gently as glass, using just the tips of my fingers.

I felt like I was holding history here in my hands. All of history, from the Bible on up.

I could smell the inside of the case better now without the binoculars in the way. Wood, leather and lint, the pine-scented floor wax my mother had always favored. Smelling the floor wax made me smile. It made me remember being 3 feet tall and watching my mother buff the floor, her elbow stuck far out and her mouth twisting around with each hard scrub of her hand.

I brought my face in closer to the case. I barely breathed. There were more smells here, things I did not recognize. The fast-growing mold of the tropics and unfamiliar cooking spices. Gradually I rested my forehead and cheeks against the edge, entrusting my face to the dark of the case, the shadow of the leather, so old, so foreign. I tried to ignore what I probably would look like if anyone were watching me, hunched over like a lamppost. I did not suck the air in, but just let it circulate passively through my nose and slightly-open mouth, taking its time, letting the subtleties develop, the distinctions.

I must admit I had fought some of my mother's stories, found them overstated, thought them unlikely. Now, with these binoculars here in my hands, I found myself thinking about things the other way around, having seen Victor's photos, Egbert's publicity slide.

How much, I began to ask myself, was true?

With my face still in the case, I smelled the clear breath of trees and the rank heat of animals. I smelled human sweat and loamy earth, canvas travel bags and horses' bridles, the sharp report of gunfire. I heard the wet clap of the bullet, the slap of fear, and life full and short and furious. I heard monkeys hooting and macaws screeching and pure white butterflies large as kites fluttering down toward the richness of any motionless animal product, be it a body or feces. I smelled the heart of a southern continent I had never visited, the size and power of the life my great grandfather had walked through, step by step, league by league.

I blinked, took the case away from my face, stepped over to the door. 3 of the cats were lined up on the kitchen counter staring at me. I ignored them, hefted the binoculars instead, glass and metal, up in my hand, facing out to the fields behind the house. These binoculars and the case were the only things I had of Cessil. They were just about the only things of his that anyone had. These 4 pounds, this smell. These were the sum total of his life.

I held the binoculars up to my face, put my eyes to where my great grandfather's had gone, fit my nose into the area where his had been, cupped my hands around his life. I swivelled the eyepieces out to fit my head, opened my eyes and saw the size of the life my great grandfather had lived.

In their last few years together, Celia and Egbert were happier than they had ever been.

Oh good, I said. Celia again.

My mother sighed.

They had money and fame, and since Egbert had turned himself in for amnesty, they also had lawfulness. To the alien societies of wealth and show business that they now travelled within, they reacted with bemused delight.

Egbert was a natural ham and the fame he achieved on the stage brought out all the pretty philosophizing and eloquent turns of phrase he had always meant to shower upon those women he had tried to flirt with in grocery stores or at baseball games. The Great War was underway, and Egbert would steal gun belts off Germanic-looking extras, would sneak bombs off women dressed in Turkish flags. The crowd loved him. They would applaud and applaud. Egbert would bow, graciously, seductively, lusting for more. He came off the glare of the stage each night with a high pink glow to his cheeks, searching desperately for Celia. She would take one look at him and they would run off to the first home they had ever owned, the home in the first town they had ever felt safe enough to live in for more than 2 weeks at a time, the home they had bought just like a normal couple, a normal couple who lived well within the law. They would run off after each show, hand in hand, cutting the autographs short, and just within the door of their home they fell on each other with the open mouths of babes. 2 pale aging bodies tousling upon the front hall rug with the same shamelessness and strength they had had upon their first meeting, magnified now by almost 3 decades of love and understanding.

Celia saw that the promise that she had felt when she was a mere 13 years old had finally been fulfilled. As a reward for her life of successful crime, she dressed and re-dressed 5 or 6 times a day, changing her clothes for breakfast, a walk, lunch, tea, the evening meal, a party at the Crumley-Norwells'. She wore silk, taffeta and lamé, had her hair tossed high, and each morning applied a facial made of avocados and yak's butter.

With each new outfit she wore, Celia's desire to show herself off to her siblings grew hotter within her quite substantial breast. And after the second year of high society, fame and new dresses, Celia felt it was time to act on this desire. She took Egbert, 3 of her best Parisian gowns and her chinchilla coat, and rode by train from Boston back to that lonely house in eastern Ontario. In her hands she clutched tickets for the return trip home the next morning. The whole trip she sat by the open window and looked into the distance with a sharp absorbed gaze, her face strangely younger in the growing chill of the air that poured in through the window. Egbert sat beside her, uncomfortable, touching only the edge of her hand, wondering what Celia had in store for them and why she carried her Colt .45 in the purse on her lap rather than tucked away in her thigh holster.

They arrived on a cold winter night. The air was laden with the sharp taste of an oncoming storm. The date was almost exactly 30 years from the night Celia had crawled out the downstairs window with a broken rib and toe, and a mild concussion. 30 years since Celia had spoken to her family, even once.

Because of the darkness of the evening, or perhaps the single-mindedness of Celia's stride, they did not see the signs as they stepped in the front gate. The price of admission went unnoticed, as did the sign-up sheets for the petition for canonization.

And Celia, out of a complete appreciation for the complexity and size of the great circle she had been travelling all her life, or perhaps in fear at this last moment of her upcoming family reunion, headed first for the quiet barn of her childhood. She moved across the yard with long sweeping steps, an apparition gliding across the scene of the crime that had been committed against her long ago. Egbert followed, small and nervous. After a moment outside in the moonlight, listening to the sleepy clucks of the chickens in the shed, she stepped into the barn to stand among the stalls with one hand to her collarbone. Egbert closed the door behind them without a word.

She stood there with her eyes closed, listening to the warm shuffle of the horses in their stalls and the placid grind of the cows, smelling again the rich aromas of the Canadian farm, the hay and horses, musty dogs and wood, the smell of leather weathered by both sun and rain, the wet metallic taste of long-term snow in the air. And then Celia's face became clouded. An unexpected smell was coming to her and it was only with the greatest of difficulty that she recognized—in the tail end of winter—the heavy velvet scent of lilacs.

She stepped back a bit and turned her nose to the east and then to the west. Pausing there, she opened her eyes slowly to see, by the illumination of the night light left on for the horses, those wide carpeted stairs where there used to be just a peg and board ladder, those wide stairs rounded by the weight of so many feet. Sniffing again, Celia began to ascend the stairs. With the greatest of grace, she maneuvered her large and tightly-corseted body up toward the loft, which she had not seen since she was 14 years old. At the top, the sweet smell was overwhelming, almost tactile, pressing against Celia in the dark. At her entrance, a sound also began. This sound started so low and rose so smoothly, continuous as the very buzz of life, that Celia wasn't even completely sure of its existence.

She fumbled back along the wall until she touched the flashlight that had replaced the hurricane lamp and matches which had been there when she was a child. Egbert, ascending the stairs behind her, heard the crisp snap of the switch. There was a flare of light so bright and close that Celia was momentarily blinded. While her eyes blinked and returned to normal, she played the light over the walls.

By this time Egbert had made out the body and the signs above it. With a quick instinctive understanding born from the speed of horror, *he reached forward to stop his wife, but she was already gone, already stepping forward with a slow measured tred toward the sleeping body she saw in the flashlight's beam. With her first step she could see it more clearly, a small person, perhaps even a child, no hips, quite thin, wearing an older-style dress and some type of cap or bonnet. Celia stepped forward again toward the bundle lying there as if deep exhaustion and the powerful sweep of sleep had just knocked her over onto her back with her hands half-extended, reaching out for the ground.*

Celia stepped forward then that third time. She heard more clearly now the buzz of life rising as a sort of hazy power within the air. This was the moment when the body abruptly coalesced before her eyes and Celia stood in front of her sleeping mother, dead these 30 years. Her mother, small and thin and exhausted in the barn where she had worked her body into a deep sleep caring for 14 small children. A single gasp escaped Celia and the air she exhaled was so deep it must have released the pressure which held her up, for her knees buckled beneath her and she started to fall down toward the body. As she fell, she reached out one hand toward her mother's face; she did not know why, perhaps to wake her. The flashlight in her other hand descended with Celia, making detail more obvious: color, texture, that increasingly familiar dress. The light blazed across the body's forehead with an unreal shine, over the stiff limbs, skated across those long-ago hands, and it was all too fast for Celia. She still reached out for the side of that almost plastic face.

Her hand came down firmly on the waxed sheen of what so many years ago had been her mother's cheek. The flesh not any more giving than the side of a milk carton.

Egbert watched Celia stand up and walk by him, her pupils black with horror.

She flowed down the stairs and across the yard to the front door of the farmhouse; from inside the house came the sounds and lights of a large, noisy family sitting down to dinner. Celia knocked 3 times hard with the butt of her .45. The first knock quieted all inside. The next 2 knocks echoed in a silence that was almost peaceful.

Inside, the family that trustingly stood up was slowed only by a slight confusion at who could be calling so late. They could not have suspected the answer even in their wildest dreams. For 30 years the 12 remaining siblings had not mentioned Celia's name, had not alluded to her. They had not even crossed out her name in the family Bible because they would've had to admit there was a name to cross out. Instead the Bible had simply been misplaced. So time had passed and the 12 original siblings, with their artificial innocence, had added to the family the actual innocence of 9 spouses and 17 new children. Thus it was that 38 people now stepped, with the simple curiosity of country folk, toward the door.

It was Samantha who opened the door, she who had been but 12 those 30 years ago. Samantha's face was middle-aged and a little compressed from her constant constipation. Instead of being chinless, she now had the start of 3 chins, which hung from the bottom of her lips like a turkey's wattles. Each night she cried with the irony of it all. Her body was the iron-thin of the close-to-old, and already she had a hump within her back, the hump which in later years would fold her over farther each day, until the only things she could see were the ankles of her nieces and nephews, whom she slapped routinely for their dirty socks. During this time her face, so inconveniently lowered, was never seen clearly and fully by another human eye, though her nieces and nephews all told stories to each other about its various deformities and protrusions. When she died in 1962, the undertaker finally broke flat the small crooked body which had not lain straight for over 20 years. Then every mourner who passed her open casket was startled by the soft and hidden beauty of her contentment.

For now, the 2 sisters stared at each other. Nothing was said. Celia pushed her roughly aside, Egbert following uncertainly, and

Samantha was left still facing the direction of the open door, a confused and awkward expression on her face as if she were wondering about an unexplained smell.

Celia swept into the front hall to stand there looking one by one at the countenances of each of her siblings, ignoring the strangers. One by one the faces of her siblings went blank and their hearts were filled with a sudden dread as they looked upon the regal figure of this city woman with her cold expression of complete hatred. After a moment the woman swept off her chinchilla coat, revealing a glittering dress few had even dreamed of. And as they were all involved in staring at that dress, with eyes that squinted as though against the sun, she pulled out from somewhere in the furs, with the light rustle of silk and perfume, a long dull gun that sucked all the light, as well as the rest of the fading ignorance, from the hall.

Celia held the gun loosely in her right hand, gesturing with it to the back of the house. When she spoke, it was so quietly that at any other time, from any other person, with any other implement in her hand, her family would have ignored her, thinking she was speaking only to herself. Yet, under the circumstances, her four words echoed brilliantly in the close air of that moment.

Get the others out, she whispered.

Her siblings, watching Celia with something similar to the attention that they had given her that winter so long ago, pushed all the newcomers out, creating not much more than the creeping noise one makes on early Sunday mornings. Perhaps the only thing that made all the indignant spouses and curious children leave—aside from the gun—was the stubborn and silent front of the 12 siblings, clearly united as though they had done this all before.

The kitchen door swung shut behind the last of the outsiders, leaving only Celia, her siblings and Egbert together in the hall.

Celia stood, every eye in the hall on her. She held her coat out

*with her left hand and shook it a little impatiently. When Matthew,
the second eldest brother, stepped jerkily toward her like a sleep-
walker, reaching out to take the furs, she dropped that loaded gun
toward his head, aiming directly at the hollow at the top of his nose,
aiming with a speed and smoothness that only comes from great
determination. She levered back the hook of the safety, the oiled click
reverberating within the house. Celia turned then to aim with the precision of a machine at each of the 11 other brothers' and sisters' faces
in turn, standing not 10 feet from the farthest of them, the dark indent
of the barrel swelling up within their silent vision until it contained
their entire world.*

*When Celia again faced Matthew, they all watched soundlessly
as her finger began to tighten.*

*This was the point when, from outside, came the small squeak-
ing tramp of purposeful feet through the snow. The sound swirled in
clearly and distinctly with the cold air through the slightly open door.*

*And even though they hadn't heard that exact sound in 30 years,
every face within that hall except Egbert's turned like a loyal dog's at
the recognition of the rhythm of those small harsh feet stomping in
from the barn. They stood staring at the open crack of the door with
their mouths slack as caught children, and not a breath was taken as
they all waited. The expression on every face was a perfect mixture of
longing and guilt.*

*The sounds outside clumped their angry weight up onto the wood
of the porch steps. They skipped every other stair, just as they'd done
in life, because they'd never had the time to do it otherwise. All 13 children could now hear the rustle of that dress being grabbed and hiked
out of the way for the last furious steps to the door.*

And then the footsteps faded.

Faded just like that, as though they had never been.

Still, the siblings all waited for a full minute, heads cocked and eyes narrowed. Only after that full minute did the 13 middle-aged brothers and sisters turn back to one another in a hall made abruptly quite a bit smaller.

Celia, with the petulance of a child, slapped her fist against her hip and, without any satisfaction at all, shot the hall mirror that contained the image of them all. The thunderous crash of the bullet into glass and wood deafened everyone so they heard no more impossible footsteps from outside (then or ever again). All they could do was gaze at the 1,000 twirling lights and colors puffing out into a glittering cloud that twinkled down about their astonished faces to bounce soundlessly upon the floor. The bullet left behind a hole in the side of the house like a wound, and that whole night the snow twirled through it to whisper smoothly down upon its own reflection in the broken glass.

Celia held the discharged gun casually within her hand for the rest of the evening, hugging her siblings to her hard and with love, allowing them to stroke her furs and remark on her dress. Later, she and Egbert sat down to supper with them and their new families, all of them catching up on the years that had passed.

It was the finest evening in Celia's life.

I went to sleep this night with my knees by my chest and 2 cats draped across my hip and waist. I went to sleep this night thinking of the roughly-patched hole in the wall of the hallway, the one I had always intended to repair better than with just a 2 × 6 nailed across it. I understood the hole's cause for the first time. It seemed amazing to me that the last of the siblings had left more than 5 decades ago.

This night I had my first dream about them, about Celia and Cessil, Anita and Egbert, Samantha and Victor, about Semper and all the rest of the 14 original children, complete with their innumerable procreating descendants. I saw them from where I lay in one of their tiny horsehair high-board beds in the Canadian farmhouse where I had been born and lived my entire life, where so many of them had been born and grown up also.

In my dream they all came home. They entered one at a time through the front door downstairs, laughing and calling, hanging up their coats and hats, racing each other up the stairs, jostling along the hall, pushing and clawing for room as they poured into my bedroom, me mysteriously so small, curled up in the tiny bed, each of them larger than life, bending their heads and jerking in their elbows to fit through the door, fighting for room and air. They pushed in about my bed and it jerked with each one of their inadvertent taps. More and more people pushed into the room. The bed began to shake and wobble, to turn and gyrate with the mass of people pushing about it. I tried to move, thinking that maybe in the confusion I could escape, but I felt even smaller now, weak, the heavy blankets and purring cats holding down my arms and legs so even my breath came out in tiny uncertain gasps.

My head lolled over in terror, my eyes wide, and that was when I saw *her* step in the door. Her, the mother of them all. I did not understand how she fit into the room. I knew it could not be managed by humans, but there she stood in the bedroom, taller than the house itself, her head touching the clouds, her back straight as the pine trees. She stood before my bed, all her descendants quieting without a word. And her face started to shift, to turn, to look down on me, at her weakest newest child, at this wishy-washy creature scared of all that lay beyond the outskirts of an empty ancient farm. The brilliant harshness of her expression carried as much power as a blow.

I woke up on the floor with the wind knocked out of me.

The 2 cats looked down from the edge of the bed with expressions of bland surprise. I held my limbs up into the air, inspecting them with worry. For the first time ever I was glad to see their span and girth. Once again, size and power was mine. For the rest of the night I locked the cats out and lay nestled tight against the protective solidity of the wall with my head completely under the covers, trying hard not to dream fearful scenes of history like a drug.

Chapter 14

What was strange about my mom calling every day—talking with her every day after all this time—was the conversations didn't have the effect I had always assumed regular contact with my mom would have. The sound of my mother's voice didn't make me blissfully happy all the time. Sometimes it made me furious, a lot of the times it made me sad.

The main thing that happened was that I didn't have to work so hard to hold onto the memories all by myself. Both the good ones and the bad.

At work I stood against the back wall of the Wearhouse each morning and watched people walking outside. I watched them closely. Their height, their weight, how they moved their hips into their stride. I wondered who they went home to at night. Sometimes now I took a step closer to catch a detail of their clothing or their smile. I stepped toward the window.

I had begun to sit on the john in my house a lot. The one on the second floor. It was a big house. I knew how many people used to

live here. Now that I thought about it, I could feel the old busy
life of it in the creak of the floor and the bend of the walls. For
the last few years, inside these rooms, it had been just me and
the cats.

I had begun to sit on the john in this house because the bathroom was a room in which I was *supposed* to be alone. The only
room. I could sit in here and listen to the creaks of the house,
pretend many people were here. That there was a whole impatient line of them just outside in the hall waiting for the bathroom, that they were also in the kitchen making lunch and in
the living room reading, out on the back porch laughing and in
their bedrooms napping. I could imagine a game of touch foot-
ball out on the back field, the field that blossomed thick with
blueberries in late summer, blueberries perfect for someone to
make jams and pies with. In the years I had lived here, only an
occasional bear wandered through, dipping its head down
through the bushes as if it were drinking.

I sat on the john, my pants down about my bony ankles,
looking at the toilet paper. I could sit here for hours. Although
the only life I could really hear in the house was Minnie meow-
ing just outside the door, I smiled the whole time.

*Cessil and Anita had 9 children in all. They were all sons except for
the final child. This girl was born 6 years after the next eldest, born
during the last year of World War I, conceived close enough to one of
Cessil's shore leaves that there were not too many eyebrows raised.*

*This baby might have been conceived from the last of the erotic
energy that the aging Cessil possessed, just before his swaying obesity
became so great that no woman could physically get hold of anything
to get erotic with. Or perhaps the baby was conceived of an infidelity,*

one quick strike back at the man who made regular trips to the poorer section of town, trips Anita had guessed about since the beginning. Maybe Anita made love with a bright and beautiful young man, not much older than her eldest sons, a quiet and blushing young wanderer with blond wispy curls that he brushed back from his face during awkward moments with a thin-wristed gesture very close to art. A man-boy who appeared in the house above the bakery shop one morning in late April and who disappeared before the week was out with everything he could carry, including all the brass doorknobs so the doors swung open and closed with every draft, and many things were revealed that should not have been.

You never asked her? I asked.

I had to say it 3 times before my mother would stop talking. I had to say it rather loud. I was sort of surprised at myself, but this seemed important. Hey hey, I said. You never asked her?

There was that silence.

Did you say something? asked my mother finally, her voice icy.

You never asked her if she slept with the blond kid?

No, said my mother, I didn't ask my grandmother if she broke her marriage vows. Does that surprise you?

Well, I said.

Well, I said, Frankly yes. You read all of Cessil's private diaries about prostitutes and how women smelled to him. You talk to Great Aunt Celia about the intimate details of her sex life, and you ask Anita many private questions about her marriage and preferences between her sons. Why do you draw the line at this?

My mother did not respond. I could see her considering putting the receiver back down in its cradle, silent and so stern. To stop talking to me entirely for a day or 2. It was how she would have reacted when I was a child, it was how she would have reacted when these phonecalls began. I waited for it, could see her looking out at the night thinking, weighing the consequences of various actions.

And this was perhaps the first moment I knew something was changing, that I really knew instead of just suspected.

For instead of hanging up, she continued with her story.

The girl child was named Anna. She was blond and throughout her life she winced at loud noises as though her skin was subject to vibrations most people could only hear. Her earliest memory was a dream about what snow must feel like, numb and wet upon the face, making only the slightest shifting sound as if the air itself was falling. She dreamed of the snow falling down on ice and glaciers and on her, the cold building up as subtle as time. And since that first dream she promised herself she would live somewhere in Canada under deep snow, where it was so cold that the few faraway noises would only emphasize the silence that had been preserved for 1,000 years.

She was never able to appreciate or even understand her older brothers. The 6 children who followed Semper and Victor had turned out to be a simple noise-loving bunch, healthy active boys who loved to hold arguments from different rooms so yelling filled the house and the window panes shook. These 6 boys laughed like basking seals and they lay all the time in the sun and the heat of Fort Lauderdale singing songs with a bass power until sweat soaked the blankets they lay on and their dark pretty eyes cried with the salt of it. These 6 boys had so much fun making noise and not listening to others that in later life they found themselves continuously stunned into good-natured disbelief at the surprising range of other people's actions.

In every family picture I have ever seen, the 6 boys are standing together in a crowd. They are the crowd. 6 of them, even-faced, even-

tempered and they are shaking their heads, waving their drinks, sheepish with incomprehension. They became old men quickly and talked a lot about how things used to be.

Anna's voice was never loud. It was small and soft as the clasp of a seabird's foot, a bird who roosted lightly if at all. Throughout her childhood her brothers didn't even hear what she said, but were always asking, "What? What? What'd she say?" over her head and inventing their own answers. Creating their sister without much concern for the reality. They made up her wishes, her thoughts, her feelings, like the time she developed a crush on the highschool rugby coach who all the brothers rather admired.

One day Anna (having been thinking lately about the relationship of her mother and father) asked her brothers why men and women got married. The brothers, red-faced and with hanging heads, explained their cleaned-up version of sex without once looking at her so they never saw her expression of utter disgust at their belabored ramblings of blooming flowers and tidal waves.

Needless to say, the brothers were completely stunned the day she ran away. She had been so happy, they said, so content.

It was from her brothers' volume that her whisper picked up a slightly harsh quality, a bit like a person with laryngitis trying to shout, a learned tension. And whenever she looked at her large brothers, her face filled with a silent frustration as if she were a visitor from France preparing to ask for directions.

Yes, it is clear that the events leading up to the day Anna finally ran away were in motion from the time she was born. Looking back on it all, it is so clear. I can see how it would happen, how it had to happen. I can trace out the straight and crushing force of time upon events, the tracks leading from the birth of Anna into a family of dark-haired boisterous boys, the tracks leading straight to my own birth.

A House Named Brazil

Really, the events were in motion even before Anna's birth, even before the arrival of the blond waif.

3 years before Anna's birth, during the height of the U.S.'s advertising budget for World War I, the power of Uncle Sam Wanting You, Cessil got nostalgic about the shipboard adventures of his youth and somehow talked himself into the Navy. True, there was a world war on and they were looking for almost anyone, but Cessil was an obese 40-year-old man, a man who weighed so much that even the effort of sitting upright made him breathe loud and raspy. Later on, Cessil told his sons his job on board the ship was as a munitions expert, but Anita said he had just been a prep cook and a bad one at that. He was still in the Navy the year Anna was born, and it was that year, 1918, that Cessil's boat stopped in Montreal and Cessil went with 2 buddies to see the old farmhouse where he had been born.

Then when he returned from the war, he sat his whole family down at the diningroom table (excepting of course Semper, who was still in hiding) in order to tell them the triumphant news. With a grin as wide as his quite wide face, he told them how on the last shore leave he had been reunited with his 12 younger siblings. He told them about the surprise and joy of that reunion, that baby Marthe was a grown woman, that Samantha had 3 chins and Matthew had 4 children. Cessil told his family that in 9 months, once his siblings' families could settle all their many and varied affairs (such as finding someone to run the shrine and the farm in their absence), all 38 of his relatives would be moving down to live with them in Fort Lauderdale. Yes, he announced, he was going to move them all, his children, wife, siblings, etc., out to a huge house he would build for them on 47 acres of swamp by the back end of town. He had bought the land today with the complete savings from Anita's shop.

It was true, he said. He had taken all her money out from their joint account that morning and given it to the farmer, who agreed it

*was quite the surprise. Cessil concluded in his breathy gasping voice
that he hoped Anita was pleased.*

*Like so many things in history, his complex unspoken motives
will have to remain a mystery. Perhaps he had heard rumors of Anita
and the pretty blond boy, and he was angry. Or this could have been
an attempt at revenge on Anita for her success with her store. Perhaps
it was simply a burst of post-war euphoria, or even long-overdue sib-
ling affection. We can only imagine his smile at the end of his speech.
We can only wonder.*

*Cessil tilted his head into his smile, looking across the din-
ingroom table, across his 7 present sons and one daughter to Anita.
There was a pause. Everyone slowly turned to look at her. No one
knew if she had slept with the little blond waif or not, and if she
regretted whichever decision it had been. Now her neck began to
darken and a vein pounded visibly on her temple. Anita opened her
mouth. She seemed confused. Finally her voice emerged. It coughed
once like an old engine and then began to scream. Her mouth became
a dark enormous cavern from which her anger poured out. Her
abuse, thickened with disgust, rolled across the table and the heads of
the 8 children, in a weighty mixture of Portuguese and English. It
shocked everyone there in that room and burdened their souls. It
threatened, it insulted, it swore.*

Idiot, Anita screamed, Craven asshole! Rasgarei teu fígado den-
tro teu corpo vivo. *Dolt, dummy! What were you thinking?* Porco!
We will get the money back. You will give the land back. Picado!
Fatso!

*All 6 younger boys started arguing, waving their arms and
yelling, "Wait a minute. Now, wait just a cotton-picking minute."
Newborn Anna began to cry at all the noise, her breath catching, her
red fists clenched. Victor quietly moved his chair out to the hall, from
which he could see the whole thing in perspective. And Cessil, my
grandfather (he who in the almost 2 decades in which he had been*

married to his small and domineering wife had never done anything without her expressed permission, aside from sleeping with prostitutes and eating whole trays of candies; he who had never argued with her or even talked back; he who was always nodding his head emphatically, quickly, without his own will at whatever she said), still did not speak a word in argument. He just moved in response. He rolled his hands around in aimless brittle gestures, his left eye wandered. His mouth jerked about in half-smiles.

And he shook his head No over and over again with such determination his jowls swung.

After that things changed.

Cessil got his wish. His relatives moved down from Canada after 9 months into the skeleton of a house being built to hold them all, to hold all Cessil's 12 siblings, their 9 spouses, and what was now their 19 children, as well as Cessil, Anita and their 7 sons and one baby daughter. And the house was destined never to be finished, for just before a room could be done, before all the wires plugged in or the toilet moved to its final spot, another baby would be born or started, another child married or another couple broke up, and the workers would have to move on to the next, more pressing priority. The section left the way it was, the wires hanging like confetti and the toilet in the center of the room like a throne. The house was built and built and continued to be built by Cessil and the boys and the relatives until it backed off into the swamp behind them, uncurling like a snake, its body uneven, unfinished, always growing, the sounds of hammers, the smell of paint, voices cursing.

Yes, a small town was built upon the land that Cessil had bought with Anita's money, and it was a lopsided, unfinished town filled with so many many people that few of them were certain of everyone else's names. The spirit of the whole place was that of a constant party.

And the house Cessil named Brazil.

But although Cessil had been granted his wish, like being tossed some small consolation toy, Anita was the one who actually won the argument. It happened that night after Cessil had announced the buying of the swamp. It happened after those 2 long minutes during which her mouth had poured out that furious cauldron of Portuguese and English insults.

Abruptly, Anita went silent. She exhaled.

And in that moment after she exhaled, her mouth smoothly closed and her face went all flat. This was the first moment when her children felt real fear.

Every one of them turned to stare at her, all of them falling silent also. None of them could remember her ever being at a loss for words. They watched her stand, draw herself up to her full 4 feet 9 inches of height. She strode quickly, firmly around the diningroom table, around her many children, up to Cessil's beachball belly, to jab her finger twice deep into the softness over his sternum, as she declared in her imminently Roman Catholic way, JAB The marriage is JAB annulled.

Mom, why are you calling?

What?

How many times do I have to ask? Why are you calling me, telling me these stories? Why now?

There was a pause while she considered my question. I heard her scraping with a spatula against something metal. There was a slight echo to her work. Perhaps she was cleaning the inside of the oven.

Dear, she said into the echo, Let's just say that to tell you why would be skipping ahead in the plot.

For a brief moment I imagined again her returning, not just her, but the whole family arriving in cars and vans and on motorcycles, a curling honking caravan of gypsies. Our restless generations had perpetually moved south and north and then south again, always searching for something just one step removed from here, from now. I could picture the jeeps and mopeds and trailers pulling in. The dust rising and the neighbors' dogs barking. I imagined myself standing there on the doorstep, mouth ajar, hands slack by my sides, while all those vehicles rocked to a stop. Then, across the caravan—the whole string of 20 or 30 vehicles, even a small school bus in the back— doors began to open, people running out toward me.

The next afternoon I took my first long walk. Normally I drove into town, walked slowly when at home or at work, one hand at all times on the wall or stair railings. Even when I walked in this way, holding on, I still listened for things inside my body straining or cracking.

I took the walk in the middle of the day, Cessil's binoculars slung over my shoulder. I walked outside, up toward the woods. I walked cautiously, but still I walked. My knees popped occasionally, my hips creaked. I'm not sure why I went this day, why I brought the binoculars along. I was feeling restless and couldn't seem to quiet down. Perhaps sitting still, next to the phone, listening to my mom each night made me want to stretch my legs during the day. And I thought I might as well bring the binoculars. I thought I might want to look at something far away. I thought if someone saw me walking, the binoculars would give my stride a look of purpose.

This afternoon I walked up the back pasture and across the hill, past the old maple-sugaring hut and into the forest. I went a fair amount farther than I had ever gone, found a rock high up the hill from which I could see clear to the water tower by town.

I stood there for the longest time.

Mourne Family Tree

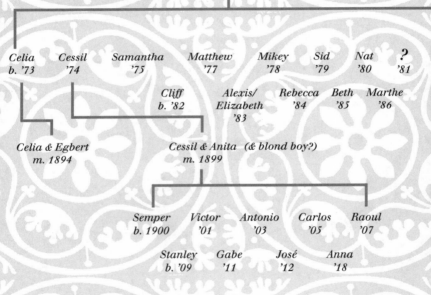

Great Great Grandmother & **?**
b. 1855 d. 1887

Celia	*Cessil*	*Samantha*	*Matthew*	*Mikey*	*Sid*	*Nat*	**?**
b. '73	*'74*	*'75*	*'77*	*'78*	*'79*	*'80*	*'81*

Cliff	*Alexis/*	*Rebecca*	*Beth* *Marthe*
b. '82	*Elizabeth*	*'84*	*'85* *'86*
	'83		

Celia & Egbert   *Cessil & Anita   (& blond boy?)*
m. 1894   *m. 1899*

Semper	*Victor*	*Antonio*	*Carlos*	*Raoul*
b. 1900	*'01*	*'03*	*'05*	*'07*

Stanley	*Gabe*	*José*	*Anna*
b. '09	*'11*	*'12*	*'18*

Chapter 15

After the walk I was a little sore, but just along my hips and the backs of my thighs. Nothing hurt so terribly. That surprised me a little bit. Sitting in the kitchen, waiting for Mom's phonecall, I found myself clenching the muscle of one calf experimentally. I swirled the foot around, in every direction, testing.

The calf was just tired, nothing more.

I stood up, clenched every muscle in the thigh also, then in the other leg. Clenched the muscles as hard as I could. I was fine, nothing wrong. No strange clicks or the feel of anything starting to rip deep inside.

So I tried stretching. I swung my arms wide about in their sockets, every which way. I rolled my head all the way round, trying to touch my ears to my shoulders. I bent over, keeping my knees straight, to get as close as I could to touching my toes, about halfway down my calves. Standing up, I breathed for a moment. Still nothing wrong. So I put one heel in my hand and held my foot up high in the air while trying to straighten the knee. Of course I couldn't, but also nothing gave. There was just a bit of soreness and my hips popped once.

As irrational as it sounds, I was a little irritated.

After long enough, you get so used to a set of rules it doesn't matter what the rules are, or how bad they are. You come to expect that world, get used to it. The limitations begin to feel comfortable, homey. Any change seems unfair. I felt a strong desire to keep stretching until something snapped.

The phone rang. I picked up fast. It was 6 o'clock exactly.

Mom, I said without waiting for her to speak.

Mom, I declared, Do you know you can call me at times other than 6 in the evening?

I heard her pause, her surprise. I listened to it hard.

Then she decided to just ignore me.

Tonight we talk about how Anna left Florida, she said, Leaving her family and never going back.

Mom, I said more determined, These stories are fun and all, but I want also to just talk with you.

We *are* talking, said my mom slightly defensively.

I lay back on my pillow on the kitchen table, the phone nestled in against my head.

No, I said taking in a deep breath, We are not talking. I want to hear what your life is like and I want us to communicate more, you know, in both directions, like other mothers and daughters do.

Well, she said, That's not what I want.

She had always been blunt. In a way you've got to sort of admire her bluntness, her self-knowledge.

If we don't tell each other about our lives, I threatened, I won't listen to your stories.

I tried to speak clearly and strongly. I tried to sound determined. The first part of changing your personality, I thought, was simply impersonation.

My mother thought my threat through carefully. Both of us wondering how serious I was.

After Anita announced that the marriage was annulled, she said, *Anna's parents—*

And I hung up on her. Just like that. I can't tell you how I surprised myself.

I can't tell you how good it felt.

Chapter 16

So, said my mom, You've graduated, then. Third in your class, huh? You must be hardworking. You must take after Anita and Victor.

It wasn't exactly a difficult highschool, I said.

(My voice, I am pleased to report, sounded rather blasé. I lay back on the kitchen table, tossed my feet up on the wall, stared at them with enjoyment, so high above.)

So, Mom asked with a slight awkwardness (normal conversation had never been her strong point), Where you working now?

The Men's Wearhouse, I answered.

The what?

The Men's Wearhouse. The Oldtyme Men's Wearhouse. On the corner of Embry and Route 16. Across from the Mobil.

Don't know it.

Oh, I said, Yeah, actually it wouldn't have been here when you lived here.

Well, whatever it is, you'll end up owning it.

Hey, I said with my voice all warm, That's nice, Mom, thanks.

It's because you'll work there so long.

I will not, I said, my voice back to normal. I can be spontaneous sometimes. I can do things I've never done before.

You're an old lady, Mom said. An old lady at 18.

19, I corrected.

Whatever, she said, Enough chitchat. Permission to continue with the stories?

Wait, wait, I said sitting up straight, Not yet. Tell me about you. Where do you live?

Jesus.

Come on.

An apartment complex, she said. Modern, brick, every apartment laid out exactly like the one below. The kitchen is square and badly lit. Not enough counter space. The only saving grace is it has a gas stove. Electric burners are just impossible to cook with. That enough?

I greeted her with silence.

Ok, ok. It's outside of town, an area intended mostly for old people. Speed bumps everywhere, the buildings are overheated and pooper-scooping is mandatory. These people get bothered by the smallest things, a lunch delivered late, graffiti, a missing brick in a walkway. They post signs, they fill out petitions.

Do you have roommates, friends?

There are people I spend time with. I wouldn't call them friends.

Would they?

What?

Would they call themselves your friends?

Permission to continue with the stories?

Well . . . I said.

I'll tell you more about Celia.

What about Celia? I asked.

. . .

A House Named Brazil

After Anita announced that the marriage was annulled, Anna's parents no longer slept in the same bed, not in the same room. Frequently they didn't even sleep even in the same wing of the house. Upon moving into the new house Anita placed a single cot for herself in the pantry. She did not talk to the man she called her ex-husband, except about fundamental safety and etiquette issues, in the way one would lecture a child. She lived within the kitchen area, bustling efficiently about, having vowed to accumulate even more money than before.

I want you to know, I said, I realize this isn't about Celia.

She comes in later on, said my mom.

I'm being quiet just for you.

Oh honey, shush up and listen.

Anita said she slept in the pantry in order to be near the ovens where she worked and to be closer to her children during the day. It was true the kitchen was the central room of the house for her children, because eating was the main occupation of Anita's sons and cooking was Anita's only occupation. Cooking was also the only occupation of the 15 new helpers she hired. After the store's kitchen moved into the new house called Brazil, her shop took over all 3 floors of their old house in town, selling the sweets she cooked at home. Her business began to deliver to states other than Florida, the name Anita became registered as a trademark, and all the money she made she kept within a 5-ton vault that was constructed in the basement of the store. Not one person in the world knew the combination of this vault except for Anita, nor was anyone else even allowed to see the room where it was stored, but every person in town and in her family opened that safe each night in the brightly-lit room of their dreams, running their fingers through the fabulous riches they all assumed it contained.

After the swamp land was bought—after Anita stopped talking to

Cessil—he in turn became bitter and even fatter. He tried to re-develop the secretly hurt look he had had as a youth. He put on a cynical smile and added an ironic twang to his voice, but within the balloon that was his face it only came off as self-pity. At this point he changed from a man of few words. He now began to talk, to blab.

And people stopped listening. He lectured to the boys about their studies and their sports, about their hobbies and their girlfriends. He told them each day which new room to build and how to do it. Yet the boys accepted advice only from their mother, ignoring their father while he jabbered on from his seat in his corner chair made of Brazilian ironwood, the only chair large and strong enough to take his mass, the chair he had them carry from one area of new construction to the next so he could continue to advise them, the chair which he soon began to sleep in as the walk back to his lonely bed was just too much, his body slumping comfortably down against its own fleshy pillows and rolls.

And then, late at night, in a hall dark with absence, his sleeping mouth would open again and new words would slip out, these words more deliberate and softer, quiet words about tall women and black hair, about the jungle and the proper way to use a machete, about the meaty breath of leopards and about wide hips that rolled like waves.

Each morning he woke with a start at the first step of someone on the stairs. His mouth clicked shut and he looked around, so surprised at the world in which he found himself. He was silent then, for a moment or 2, while he cast about for the reductive maxims that he would lecture on that day.

Thus was created the house and family in which Anna grew up. A family of noise, heat and separation. Some people's nerves are just tuned higher than others. Things grate more easily against them. And it was always the noise that Anna thought of first when she remembered that house. Noise everywhere, the boys yelling, her father rambling, her mother roaring out orders to her staff like a sea captain in a storm. The sounds of hammers and saws and things falling, instructions cried out and questions bellowed back. And the animals, the pets that her brothers were always adopting because they were lost, wounded or cute, and then they were ignored. The animals cried for food or attention. They fought with one another, dogs, cats, parrots, baby gators and full-grown snakes; barking talking mewling and dying. And there were the other people within the house: the relatives, the friends, the girlfriends, the visitors. Anna's home was filled with the heat of a great steamy cloud of close bodies in a tropical temperature, the cloud rising all around and about them, pulling them tight and near into a moist knot of thick air strengthened by the heat of those giant ovens that were always cooking, spewing out peanut cakes, beijinhos and cocados, tray after tray. The trucks taking away in loads whatever the boys could not manage to eat.

Anna was raised in the huge pile of people and animals and food and movement on the edge of a swamp, and she hated every movement and creature within her hearing with an intensity that gave her an ulcer when she was 10 and made her run away when she was 13. She headed toward Canada without money or food or a map.

There was nothing special about the day she ran away. Some coconut macaroons were cooking, all 17 commercial ovens full-on, the air thick with the smell of coconut and sugar as it always was in that ramshackle mansion, even late at night, even on holidays. The boys were starting a new wing of the house, tearing down the wall in the diningroom where the wing would be attached. Cessil was shouting advice, something fell, the walls shook, the boys hooted with laughter. Two half-grown gators in the living room were roaring over a baby rabbit they had killed upon a couch and Victor, at the age

of 29, was sitting upon the kitchen counter with the yellow and unerr-
ing gaze of a vulture, watching Anna as it all built up within her, him
saying only small things. "You ok?" "Look a little tense." "Tummy
hurts, huh?" She had begun to chew slowly on the knuckle of her right
thumb, pausing only to sip from the fifth glass of milk she'd drunk
that morning as part of her attempt to quell the shards of pain jab-
bing inside her.

She kept her head down and her movements slow, trying to bore
Victor enough for him to look away, to leave her alone. She was try-
ing to keep her back straight while he watched her, to keep fear from
her eyes, when suddenly out of the pantry swept her mother, 4 helpers
in tow. They ripped open the first of the great ovens, a blast of heat as
from hell swirling through the room, and the workers bent their bod-
ies eagerly into that inferno, muscles bulging and streaked with
sweat, unloading each of the 170 trays of macaroons from the ovens
which hissed great clouds of steam into the already saturated air. The
edges of the kitchen became hazy, leaving only the outlines of the
workers' stooped backs and the unending trays of sweets, the merry
bellows of advice from worker to worker, her mother's raspy
demands and the glowing point of her cigar.

And Anna simply stood up and left. She walked out of the kitchen,
out the front door, down the driveway and across the road into the
swamp, walking straight off the land her father had bought in the
year of her birth, taking with her only the glass of milk which she had
been holding at the time and which she did not put down as she con-
tinued to tramp unerringly north through the heat of a typical tropi-
cal day in Fort Lauderdale. Her face flat as someone hypnotized.

No one (aside from Victor) noticed she had gone until breakfast
the next morning, so the hunt centered 20 miles short of her actual
location as she steadily walked north.

She did not let go of that milk glass until she was checked into the Mortimer Fink Memorial Hospital in Atlanta by 2 policemen for exhaustion, exposure and without any ulcer at all. There in the Atlanta hospital she met the first person to whom she had spoken since she started on her journey, her whisper hoarse and uncertain at first, then later gathering speed and confidence until she was talking so quickly many of the words were no longer fully-formed. She was just talking as quickly as she could to the only listener she had ever had, glorying in the sound of her own voice and the long-delayed expression of her thoughts, glorying in the way her words changed the visitor's face from moment to moment, producing smiles, surprise, frowns. Glorying in the power of her words on the attentive kindly silence of her listener, a doctor, a man who sat very still, who had a low voice and never made loud noises, a man who had pale cool fingers which were always a little damp from his frequent washings, a man who let her adjust the room's air conditioning to be as high as she wished and who later married Anna to become my father.

Anna married her doctor? I asked.

Yes.

Yuck, I said, imagining my general practitioner and all the medical experts on growth he had referred me to, their look of professional self-satisfaction, their habits of checking their watches every few minutes.

He was my father, my mother said, with that warning tone in her voice.

Oh please, I answered, You barely even knew him. I know that much.

Well, said my mother sternly, and then surprisingly enough, she giggled. Well, she said again, Yes.

· · ·

After my mom's phonecall I went on a walk again, this time crossing the road and heading down through the forest toward the town dump. I was feeling good. It was about 7 at night. Halfway down the hill I discovered an old outhouse, half-fallen over, with a moon-shaped window carved in the door. I did not know which of the 3 nearby farmhouses it belonged to. It might have been quite old.

On the way back, walking among the trees, there was nothing in my mind but the image of Celia clambering over snowdrifts 20 feet high while striding on to the nearest town during the longest winter in Canadian history; there was nothing in my mind but the image of Cessil walking through the moist heat of the Brazilian rain forest, the glimmer of silver railroad tracks pointing the way through a jungle as shadowy as a closet.

I could see each step that they took.

Mourne Family Tree

Great Great Grandmother & **?**
b. 1855   d. 1887

Celia
b. '73

Cessil
'74

Samantha
'75

Matthew
'77

Mikey
'78

Sid
'79

Nat
'80

?
'81

Cliff
b. '82

Alexis/
Elizabeth
'83

Rebecca
'84

Beth
'85

Marthe
'86

Celia & Egbert
m. 1894

Cessil & Anita (& blond boy?)
m. 1899

Semper
b. 1900

Victor
'01

Antonio
'03

Carlos
'05

Raoul
'07

Stanley
b. '09

Gabe
'11

José
'12

Anna
'18

Anna & Doctor
m. 1935

Chapter 17

Like I said, I bought groceries more often than I needed to, in order to see Ned.

I could never look at him directly. I barely had enough courage to say good morning to his mother, Mrs. Holt (whom I've known since I was a child, who had always loved my mother and been consistently kind to me). I got breathless from the moment I stepped into the store. Sometimes just the smell of fruit stacked high, in some other store, in any other store, would make me breathe high and inefficient. Fluorescent light glittering down aisles made my eyes jitter with the need to find him, and then to look away.

Today he wore a lumberjack shirt, which his skinny frame didn't quite fill out. He had a big inflamed zit right between his eyes; I could tell he'd been picking it. It had that kind of puffy irritated look. From the way he wouldn't look up from the counter, away from the grocery bags and my frozen foods, I knew the last few days with the zit had been difficult for him. He was not a terribly confident boy; that was part of the reason I liked him. I knew he would assume the shame of his zit in a deeply personal way. The pain of that smote my heart deep for him.

While he packed my groceries with his head down, I took the risk of looking right at him, at his zit and the features of his face. I was trying to memorize things. His nose was a little like Egbert's, a bit too hooked and bony, a strong nose that a man older than Ned might carry off with more grace. I reached for the bag he had just finished packing.

Seeing my oversized hands suddenly appear in his frame of vision must have startled Ned a bit, for he jerked his face up quickly, blinking, with that zit like a third eye between.

My eyes were trapped. We stared at each other.

And I smiled at him. Directly. I didn't plan it. It just happened.

For the smallest moment, he looked surprised.

It was such a fast shimmer of surprise that I'm sure many people wouldn't have noticed. Just a quick contraction of the eyebrows, puzzlement. Not disgust, not amusement, not embarrassment. Just surprise.

Then he politely smiled back.

But because of that single movement of his eyebrows, and because of the politeness that followed, I decided I would never shop here again. From now on, I would shop down at huge generic Dominion Supermarket. Go only once a week. There, I wouldn't have to talk to a soul.

Mom, I asked, Do you love me?

Since I was 7 and past the point of being dependent on her for every bath and bite of food, she had not told me she loved me. Not straight out in those words.

What? Mom asked.

Do you love me?

Oh, oh honey, she said, and I could hear her working at this, understanding I was serious. She asked, Isn't that a little besides the point?

How can that be besides the point?

She sighed then and I heard her hair rustle. Perhaps she was brushing it behind her ears, perhaps scratching her head in thought. She said, Would I make you listen to these stories otherwise?

I tried hard to make that into what I wanted it to be.

Look, can't you just say it, I asked. Just say it once so I can hear. You don't have to mean it. Lots of people say it all the time without meaning it.

Mom inhaled, then started coughing.

It's those cigars, you know, I said, relieved to be able to back down. You're smoking too many, trying to copy Anita.

Well, she said, I don't really inhale.

Aww Jesus, Mom, I said. Don't you know they're what's making your voice all raspy now?

Speaking of which, she said defiantly and she fumbled with something for a moment before I heard the match flare and a few hard puffs of her breath.

The breakfast on the day that Egbert was murdered ...

How come you're not cooking tonight? I interrupted.

She just paused for a moment, then started over.

The breakfast on the day that Egbert was murdered ...

Her voice sounded a little louder tonight, a little faster. Her voice perhaps even more intent than before.

Mom, I said, Mom, I pulled out my highschool history book last night to look for the stuff you've been talking about. None of these things are in it. Not the riots after World War I, not Florida filled with Indians, not how much wildlife used to exist, not any mention of Great Uncle Victor. Not even the winter of 1887.

The major purpose of school, said my mom, Is to bore all the questions and rebellion out of the young before they can get any power. Teachers don't inform you that one of Faulkner's greatest books is about having sex with cows, or that during the American Civil War more soldiers died from their own doctors than from the battlefield. Or that after Saint Theresa D'Avila's death, her body didn't decompose, so nuns hacked good-luck hunks of flesh out of her arms with dinner knives, a monk plucked out her eyeball as a reliquary, a bishop tore off her arm. The Pope fought bitterly for the rest of her one-armed one-eyed gnawed-on body.

A little bit of that kind of info, she said, Would give us bravery. It would be food for the heart.

And my mom took advantage of my silence to move right into the story.

The breakfast on the day that Egbert was murdered, Celia remembered perfectly for the rest of her days.

Oh, I said. Oh, this story's gonna make me sad.

Shush up, hun.

It was as though somehow her life had stopped at that meal and breakfast was always just finishing. Days and years passed, but the food stayed heavy in her gut. She hadn't felt well that morning. There had been a sharp stab of pain low within her torso when she awoke, a twisting moving fear that made her think she might have the flu, so she chose only oatmeal for breakfast.

Egbert, on the other hand, had 3 eggs, 6 sausage links and 2 muffins, and he was smiling quite a lot. The Great War had ended 2 days before and he believed things would be different now. Humanity, he said, had gotten too powerful and civilized for such violence ever again. Woodrow Wilson was right, the League of Nations was the only way, the future was rosy with international love. She remembered the way Egbert scooped his eggs up whole, his mouth open to accept them like a child's.

Egbert and she had had sex early that morning and she could still feel the lazy warmth between her legs like a gift. She sent the maid out for more muffins and then lifted both of Egbert's thin and so clever hands to her heat there, apparent through the silk of her gown. She looked down on the veins twisting across the backs of his hands, saw with tenderness how his narrow bones were increasingly bared by age. His dear sour face lifting with surprise.

That night Egbert was giving a special performance to celebrate the end of the war. Egbert had figured tonight was the right timing: the victory was still fresh, but the dangerous frenzied celebrations of a whole country drunk with victory were winding down, the riots and mob robberies. Every liquor store and fireworks store in the city had been looted. Five flag stores had been broken into, the American flags stolen for parades and all the other flags either urinated on or burned. Someone had discovered that if you didn't have fireworks to set off, talcum powder thrown into the air could look like glistening smoke for a moment, so now every one of the 147 spontaneous parades in the city had had so much talcum powder thrown that people were left dusty-white as ghosts and coughing, and 2 babies had died from respiratory distress. An old woman had been hung from a lamppost downtown for her accent (an accent that turned out to be Danish), and every diner that served German sausage or Hungarian goulash was burned to the ground, twice with the owners in them. There were worse stories from New York and San Francisco.

Still, now people had hopes. The war was over. Everything would get better.

Celia, who was filling out a little too much from all the richness of this easy life, had the 2 maids who dressed her after breakfast pull her corset in extra tight, in the belief that it might help her to diet, or at least help stop her gut from hurting.

That last show was the high point of Egbert's life. The crowd's appreciation was hard to contain. Egbert wore a red, white and blue costume and stole the volunteers' ammo belts, suspenders and the deeds to disputed parts of Germany and Austria-Hungary. He was applauded at the start of every number, at the end of every number, during every number and whenever he tried to address the crowd. The audience beat its hands in unflagging senseless energy, and halfway through the show someone with good lungs in the back started the Pledge of Allegiance. Before the third word was out, every red mouth within those 1,000 heads took up the vow. The beat of the words came in waves, the combined power hitting the stage in solid pulses.

. . . AND TO THE REPUBLIC FOR WHICH IT STANDS . . .

Each syllable of the pledge in sync, together even to the breaths, so it was just one voice, one person, one mind.

After the Allegiance ended there was a silence, almost an embarrassed silence. The crowd breathed out. People began to sit back in their seats and one woman coughed. Then the nameless voice from the back called out again, this time Egbert's name, and the crowd immediately picked it up like a hammer, pounding it out in rhythm, repeating the 2 syllables without meaning or reason again and again, until it was no longer his name but merely the beat of power united in the pledge of a completely different sort.

. . . EGBERT   EGBERT   EGBERT . . .

Egbert stood there at the end of his show, holding up those pale thin hands, palms forward, so fragile and aging, trying to get silence, attention, civility, being rocked back upon his heels like a puppet with the breath and power of the crowd's voice. He grinned, not under-standing the mob mentality, the danger, confusing the enthusiasm with his own success.

Celia, standing in the wings, could see the pink blush high on his cheeks. Turning toward the audience, she could see a small child in the front row who no longer even faced the stage, but who had turned back to the crowd, punching the cushion of her chair with her fists and screaming with all the strength available within her. And again Celia felt the jolt of pain/indigestion from down deep within the base of her torso. For a second she could almost name the pain and why it came, but then she got distracted by Egbert stepping off the stage. He could not wait for the encores to be over, his whole face a brilliant rose, his soft palms now reaching for her, the curtains swinging shut and still the hands on the other side of the curtain were raised and blurring the air with their power, still that one united voice used Egbert's name, screaming it out like a demanding giant crouched down on the other side. The closed curtain swayed with the continu-ing beat of those 2 syllables.

The curtain brushed up against Celia and Egbert holding each other in the darkness. All the energy and hope of the 2 days since the Central Powers' surrender were solidified in that single embrace, so Celia felt her heart crackle with desire. Not a word was said. Egbert quickly changed into street clothes and they stepped out the back door of the theater with the simple thought of snagging a fast cab back to their own front hall.

But the crowd was already out there, abruptly materialized, milling and jostling, waiting.

Celia and Egbert stood in front of the milling mob, which extended off into the darkness without end or meaning and they were awed. Again its single voice boomed out, this time:

—SIGN MINE—

As a single unfolding arm, 1,000 hands unrolled forward for

Egbert's signature, each containing a sheet of paper, sometimes 2 or more, and a pen. Signing this many would have taken all night. Egbert looked back at Celia by his side, his cheeks glowing even brighter with what he took as this new proof of his power. He touched Celia lightly on the arm, a single touch on the soft soap flesh that he still loved so much, before he stepped away into the crowd.

(His touch was a touch that was designed to hold her for only a moment while he handled this crowd. The warmth upon her arm from his fingertips faded even before he did. When she returned home an hour later that night under police escort, she got down on her knees in the front hall immediately—not in amorous desire, as she had intended to before with Egbert—but instead she knelt all alone to sniff the rugs for some small proof of the love she and her late husband had shared. Only then did she remember that touch, that last touch near her elbow, and her fingers sought it out again and again, but could not quite find it, could not quite touch it, not feel that warmth ever again.)

Egbert stepped up to the edge of the crowd and spoke in a confident voice. He said a sentence or 2 about the lateness of the hour and his own increasing age. His voice rang clear and loud with his joy. He said they had been the best audience possible and some other day perhaps . . .

"Perhaps" was the last whole word Celia heard him say.

The crowd had shuffled in loosely behind him, still holding out their papers, still extending their arms out toward him.

Celia had to step forward and a little to the left to see him around the shoulders and heads that separated them now. A few people in the very inner circle that surrounded Egbert must have dropped their pens and papers without realizing it because now their hands were vibrant with emptiness but still they reached out toward him, their fingers spread.

Celia felt again that stab within the lower portion of her belly *that she now realized was her womb, was the ice within her womb moving for the first time in 31 years. Her breath began to slow as she heard—very far away, as if in a dream—a word that started with one voice but moved like a wave to be picked up by 1,000 voices, the word which would echo ragged and insane within her ears for the rest of her life, so Celia would always have to ask anyone who spoke to her, as if she were hard of hearing, What was that you said?*

And that word spat out into the air:

—THIEF—

Celia began to yank up the front of her skirt, her arms moving like molasses, her iron-curving sides not bending, the cruelty of the old-fashioned whalebone corset biting down and through the softness of her flesh. Her right arm reaching, reaching down beneath the skirts and petticoats, beneath the slip, moving past the place where the ice within her womb now twisted and tore like a mad dog in her guts, past where her husband's hands had pressed only that morning. Her right arm moving down for the gun she had carried in a thigh holster for 24 years and 7 months, and which she now knew, even before she tried for it, she would not be able to reach.

Ahead of her she could still see a bit of her husband's face, the saucer eyes she had loved so much. He had turned toward the place where the word had first started, and his expression was that of a small child. He did not understand what was happening and it was with real confusion that his body shook, hit somewhere from behind. His face twisted in pain and he was turning to her, turning to look to his powerful Celia for explanation, when he was snatched from sight, his hand floating after him like a handkerchief.

Celia pounded after him through the crowd, reaching beneath her skirts, shoving, pushing through the people, slamming her way between the bodies. Heads and arms and sticks passing by her, all poised in forward motion like the sea, and she saw faces and fists and then there was blood. Each time she reached the place where she thought he should be, there was only the crowd pushing in another direction, an endless pressure on her from all sides, an endless shifting. Things clutched in people's hands. The roaring of a bull gone mad. And the high mindless screaming in her own woman's throat never stopped, never paused, not until the crowd finally slowed, slowed and stepped back, stepped back and walked away, breaking up from a furious giant into a mass of slightly befuddled individuals walking to their homes in all different directions, wiping their hands on their clothes.

Celia wandered about alone then, down the quiet street, a woman left with nothing at all in the dark, nothing more than the trash and stains common to any city street, on any given night.

The only thing left for Celia after the mob dispersed were the late-arriving policemen, who began to ask questions, and the reporters. The reporters who reprinted Celia and Egbert's history in the papers the very next morning. People wanted so to understand. Egbert had not had a suspicious accent or Hungarian roots. He did not have a German name. The crowd had been good Americans out for a night of entertainment in a normal American city only 2 days after America had proved itself to be a country always in the right. There had been children in the crowd. There was such a need to understand.

The newspaper stories reminded people of Egbert and Celia's criminal past.

Public opinion turned against them within 48 hours.

Within 2 weeks, 14 cities on the East Coast were suing Celia for the amount of money they claimed she and Egbert had stolen from their citizens.

For a year the names of Celia and Egbert were in the newspaper even more than they had been in the years when Egbert had had his show. Stories were told about Egbert, things were said about her. Mutterings of mob tie-ins, random violence, unpaid bills, orgies.

Celia put up a marker in Mount Auburn Cemetery for Egbert, so there would be at least something she could look at as proof of his life, a 10-foot-tall marble monument that proclaimed loudly to the world his name, his birth and death dates, her love for him. But each time it was raised, someone would knock it down, paint over it, crack the center column. She kept having it repaired until the last of her money was taken away by the court. She was declared bankrupt and the stone lay like a body, more of it carried away each day by souvenir hunters, Egbert's name shattered, disintegrating.

Thus, within a year of Egbert's death, still dressed in the black that she would wear for the rest of her days, Celia sat upon the doorstep of the house that was no longer hers, holding an empty purse, wearing a plain cotton dress. The only 2 things she could think of that were solely hers—that no one during the bankruptcy hearing had made a claim on or bickered over—were her body and the way she mourned her husband without pause or thought every moment of her life, in the same unconscious way she breathed, as if her grief were a small fast animal within her chest, whirring around and around in a circle with the high-speed whine of terror.

Sitting on the doorstep of her former house that day, she thought long and hard. She evaluated the world and her life with an objective distance few people can master once they're pulled into all the harried busy-ness of adulthood. She regarded the world in a straightforward and uncharmed way and found it lacking. She found it brutal and cruel. And from that day forth she set about to master this new world with all the power of her so considerable will. She set about to get all she could from it.

Thus she disappeared from the sight of those wealthy socialites *who had known her when Egbert was still alive. She sought out an appropriately cruel life. At the age of 46, she became a prostitute. She vanished into a world that richly illustrated, in violence and petty ugliness, everything she now felt about her life and the people within it. She was not young enough to avoid the worst parts of the business, was immersed in the very dregs of it. But she revelled in that ugliness. She sought to have the ugliness of her heart mirrored in the ugliness of her life. She liked seeing people prove themselves, again and again, to be as bad as she now believed them to be. And for 4 years she managed her new profession as competently as she had managed the rest of her life. She did not become partners with any man who would protect her and take half her money, not while she still had her gun to protect her instead. She worked night and day at her career, for there was nothing else in her life that interested her. For 4 long years she soaked in enough cruelty to fill her heart, enough cynicism to last her a century, enough money to dress herself in black silk for the rest of her days and enough semen to father a new world. Enough simple friction to warm up even her cold womb just a little bit, just enough.*

Early one morning, at the end of those 4 long years, she rang the doorbell of a house in Fort Lauderdale where a private investigator had told her she would find her entire family assembled. She stood on the doorstep with the Colt .45 once again loaded and visible within her hands, stood there in the doorway of her brother's house, at the age of 50, with her condition quite apparent in her heavy-heeled wide-bellied stance, her past profession advertised by the cut of her dress. She stood there tall and proud as a very rich prostitute, pregnant with the child of some unknown customer. She stood there in the doorway of the house of her brother, her brother whom she had not seen since he had tried to kill her when she was 14 years old.

And the first thing she told her siblings—in a voice measured out with exhaustion and a grief just beginning to be expressed—was that she was home to stay.

The first real fight between me and my mother came upon us rather suddenly. And we had been getting on so well. It started simply, with a single sentence.

Mom said, I've sent Celia's gun up to you through the mail.

What? I asked and stopped patting the kitten beside me.

It was not that I hadn't heard; it was just that the words didn't seem to me like they could be English.

She repeated that she had sent Celia's Colt .45 up to me through the postal system, that it should arrive tomorrow or the next day, that she'd even sent a box of the original bullets with it. She sounded rather excited about the bullets. She said she didn't want the family to get their hands on the gun. Whenever she died.

That's illegal, my mouth said abruptly, loud and clear. I could see her eyes narrow as though she were in front of me. The eyes narrowing smoothly, exactly, the mouth tight.

Excuse me? she asked. Her voice warning.

Transporting arms across the border, I said. It's a federal crime.

I tried to speak as clearly as possible, to put the importance of the issue into my voice. When they had lived up here in Canada, both my parents had been illegal aliens. My earliest association with policemen was a sense of unease, of fear. Now an image was closing in on my mind of cement grey hallways and iron bars, twisted hands reaching out.

We could both go to jail, I said.

Child, she said, her voice curt. I called it Books on the declaration form. They won't know. They won't check.

Let's say the bullets rattle.

Child, she said.

Let's say the postman decides to ask some questions when he delivers the package, I said. I was having a problem breathing through my fear, through my desperate need to communicate.

Child, my mother clucked.

Let's say he finds out I have forged hundreds of signatures on checks for my mother who hasn't lived on the farm for almost 5 years. That I've lived here on my own without an adult since the age of 14.

Has it been that long?

The farm which I don't even know who legally owns, or if taxes have ever been paid on it.

Child, she clucked a final time.

I AM NOT A CHILD! My voice was a scream that for a moment stilled all the crickets in the field out back and made the static on the phone line die down.

After a long and lingering moment of surprise, my mother's voice came quietly. You will always be my child, she said. I am your mother.

Neither of us hung up. I realized about this time what was happening and everything in the kitchen suddenly snapped into focus, the 12 10-gallon pans on the wall, the 4 wood stoves, the 25 empty breakfast chairs. I breathed twice. My body felt thin and muscular. The air rumbled around in my lungs distinct as marbles.

While I'm at this, I said, Why did you send me the thing with bullets in it? I don't want the bullets. I don't want the gun. I don't want it loaded. The gun could go off, in my face, at a cat. I have no practical use for it. I don't shoot the lids off jars when I can't undo them.

My words were strangely easy to pull out of myself. They

burbled up into my mouth sweet and light. On the other end, for once, my mother was listening to me. Fueled by words, my mouth was humming like a new car, spare in its movements, fast and responsive, channeling all its energy down the phone line that stretched away from me into the wall. Gone from sight. A thin black line, a universe for the 2 of us, twirling in darkness, in orbit.

And, hearing her silence, I just kept talking. I had so much to say to my mother who had never really listened. I was no longer asking questions about her or her stories. I was starting to talk instead about myself, about all that I had always wanted to tell her.

Guns, I said, Make me ill. They have for as long as I can remember. What are they but a way of handing out death? Last summer Rita died—the hairless chihuahua, you remember her. Not from a gun. One morning she just stayed in my bed after I got up, and she seemed to be more and more impressed with the act of breathing. Then she stopped. It was a perfectly cloudless day. That surprised me. I wished afterward it had been at least a little cloudy. For Rita I cried 2 straight weeks. Death and things dying make me feel bad. Guns make me feel bad. I don't like them and I have every intention of living happily, fully, richly, until I reach the ripe old age of 105. Loving every one of those days, every one of those years without ever killing anyone, or even threatening to, and I am going to have many friends and children also and teach them all to laugh rather than cry. I am not going to live on this farm for much longer, not much longer, and once I leave—once I leave, mind you—no one will be able to hold me.

Of course, this is when it happened. Just when I was doing so well, when I was feeling so good. When I was finally talking. My voice was so strong and the excitement in my body boiled up in a fast even rhythm as though I were running quite hard. This was when I heard a small mechanical voice in the pauses of my breath, in the staticky background on my mother's side of the line.

The background voice said, Dr. Hadley to O.R. 3 stat, Dr. Hadley.

No one, I repeated out of confusion, No one will hold me.

The rhythm in me was all wrong now, my breath couldn't seem to be pulled in deep enough for my heart. I pushed the kitten off my lap.

Mom, I said, Mom.

Yes, yes, she said in her raspy precise voice.

Mom.

I'm ok, she said, That wasn't for me.

You're in the hospital. The words came from the back of my throat, far down, once again so difficult to pull out.

When she responded her voice was slow and matter-of-fact. Little emotion or struggle.

I checked in today, she said. I've known for a while. My belly. My belly's been hurting. Her vocabulary was that of a 5-year-old.

The operation is next week, she said. I think I'm going to have to speed these stories up.

Chapter 18

At the end of my shift, I asked Roberta out for lunch. She's the only other woman at work. When I spoke she seemed to have a problem locating me for a moment, finding my face above hers and then focusing on it. She put on the smile she used on the customers and said lunch was a lovely idea but maybe it would be better to do some other day when she was a little less busy.

I nodded, looked away toward the display window and the long afternoon stretched out in front of me. I was breathing funny, had been all morning. Then, surprised I was speaking again, surprised I had even spoken the first time, I said, I think sometimes things are better to do today. Who knows what will happen tomorrow?

She blinked, and for a moment her public smile went all still. I had a glimpse then of how she looked when she was alone at night. Then her smile came back, smaller but less artificial.

You're right, she said, You're really right. She looked down at her receipts for the day, then outside at the street. Ok, she said impulsively, Let's go.

At lunch, I suddenly felt shy, so I mostly just asked her questions. In the years since then, in the friendships I've had, I have found that almost everyone likes to be asked questions about their lives, likes to talk about themselves, to be of interest. Within 15 minutes Roberta was telling me she'd broken up with her husband 6 months ago and since then she'd been lonely every day. She was amazed by that, that the loneliness can go on that long, that it can get worse each day instead of better. I nodded, surprised that she had lived into her late twenties without understanding that. By the end of the meal, as she talked, her face had gone loose and flat, not at all like it was in the store. I realized, for the first time, what effort it must take for her to smile at the customers in the store. Over dessert she asked me if I thought she should go back to her husband, then looked at me with her face all bare and waiting for my answer.

Through my surprise, I told her, I'm not the best person to ask for love advice.

When we left the restaurant I mistakenly took a left turn out the doorway so we were heading back toward the dumpster behind the restaurant instead of toward our cars. She followed me for the 5 steps it took me to realize my mistake. She had her head down and was just walking. I think she would have walked on much longer, following me.

I'd like to make it clear I had idolized her for a solid year.

When I got back home, I slept deeply for the rest of the afternoon. Not one of those naps you gently ease into. This one I *fell* into. I don't know where I went, somewhere far away. I wasn't feeling anything in particular. At least it didn't seem like I was, not about my mom, not about Roberta. I just slept, deep deep down.

When I woke up, my body lay there sort of heavy, a bit sweaty.

I stayed there for the longest time, with my arms down at my sides, too tired even to hug myself.

. . .

Breath, I'd begun to think about breath.

How it happens all the time. How it has to happen.

Air pulled deep into your lungs, swirling around into your veins. Spinning off around the body, up each little driveway, to the cells and organs.

My whole life, my mom had been telling me that she would die at an early age. She had not stated it as a threat, not melodramatically. She had just stated it. As a fact.

When Mom called, we both said hello. There was a quietness to our voices. It was like we were both at work, not at a good job but at a necessary one. The kind where you bid hello matter-of-factly, almost under your breath, Hi and Hi, then got right down to work.

There was no mention of the hospital.

About Victor I can't tell you that much.

For this story, Mom's voice was less sure. It was clear she had not told this story as often as the others. She had not practiced it as a public performance.

I never met him. He didn't seem to have confided all that much in anyone in the family, and the family was loath to talk about what was known about him. Just the mention of his name made his 6 younger brothers uncharacteristically quiet for hours. Only his ex-girlfriends seemed to like discussing him, at least discussing the younger years, when they knew him. I called them out of frustration at my family's silence on the subject of Victor. The ex-girlfriends, I found, would enthusiastically arrange to meet me, away from their husbands, the ones they'd been married to for 20 or 25 years. At the coffee shop or in the public park where we met, each would sigh a lot and touch her collarbone as she reminisced. Each showed me some dried flowers pressed for decades between the pages of a diary or photo album, complete with faded cursory notes concerning dinner reservations or movie times, the notes signed with just a dash and then Victor. Never Vic, never Love, never Your Sweetie.

Every one of the girlfriends blamed what he did during the war on that woman he ended up marrying. She'd made them uneasy, so still all the time, always listening, her head cocked just so. They said she must have made him do it, do all of it. It could be the only explanation.

He left no journals. I can only list his actions. Make suppositions.

Yes, he had many girlfriends, but from his brothers I learned that most of these relationships were initiated by the women. His brothers were quite jealous, always wondered how he did it. The prettiest women in the state would meet him once and then set out to court him, chasing him as aggressively as women were allowed to back then. Each woman would relentlessly frequent the places he frequented until she finally bumped into him. She would act surprised, ask him how he was doing. At some point during the conversation she would mention, trying to sound casual with her complexion so high and her hands slightly shaking, that she had not been bowling in years. That she had not been bowling or hadn't seen the new play in town or loved walking on the beach, just couldn't get enough of it.

Victor would look at her. He was, I've been told, the kind of person who didn't mind pauses in conversation, the kind of pause that made other people start rambling on about anything, off balance. The kind of pause that he stood through so calm. He didn't mind staring, seemed almost to be somewhere other than behind his eyes. He would gaze at whatever his eyes had landed on: the woman's teeth, her earrings, the part in her hair, her chest. His brothers never could under-

stand why the women didn't seem to mind the stares from him, seemed instead to get even more breathy and fixated.

Sometimes then—sometimes but not always—he'd say in his careful slow voice, Well then, would you care to go bowling?

He occasionally took the same woman out for a few weeks or months at a time. 3 months at the most. Then he would break up with her. I found out from talking to these ex-girlfriends that he had broken up with every one using the same speech. He would confess to the woman that Semper, his brother, after almost 2 decades of fighting, had finally become the head crime boss in town. Victor would say that early on during Semper's career a bomb had gone off in the kitchen, almost killing his whole family. And now Semper had finally won the battle for control of Fort Lauderdale and had moved back home again, even though the old Mafia head, 3-Fingered Vargas, was still bitter. Victor would tell his girlfriend that the situation was quite dangerous. He would say he could deal with the danger to himself and to his family, but not to her. Anyone in town could find out how important she was to him, anyone. He couldn't be brave, couldn't be strong, not when she was in danger too. Did she understand he had to protect her?

None of his girlfriends knew this was the same speech he had used on the others. Each had just innocently, proudly, sadly repeated it to me, whole phrases that were the same, from woman to woman. And each had believed his words in spite of being deeply hurt and furious (even more furious when he kept his word and never again spoke to her on the street).

Few people who met him seemed to question much of what he said or did. He didn't talk a lot about what he was thinking or feeling, and people filled in the blanks with their own assumptions. He was a pretty man, with wide cheekbones and a jutting chin. If he was an actor, he would have been cast every time as the good guy. He had done well in school. He had high marks from his teachers at Columbia in physics, in chemistry, in studying the science of surface tension.

But he did have one strange habit that I heard of. Sometimes he would be walking home—with or without other people, it didn't matter—and he would just stop in midstep. Stop dead in the street, on the sidewalk, or halfway in a door. This didn't happen a lot, but it happened enough and it was strange enough that people remembered. He would stand there staring at whatever it was his eyes had been fixed on when he had stopped, standing there for 5 seconds, 5 minutes, for long enough for whatever it was that gripped him to pass: the thought, the feeling, the spirit. Then he shook his head, rubbed his neck and walked on as though he had not paused at all.

People made assumptions. There were many who believed he was brilliant: his brothers, his girlfriends, one or 2 of the teachers from Columbia. Just not his parents, not his mother. Anita still lived for the moment each night when Semper would return home from his long day at work, changing his clothes immediately, right there in the hall, from a white camel-hair suit to a white camel-hair suit, as though the first had been dirtied in some irreversible way. Anita never believed that he did the things he was rumored to have done. She never pictured him with a gun in his hand, the gun dark against his white suit, his eyes reflexively and involuntarily clenching shut every time his finger tightened on the trigger. At home again, in his fresh suit, Semper would sneak into his mother's room, no matter what the hour, and give her a quick kiss good night on the lips, along with a single sentence of advice, just like in the years when he had only visited one night a year.

But Anita was in the minority in her preference for Semper. So many others believed in Victor, believed in his future.

So, life passed by easily enough for Victor. In his thirtieth year there was even one woman whom he had agreed to marry. She was the daughter of the owner of the chemical manufacturing company Victor worked for. Victor's doctorate was in researching surface ten-

sion, the skin on the outside of every liquid that allows water spiders to skate across ponds, that allows oil to separate so perfectly, that automatically encloses a droplet of any liquid to separate it from the air by the narrowest scrim, leaving everything inside unknown. Although Victor was just finishing up his post-doc at the company's research lab, it was assumed that if he married the daughter, the company would let him run the lab. She had first spotted him in the cafeteria. Arranged to have him ask her out within the week.

So Victor was taking out this woman, his fiancée, each Saturday night to go roller skating and each Wednesday to the movies, smiling as he held her hand, his handsome face already grouped so easily with her own, his academic record, his mother's not insubstantial income, his own shining future as clear to them all as if it had already been accomplished.

Yes, everyone was happy with him indeed, especially the daughter, for each Monday night while her parents played bridge, Victor had one of his younger brothers alley-oop him up to the trellis she had had nailed beneath her window for just such an occasion. Inside her bedroom, he petted her squirming pleading flesh within an inch of satisfaction, while rubbing the length and breadth of his still-zippered-up-but-inhuman pressure against her, so she was left moaning and dizzy upon her bed, incoherent with unmet desire, incapable of thinking of anything but her wedding night.

Yes, it was assumed that he would get both her and the research lab—it seemed such a certainty it was almost regarded as already having occurred—until one late night he climbed down the trellis to lay his eyes on Clara for the first time.

It had been a particularly intense evening, so even his hips were experiencing a mild dissatisfaction. (And I know about this evening because it struck him so strongly that when he got home in the predawn light he told his mother all about it as she was starting the dough for the next day's bread. I guess his description of the incident and his talking so quickly, in such detail, was strange enough that she remembered what he had said 15 years later to tell me about it.) That late night, as he let go of the trellis to fall the last few feet to the ground, he saw below him a young woman standing in the dark night by the white Easter lilies.

The part of him used to judging women saw instantly that this woman was not very beautiful, that in the normal light of day rather than the pale glow of the full moon, her features might even be considered plain. But it was not her features his eyes were noticing. It was her skin and the way she held her head. Very white skin, contoured, almost hard. In that slight light of the moon, her skin was clearly and radiantly white, exactly like the wet flesh of the fibrous flowers she was touching. Hers was a foreign face, a near motionless face. When she did smile (such a rare event he would not see it for almost 2 weeks), her skin glided back as though it were on rollers and her mouth was red.

Based on her actions, Clara had always been judged a good and kind woman, yet there was something about her that made most men stay away, except in their dreams. The night Victor first saw her, she was pressing one of the Easter lilies lightly to her cheek, one white curve melting into the next.

Victor landed on the ground and stepped away from the trellis toward her. He could tell from the shift of her shoulders that she had heard him. Still she did not look at him. He bluffed the only way he could. He made his voice lean and righteous as he stepped forward into her line of vision and asked her what she was doing here in this private garden.

And this, this was the second thing that got him. The first thing had been her skin and the way she held her head, as though she were not quite sure about life yet, was still reserving her opinion. This first impression ensured that he was watching her closely, as he watched few things outside of his lab. But the second thing was what got him. What made him give up his life as he knew it, give up the future that he had always assumed was the most completely acceptable future he could have.

It happened when he stepped into her line of vision. Her face did not register any shock or fascination. The eyes did not snap into focus on him. He had seen the power of his looks on people's faces since he was a young boy; he had seen from people's expressions how many things they already assumed about him. How much he had already won. Her face instead just regarded him, her eyes pointing straight at him.

No, she was not his from the moment she turned to him. And her face, her face. He was looking at it full on now, oblivious to whatever she was saying. He only saw her red mouth open, those small round teeth flashing in the night as she said something, said something while reaching for the white stick beside her, holding the white stick in order to walk across the yard to the house next door, walking so gracefully and confident and tall. The bone white of her stick sweeping before her in arcs that trailed after her through the darkness and left no sound at all.

In a single fluid moment he was left only with the imprint of her face upon his memory as he stood there at night in a garden filled with tall and nodding flowers. Her face in which there was a clarity of strength and emotion such as he had never felt, that made his heart know he was born to live and die with this woman, to make love with her and feel his body quiver in her orbit.

His face became drenched with sweat. He came back the next night (which was a Tuesday, so not one of his standard visiting nights) dressed in his very best to find out that, yes, she was blind. Yes, she was one of the cooks for the judge next door. And, yes, she was only 19.

That night he asked the girl's father, the butler, for her hand in marriage. Victor was refused and refused—refused every Tuesday, Thursday, Friday and Sunday nights for 3 solid months—while on

Monday and Wednesday and Saturday he continued to appear next door for dates with the chemical manufacturer's daughter, to whom he was still engaged. He was refused by the butler, on behalf of his daughter, and refused by the 19-year-old daughter herself without her once blushing or acknowledging affection for the jut of Victor's chin, which until then had won women over in an instant. I imagine it almost made him smile every night at the inevitable no, for he was refused normally, in a normal voice, with a normal expression, one of her hands placed kindly on his wrist.

Yes, it just about filled him with joy at how calmly she denied him, without any great expectations or emotions. He was refused politely and with amusement while she continued to allow him near her, listening to him, letting him peel carrots beside her, talk to her, until the young woman, whose name as I said was Clara, finally began to believe in the endurance of Victor's emotions and to depend on the strength and handsome feel of his wide and capable wrist beneath her hand when she said no. She began to depend on his declarations of love and the heat of his constant nearby presence, began to depend on his low voice and long pauses, his careful words and peculiar smell of lab chemicals and cookie dough, began to depend on what she thought of as him, until finally she said yes to him with as much impassive certainty as she had previously said no. She declared he was a good man and her red mouth rolled back smooth and wide at the surprised, Oh, in his voice.

She reached forward then to find his hands and press them to the white thin skin of her face. She said, I am happy now. She said, I will be happy until my dying day. The way she had made this decision was similar to how she walked through her dark world; she considered the options carefully before she moved: listening, smelling. But once she committed herself to a path, she did so fully, swinging forward into her stride.

They were married to the righteous rage of the chemical manu-

*facturer and to the incomparable horror of his daughter, the daugh-
ter who jounced each night alone and angry upon the heel of her
hand, thinking of Victor and the words he had said to her and of
that animal pressure that had pushed against her from within his
pants.*

*It was then that the chemical manufacturer and the daughter
joined forces for the first time since the daughter had reached puberty.
Together, they blackballed Victor at all 8 of the major chemical
research labs in the continental U.S., so Victor found, despite his Ph.D.
from Columbia, no company would even interview him.*

*This was when Victor and Clara decided they would go to
Europe for their honeymoon, and this was when that picture of him
was taken, the one at his wedding. Clara is not in the picture. She isn't
in any of the remaining family pictures. All the photos which showed
her or the children were destroyed by the family at the time of the
trial, at the time of her death.*

*The pictures of Victor were not destroyed. The family, in spite of
everything, could not part with them.*

*When Victor and Clara left on their honeymoon everyone
assumed they would be back within the month, 6 weeks on the outside. Perhaps even Victor and Clara assumed it. Perhaps it was only
once Victor read some of the trade magazines there in Europe that he
became curious and toured a lab or 2.*

*Within 5 weeks in Europe he had his search narrowed down to
Germany. In the letter he wrote to his mother describing his decision,
he said that the German language was close to that of modern science; many of the German words for chemicals were the same as in
English. The language gave his throat pleasure and its logic fit easily
in his mind. He saw promise in the people's desperate attitude toward
the extraordinarily depressed and grey country, the promise of swift
change. He appreciated the country's desire for efficiency and for the
scientific method, the people's innate respect for authority. And he*

admitted he had never felt at home in the lackadaisical American South.

Perhaps he felt as though he had finally found a country with which he could identify. He saw quite clearly that things were going to start happening here in Germany, and he told Clara that he thought there would be a need for colloidal scientists to create those changes.

Perhaps Clara reached forward at that point to touch his face, to feel his expression; maybe her hands moved softly across his mouth and eyes. She seemed very serious and did not say much else that night. The first child would be born within 10 months of their wedding. She might already have known she was pregnant.

Clara and Victor settled down in Berlin without ever returning to the States. The year was 1932.

There in Nazi Germany, Victor behaved no differently. He had always loved success. Worked for it. Before the war started he would send back short but confident letters to his mother of how well he was doing, moving up the ranks, rewarded by his new country, beloved by his new boss. Perhaps his success made him work even harder than normal. He wrote home about how interesting his new research was, the intersection of the study of surface tension and the exact combustion point of certain common oils. Later on, he began to work with other combustible liquids, liquids that unfortunately he was no longer free to name in the interests of national security.

Once the U.S. entered the war, his letters became more rare. Each of them bore the official stamp of the censor, and Victor's wording was so careful. He told his family he was quite busy. He told them he missed them, that he was working hard, that Clara had a new child. He told them he hoped they all had a strong bomb shelter nearby, one

that had its own air system and was inflammable. He said he had
nightmares about them sometimes.

My mother told me that she knew nothing about the trial, really. She'd heard it just that once on the radio when she was a child, 5 maybe 6. She'd forgotten most of it.

This time I did not bother to ask her why she had not researched this part of the story, why in fact she had even seemed to *forget* some of the story, my mother who forgot nothing ever told to her about her family.

She had actually heard the trial along with the rest of the family, all of them sitting close in around the radio in the living room of that house named Brazil, listening to the slow voice of a man who kept clearing his throat, kept pausing. At that time she did not know why they were listening to this man's voice at all, or why all the adults turned away from each other toward the window or to look down at their own hands while they listened to the man's technical explanations of the field of colloidal science and its applications: meteorology, commercial food preparation, anthrax bombs, the flamethrower. As the evening progressed, as the man's voice moved onto his own personal breakthroughs, she did not know why each of the adults came up with an excuse to leave the room. She did not know why the adults, one by one, returned to their own rooms of the house, shutting the door before turning on their radio, listening all alone where their public faces could fall away and the emotion could be slow and honest.

Adult by adult, the living room emptied and the rest of the house filled up until the man's increasingly cautious voice crept out from under every door and down every hall. It filled the house with the distorted echoing whisper of his careful confessions, the phrases of "dispersal device," "acid entry hosts," "skin loss," and "secondary results." He described the difficulty of setting things on fire other than warehouses and tents, explaining that most other military targets were made up of such high water content. You had to bind something fairly flammable to the skin to overcome that initial obstacle.

Great Uncle Victor said he was following orders. He maintained he'd always been good at his job. He explained he'd never been so egotistical as to question society's aims, that his new country had been good to him, that this was war. He said he had wanted to succeed, he wanted to be loved by his new mother country.

The dark swamp outside the house was silent with surprise at the encompassing echo of this man's amplified voice.

When the last adult left, the radio in the livingroom was shut off so that the children would then not hear the rest of the testimony and trial that soon could become only worse. My mom remembered the last adult to leave was Semper. His expression as he clicked off the radio gave her nightmares for the rest of her childhood. His face bore a look of a horror so intense that he appeared to be smiling.

The children were left in the center room with the silent big radio, its green cat's eye winked out. They were left with nothing but the newspaper articles and family photo albums scattered across the floor. They were left with nothing but the man's muffled voice echoing through the halls from behind closed doors, telling them stories that not one of them (aside from Mom) would ever discuss again, not with people outside the family, not among themselves. Stories of how much his employers had loved him, of the parade in his honor, of the chateau he lived in. Of the fascinating challenge of the scientific problem. Of how seldom he witnessed his research being tested. How seldom, he said, how rare.

From that night on, every child in the family shifted, guilty and embarrassed, as embarrassed as an adult or a criminal, at any mention of the war or the scientific method, of Jews or humans' innate struggle for approval.

And while down the hall the radios continued to whisper, my mother sat quietly in a corner of the livingroom, looking at the photo of a handsome happy man surrounded by his own family on a warm spring day, everyone dressed in white ironed happiness. The man's stories over the radio were long and confusing, and his face drew closer and closer until she fell asleep with her face on the photo.

She woke in her own bedroom, the house silent, the pictures packed away, and all the stories slipping from her memory with the speed of dreams, so when she thought of Victor's name she did not think of details, but only of the slow deep voice of a man who kept clearing his throat and told her stories to put her to sleep.

Clara's fate with the family was sealed weeks later, on that day of the newscast, the day the whole family watched the newsreel that had been shipped to them express from Europe at great expense. They played it on a movie projector they had bought especially for the event, the chairs set out in wide circles round the screen, as many chairs as for a movie audience, all the people sitting there as silent as though it were a room of empty chairs. They had been warming the projector up since early afternoon, believing it, like the radio, might have less static then. They had been sitting there, waiting. Every one of them had already known what would happen, had known it since the shock of reading that morning's headlines 2 weeks ago. Still they had been sitting so patiently, waiting to watch.

This was the newscast of Victor receiving his verdict and then leaving the courthouse handcuffed and restrained so completely 2 guards had to hold him up and move him forward, his feet dragging, his face pale and confused. Clara followed close behind, one arm cradling their new baby, the other hand held out toward Victor, not touching, for no guard would allow her to hold the crook of Victor's arm the way she was used to, the way she had walked with Victor for 12 years now. Instead a guard guided her by the elbow while her 3 older children trailed after her like a line of ducks. More guards walked between them and the reporters, between them and the crowd, between the crowd and Semper.

Semper's craggy face suddenly visible there in Germany, there on the newscast, unmistakable.

Even though every adult in the family had known for 2 weeks now that Semper had been there, still every one of them jerked up in their seats to look around for Semper in the room with them. It was as though if they could just find him sitting harmless here in the livingroom, he would be harmless there in Germany too. On the screen, the white of his camel-hair suit and the black of his competent-looking machine gun got rapidly bigger as he ran up the steps toward them, filling the screen so completely there was a juggling as the camera fell over, twisting and then crashing down on its side. The picture jumped and flickered and then reappeared all askew, showing the 2 brothers standing up horizontally across the screen. Semper much closer to the camera, his wide back to them all, Victor's startled face staring out at the viewer. The guards had fallen away from Victor on the steps, dead or too terrified to move.

Then Victor misbalanced in his surprise and in his chains, falling back across the steps, his manacled hands waving in an effort to cushion his fall. The crowd is running everywhere. Semper is yelling—Us Mournes, us Mournes take care of our own. *He is snuggling the gun down into the hollow of his shoulder, settling his body about it to fire, when suddenly and smoothly Clara is there. She is* stepping in between them, holding the new baby to her chest, smiling white and confident, not facing Semper or even Victor, not led by any guard, but instead showing her truth in this blurred moment of horror by turning an ear to each of the brothers, her eyes like the decoration they were, her eyes turned off to point at the sky, away from the earth she was risking for her Victor. A brave smile was on her red red mouth, her teeth white like stars. She must have been confident that Semper would not shoot with her in the way, so confident that she was smiling right up to the moment her 3 children leapt toward her, leapt toward her like frightened birds at the start of the gunfire.

The children's bodies were blown back instantly, the power of a gun designed for adults.

Victor's wife stood there strangely solid through the bullets' spray. Her hips wiggled lewdly once. The gunfire stopped then and she relaxed as with relief, her body rolling back, one hand still cupping where her baby had been. Her body falling backwards, twisting. Her hand reaching, striving for one last touch of her husband's body. Scraping across the cement just in front of him like a branch.

Turned like that toward the camera, the front of her body and face was very very dead. Lying down like that, Victor miraculously was fine.

And 3 guards trampled the camera in the process of tackling Semper from behind, Semper, who was just opening his eyes as he let go of the trigger.

Pictures of Victor still remain in Fort Lauderdale. He smiles out from above the mantelpiece in the livingroom, and from the painting of the family displayed in the kitchen, he smiles handsome as always.

Semper's pictures also remain. He was sentenced to life in prison, but still corresponds with the family now. Fairly senile, he writes spidery letters on prison stationery, asks how his grandmother's canon-

ization procedures are going and, in a postscript, always reminds the children about the importance of putting family first.

Only Clara and her children were lost to the family that day. No pictures of them, and what might have been, remain. Anita was the one to destroy the photos, the same day as she watched their murder on film. She took their fate so much to heart. They were her first grandchildren and she had never even met them.

Yes, Anita decided on the day she watched her grandchildren die in front of her, killed by her favorite son, that the world was headed for disaster and only she could avert it. She burned all the pictures of the grandchildren in her favorite commercial oven, number 14, the one with the steadiest heat, and then looking out at the long long day ahead of her, she followed the photos up with cooking cakes in the same oven; 4 wedding cakes for which she had no buyers. 4 cakes cooked on the same day she had first seen her 4 grandchildren in motion, there across the screen, the 3 older ones walking along in their tiny leather lace-up shoes, in their coats with the velvet collars, their mops of hair all brushed for the public.

She cooked 4 elaborate cakes with terraced layers, with twinkling blue candy streams and whole bouquets of marzipan flowers of unnatural beauty. And hidden among the birds of paradise and gardenias, among the honeysuckles and Easter lilies, hidden in each bouquet was a brightly-colored child's top or tiny woolen glove woven entirely from icing. Anita made the cakes one after another without talking to a soul.

From that day on she retreated one more step from her family, in order to pour all of the energy she had left over from her cooking into writing letters of advice to the president and heads of states, advice couched in lengthy metaphors of raw batter, necessary ingredients and things burning.

· · ·

My only other memory of my Uncle Victor was the newspaper account of his death. My older cousins secretly read it to me in the barn. They told me that he had been just as reserved and proper as always, as constrained and charming. That he had listened to the priest with an attentive and polite smile. That he had stepped up decorously to bow his head for the duty of the other man on the stage. That it was only at the first harsh jerk of the rope that his face changed and something dropped from his expression as his body rose up. He looked confused and breathless, and he cried out his mother's name 3 times as his feet dangled above the ground. Each cry of Mother, Mom, Ma went higher in tone and pain, until the last one was just a flute's hollow cry with the fading wind left in his lungs.

And even as his face and eyes were forced up, his right toe reached downward beneath him cautiously, extending, hopeful. Surreptitious.

There was a brutal snap.

After they had cut him down, his face was different in some essential way. The tension gone from around his mouth, all the skin eased back over the burden of his bones. At this point it was possible to see the hollow beauty of his face without his expression or words to confuse things; and even the Jewish newspapers covered their front pages with close-ups of his tranquil sleep.

These photos of his death were so large, so beautiful, exhibited so widely across the world, within many stores and windows, that no one knew whether the world's emotion at his execution was of vengeance, disgust or a quiet unvoiced regret.

I had waited out her story, listening so carefully now for other things, other parts. My mother's voice was quieter tonight, lacking the aggression of the previous nights. Something had unwound and her speech reflected it. For the first time that I could remember, her pronunciation was off, she slurred as though tired or perhaps on painkillers. I could hear it now and wondered how long the slurring had been going on, how much I had needed to ignore. I myself had a bit of a headache. I held a hand to my forehead while she spoke and I breathed in deeply as though the phone might smell of her.

He died, I said.

Yes, she answered simply.

She died and the kids?

Yes.

And Semper?

Prison for the rest of his life.

He dead yet?

No, Mom answered, Not that I know of.

Well, now that's good, huh? One positive thing.

She didn't answer me.

Ok, I said, I've been thinking about this. What's wrong with you?

You don't really want to know.

Oh yes, yes I do, I said. That's why I asked. That's what happens when people ask questions, they want to know the answer. What's wrong with you?

Cancer of the liver.

What?

See, she spoke flatly, See, I told you. You didn't want to know.

We both listened to my breath working on into the phone. It seemed rather labored.

Cancer, she said even more flatly. Unusual in someone of my age.

Well, ahh, I said. My mouth felt dry, my head thick.

I asked, What kind of cancer was it, again?

Liver.

What's your prognosis? I asked. Can I talk to your doctor? Who is your doctor? Are you sure the person's good?

The words came out of my mouth and I listened to them there. My face was abruptly quite hot.

My mother did not respond.

I said, Mom, I'm coming to be with you.

Once again she did not respond.

I said, Wait, wait wait. I have rights. I am allowed. I am family.

Mom snorted, not as though she was amused, more as though she was just snorting. She said, Things are rather messy.

She said, You don't understand how messy, how tiring. Look dear, I know you. You're not up to this. You cried 2 weeks over a dead Chihuahua.

There was a pause between us.

That's unfair, I answered and touched my cheek gingerly.

Please, she said, Let's not argue about the obvious. I don't need this right now. Look, hun, I've always meant to keep some secrets. I might not act like it, but I have.

I can help, I said. I can clean the mess up. I'm strong. I can grow stronger. You need me. You can talk to me in person, tell me the rest of the stories. You can act them out in front of me, imitate people so I can see.

Please, Mom, I said. Please.

The silence between us was long. I could hear her breathing now also. I lay the flat of my hands against my face, hoping to cool it. Propped the phone up with my shoulder.

Honey, she said, I don't need you. Look, she said, I will be honest. I am scared of this. And quite frankly, I do not want you to witness my fear.

Her voice was so low.

Into the silence I clearly hiccuped.

What? she asked. Hey, hey honey. What are you doing? She sounded almost angry.

I hiccuped again. My attempts to breathe normally were what had started the hiccups. The shiver in my breath became more audible. I am ashamed about this part.

I heard my mom pause, trying to remember how to be kind, trying to be polite, as if she ever was. She said, Fran, you're helping a lot just by listening to these stories. Fran, she said, I want you to remember that, that you helped the way I wanted, the way I requested. This is my only request to anyone, about anything. These stories, and you listening. I want you to remember them, these stories, not me bald and vomiting into a pan. I want you to remember you helped.

She said, These stories are all of what is best of me.

I said, You're bald?

My mother said nothing. Perhaps she was listening to my sleeve rustling as I wiped it under my nose.

Really? I asked.

Mom, I said trying to regroup, You've got to change your attitude. Attitude is supposed to help. You always believed you were going to . . . You've always believed you wouldn't live so long, ever since I was a little kid. Please believe instead you will live for a long long time. Into your nineties. Your early hundreds. Don't even think otherwise.

These stories, she said, Contain my life just as much as my bones and organs. Remember them.

I can't possibly remember them the first time through, I said slyly. You'll have to tell them all again.

I added, Maybe 3 times.

We were silent then together for a long time. Stubborn, both of us. Stubborn. Waiting. My mom's wheezy respiration. My quavering breaths and occasional hiccup.

And I think if I had to say the closest time I ever had with her, if I had to choose the moment when we were the most ourselves and yet together, it would not be the times we went blueberry picking. It would not be when we went swimming down in the pond, or the day we went shopping for my fourth-grade outfit. It would not be when I confessed to her at the age of 12 that I wanted to own my own circus someday.

No, instead it would be this moment, here, on the phone, saying nothing at all. In the midst of a fight. Just listening to each other's breath. Wheezing for different reasons.

This is not to say I wasn't furious with her. This is just to say, in that moment, I could also love her.

Mom, I said finally, I've been wondering. How are you sending the packages to me from all over?

Mom chuckled. For a while, she said, I worked in a truck stop doing the cooking. Some of those guys will do anything for a good peach pie. I arranged it weeks before I had to check in here. Those pies were objects of art.

For once, she said, I actually planned ahead.

Chapter 19

After she hung up, I called the operator to trace the call.

The operator said only the police could trace calls and she didn't think it could be done internationally at all. Remember, this was back in the 70s, before all the common options of Caller ID and Call Return. A lot of people still had party lines out in the country. Some people didn't answer the phone at all during thunderstorms for fear of lightning somehow running up the wire and zapping them.

I told the operator this was important. I told her I had to reach my mother. I asked her if there was any way.

Hearing something in my voice, the operator paused, then suggested helpfully that if my mother had committed a felony, perhaps the police in the States could help trace the call.

The next afternoon I went running. Running hard and fast. Much farther than I'd gone on the walks. At first I went through the forest, leaping over fallen trees and old fence posts. But the bushes got too much for me, so I broke out of the forest down by

Ed's Truck Repair Palace and ran along Route 16. I heard the cars slow down as they went by. I saw people's faces in their rearview mirrors. After a few minutes Mrs. Holt slowed down alongside me. I saw it was her when she cranked down her side window to ask if there was anything wrong. I shook my head, still running, imagined Ned hearing about this. I tried to smile, cocked one hand out in a little wave, the way people do when they know what they are doing. After a little pause, she nodded her head, cranked her window back up and drove on. Perhaps she thought I had taken up jogging. I was wearing jeans and a turtleneck, and I was not jogging; I was running, my knees high and pumping. Perhaps she thought this was my version of the sport.

I ran clear around Edwin's lake and back up the old forester's road. I ran up the hill and over to Route 103, I ran farther than I had ever thought I could run, I ran until my legs shook. I overtook 4 separate kids on bikes. I ran until 3 small blisters had formed on the insides of my arms, from chafing against the seams of my turtleneck. I ran until it became hard to stop, my legs trembling but still moving forward on their own as though that was all they now knew how to do. Slowing down took 10 minutes of constant coaxing, of remembering how to stand still.

Only when I finally managed to stop completely, to stand there with my head down and ribs heaving, did I realize that I didn't even have Cessil's binoculars with me.

As usual when Mom called, it was at 6 P.M. exactly and she did not say hello. I thought it would take an atom bomb to make her shift her course, a black hole, kryptonite. I pulled the blanket up tighter around me on the kitchen table, settled my head down better onto the pillow. How on earth, I thought, could she have cancer of the liver and not change at all, not one bit? Not be any more affectionate, not more angry, not polite?

And when I picture myself back then, at this moment, thinking about this question, I see myself, head tight against the receiver, eyes closed in concentration, lying sprawled across the kitchen table. I am thinking about the relentlessness of my mother, the sheer force of her will. And in my imagination, the expression on my face could be taken as a grin.

Or maybe not. Maybe I am making that up. All I can honestly say is that now I was listening to her voice on the phone as hard as I could. I was listening with all my strength.

6 months after Celia had appeared on the doorstep of the family house in Fort Lauderdale visibly pregnant . . .

Yea, I cheered a little too hard, Yea Celia.

. . . she was still pregnant. Her belly was larger now, much larger, but she gave no sign that her time was near.

The family had started to worry 3 months before this point, but Celia would not allow a doctor near her, and the Colt .45 never left her hand. Her other hand tended to rest on the sweeping crest of her stomach, fingers spread, palm down, affectionate.

She had told them the child, miraculously, was dead Egbert's baby. They no more believed it than she did, but when she was alone she tried out the name a few times. She said, Egbert, in the dark, Egbert Junior, and sometimes then the baby kicked. She saw no reason why the situation had to end and so she slept each night propped up in bed, the gun lying in her hand, balanced on the notch between her legs, whether to threaten the baby inside her body or the family outside her bedroom door, no one knew.

There seemed to be nothing the family could do but watch her girth increase like a balloon day by day. Some of the children had started betting that one day a slimy green Martian creature would split her stubborn body open like an avocado pit and peer out from the remains. Both the children and adults spent a lot of time watching her, but Celia ignored them all and swelled only larger and larger, eating her way through vast breakfasts, lunches and dinners.

Celia grew very large and ungainly, her whole body bent backwards in an arc away from the burden. She had a hard time keeping up with the exact proportions of her stomach, and would navigate her way through the halls of the house tapping the sides of her belly against the walls like a blind woman uses a cane. Her lower back ached from the strain so much that one day she disappeared for a few hours into town, then reappeared rolling gracefully down the driveway in an all new electric-blue wheelchair. The chair made a small clicking noise like a toy train, and the children could track this sound from several rooms away while they planned and schemed on how to get the chair away from her to take it on wild rides down Gator Hill and out onto the highway. From the day Celia got it, however, she never left the comfort of its ride, except when locked in the bathroom, and when, at night, she parked it around the far corner of her bed, the gun and her body propped up between the door and her wheelchair. At night she slept so lightly, her first old woman whiskers rising and falling with her snores as her partially open eyes twitched and rolled white at the doorway behind which both children and adults schemed.

By the last week of the sixth month of Celia's return, the tension in the house had become as tight as the skin and clothing across her belly.

It finally happened at breakfast. Celia had been holding up the last bite of her nineteenth pancake when her hand paused in front of *her face. She looked quizzically at her fork as though realizing she had had enough. Slowly she put the mouthful down and stood up, perhaps with the idea of going to the bathroom. Everyone looked up at her expectantly because she was standing rather than using the wheelchair. Then she was opening her mouth, beginning to turn, to turn as if to run, to run from whatever it was that was finally ripping its way free of the half-nelson her hip bones had upon it. Distracted by the intensity of this internal fight, her feet did not move and she screamed instead, screamed in pain and anger and loss as she fell over backwards onto the breakfast that they had all been enjoying, pancakes, eggs and toast flying up everywhere, the heavy wood table bouncing a little into the air with the impact.*

The thing inside Celia now began to fight its way free with solid effective movements that pulled from her enraged possessive howls, unstoppable and inhuman, her face mottled and bulging, her entire upper body slapping from side to side in the grip of whatever fight she was making to still hold on, her fists pounding down upon the table, pounding down upon toast and jam, pancakes and utensils, scrambled eggs and bacon, flipping those food bits and textures and colors up into the air as she breathed in a niggardly clenched way, trying not to cough out that thing which she knew, without a doubt, once it was out she could no longer call Egbert, for it would stop her fantasy dead with the individual set of its eyes, the short sweep of its nose, the clumsy way it moved its fat hands.

Before the doctor could arrive, the child was out.

And as the baby slipped out, in that exact moment, Celia let go also of a strange and powerful sound. A word, half sigh and half sob, created from all her considerable strength and remaining youth leaving her in a single long exhale. That sob/sigh/word which became her child's name in lieu of any other possible suggestion from Celia, because from the point at which the child slid wet and fully-formed out of her body onto the last of the pancakes (the baby clearly 6 months old at the moment of his birth), she refused to admit that the child had ever had anything to do with her, with her body or with her life.

And the sound she had made was slow and regretful. Sadly she said, Bah-bah-louuu.

From that moment on, all the muscles and bones in Celia's body relaxed into old age.

Once the baby was out (a healthy, pretty male with a pert and tiny nose, looking as Celia had prophesied not a bit like her Egbert), Celia never again used her legs. She whirred busily about the house in her wheelchair, treating the child, Babalou, as nothing more than a troublesome obstacle her chair could not go over.

On his first birthday, finally and officially, 2 of Celia's sisters— the fighting twins, Alexis and Elizabeth—adopted Babalou as their own at town hall. He became the child they had never gotten around to having with the men they had never gotten around to marrying, for both of the twins had always been just a shade too busy setting the other twin right on one or 2 matters in which she was dead wrong.

This decision was the only decision of the fighting twins' lives about which they never argued. The 2 were happier than they had ever been, holding Babalou within their old-woman arms, holding this patient and docile infant who was generally so happy and sweet and who for the longest time had not a notion of who his real mother was, for he bore not the slightest resemblance to his mother in body or personality, being small and thin, with the bones of a dancer and a head of dark wild hair. He had a quiet lost side to him which meant that whenever the many other children in the house stepped forward to take away his toy or game, he let them do what- ever they wished, without a word. As he watched the other child walk away clutching the object with glee, his eyebrows would tighten over his fine small nose and he would become completely confused.

After Babalou was born, Celia stopped overeating. Food became an irritation to her, as did almost all the rest of the habits of life. After Babalou's birth she lost interest in everything except for telling stories. She ate only enough to keep talking. She told stories of her life, of her mother and of Cessil, her sisters and her brothers, her youthful beauty and of course of her husband Egbert, her love for him and his love for her, and the way that love continued in the form of these tales, which from that day forth were delivered from her lips fully formed and alive, unstopping until the day she died. No one within the family would accept these histories from her willingly, except for one young girl-child who didn't come along for more than a decade, a little girl who sucked up the stories every morning along with her oatmeal, sucked them into her wide eyes and hungry ears. I mean of course me, who never stopped listening to my Great Aunt Celia, memorizing her plots and characters and phrases, until the night she was murdered in her own bed.

Within a year of the birth of Babalou, Celia had metamorphosized into the old and bony woman I would come to know so well. The woman who rolled around the house in a beat-up clacking electric-blue wheelchair, her freckled old-lady hands expertly flicking forward its wheels, while she drooled out endless stories about the family and poked her pushy way into other people's business.

No one is quite sure when it happened, but by the time I knew her, her face was as completely dead to movement and emotion as the bottom of a frying pan, as if perhaps she had already had some small stroke. The only 2 things about this old woman which hinted of the glamorous past she claimed so incessantly had once been hers were the enormous bust which rolled out onto her bony knees like a soft and ample shelf, and the gun which she never let out of her hand, not even for a bath. Once a week she used that gun for target practice, shooting at the mailbox in the driveway, 100 rounds each week, so visitors with any sort of love of life and limb began to take up the habit of coming around by the back door.

My mom took a long drink of water. The glass clinked twice against her teeth.

Didn't she ever worry that she'd hit someone by mistake?

What? asked my mom.

Didn't she ever worry she would shoot someone by mistake? I asked. A neighbor's dog, the postman, a child?

Mom began to laugh. Her laugh sounded so similar to how it used to. Sure, it was raspier from the cigars, and maybe a shade weaker. But it was the same timing, the same lilt and exhale.

She laughed for a while.

How's your life now? It was the first time she had asked as if she actually wanted to hear.

I had dreamed about this for so long.

Good, I said.

It felt so different from the way I had imagined it would feel.

Good, she repeated, trying not to sound doubtful.

Oh yeah, I said, Well, it's, you know, good. You know how much I love living here, on this farm. I've never wanted to be anyplace else. And, uh, the job is good, firm.

Really, said my mom. She was listening to this. I could hear that, her listening.

Oh yeah, I said with more energy. The job. Great. My boss, Oliver, adores me. And I like him well enough. He's one of those guys who smiles with his ears, you know. Nothing else moves but his ears. Also, I got friends. Roberta, for instance . . .

What about a guy?

What?

A guy, you know, a boyfriend.

For the first time I could hear in her voice the need.

Oh, I said, Oh yeah, Ned. He's nice enough. Great hair, you know, real curly. He likes me a lot. I don't know, though. We're taking it slow.

Really, said my mom, Really? And her voice slurred a little more than normal. Her voice sounded almost like she was half asleep.

Ned, she said, Brown hair?

She asked, Hair like your dad's?

Oh, I said. Oh.

Then I made myself say, Yes.

I hadn't thought of it like that, I told her. But you're exactly right. Brown hair just like Dad's.

I asked what her chances were and my voice came out creaky.

She said one in 3, and quickly started talking about her neighbors.

There is a garden, she said, Out front where I can see them hobble about. It is spring here, there are flowers, color. The sky is blue. My neighbors uniformly wear white, hospital gowns and pants. The disgust I feel for them . . .

I could feel each of my breaths being sucked in over my teeth. I could feel the blood rustling round my veins. One, she had said, in 3. After my father left, after everything else that had happened, there were times when she had prayed for death. I did not know if she still did.

I did not know if the one in 3 was for living or dying, and although I opened my mouth, I did not ask. I could not.

There are 2 other women in my room, she said. Since I checked in here they've been listening to the stories too. They say they enjoy them.

In the background I heard 2 women chuckling, delighted at being mentioned.

The room's walls, she said, Are speckled with blue, like the inside of an egg. As if we are going to hatch.

She asked me what I thought.

I asked her if she was scared, did she need help, where was she, God, just tell me where you are.

The click was soft and sneaky as a clock's.

Some things, I tell you, some things just don't change.

Celia's gun arrived the next morning, postmarked Austin, Texas. The postman gazed up at the house and at the peacocks while he put the package in the mailbox, but his gaze was not any longer or more curious than the one he normally gave the house.

The form on the package did say BOOKS. And when I picked the box up in my hand, there was an unmistakable shift of weight within, and the faintest clink of metal.

Babalou as a baby.

My mother in the only photo she ever let me take of her.

Mourne Family Tree

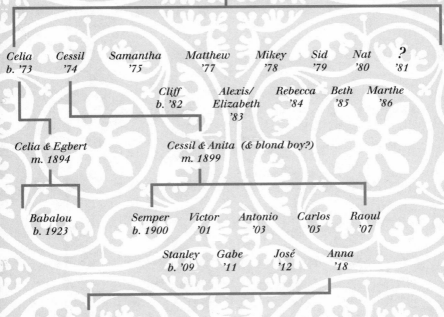

Great Great Grandmother & **?**
b. 1855   d. 1887

*Celia
b. '73*   *Cessil
'74*   *Samantha
'75*   *Matthew
'77*   *Mikey
'78*   *Sid
'79*   *Nat
'80*   **?**
'81

*Cliff
b. '82*   *Alexis/
Elizabeth
'83*   *Rebecca
'84*   *Beth
'85*   *Marthe
'86*

*Celia & Egbert
m. 1894*   *Cessil & Anita   (& blond boy?)
m. 1899*

*Babalou
b. 1923*   *Semper
b. 1900*   *Victor
'01*   *Antonio
'03*   *Carlos
'05*   *Raoul
'07*

*Stanley
b. '09*   *Gabe
'11*   *José
'12*   *Anna
'18*

*Anna & Doctor
m. 1935*

Chapter 20

Last night I dreamed of my mother standing in front of me on the driveway, hands on her hips, bald and yelling. I dreamed that blood came from her mouth and she spat it out like it was her anger. It got all over my pants, my shirt.

Last night I dreamed I lifted the disease from her belly, heavy and curled in on itself. I was holding it out to everyone in the room like a child.

After work, I walked into Holt's Groceries. Ned was in the back, among the fruits, stacking grapefruits. I stopped about 5 feet away and said, Ned.

I hadn't been in here for 3 days, since the time I'd promised myself I wouldn't come back.

He turned around, a grapefruit in each hand, his eyebrows raised in a Can-I-Help-You expression. He had a little stubble on his face. I noticed that if he grew a beard, it would grow thickest at the tip of his chin like a goat's. I wanted to hug him to me like a child.

Ned, I said, I have stopped coming here to shop. I am shopping at Dominion's over on Embry. Because I am doing this, I can take the risk of asking if you want to go to a movie with me over at the mall.

There was a pause. He looked confused. As though perhaps he was trying to reshape my words into an inquiry about vegetables.

What? he asked.

I just asked you out, I said. My voice came from somewhere high in my throat.

I, uh. He looked down at the grapefruits in his hands and then back up to me. I have a girlfriend, he said. Susan McPhee.

He took the change in my expression as an effort to place her name.

He added helpfully, She works over at the video store. Was a year ahead of us in middle school. The girl with brown hair who tripped on the way up the stairs during graduation?

Oh, I said. Oh yes.

We've been going steady for about 3 months now.

Oh, well, I said. Ah, well, then. See you. I held up my hand and turned around to leave. Perhaps it was my back that got to him. I might have been holding it funny. I was certainly considering the length of the walk I had to make now down the fruit aisle, with him watching.

Fran, he called.

I stopped, turned around.

I'm flattered you asked, he added. He gestured out vaguely at the store with a grapefruit, searching for his next words. He added, You're a good person, Fran. Anyone can see that.

Um, thanks. I think I smiled at this point. I certainly tried to. I held up a hand again and turned to go.

And I turned back.

Ned, I said, Ned. I admire how kindly you bag the produce,

no matter whose groceries it is. You look like you care, care about the vegetables. Care about the people who unpack the groceries at the other end. That kind of caring helps people get out of bed in the morning, it helps people through the day. I appreciate it. I bet a lot of people do. Thank you.

I couldn't look directly at him anymore. I think he was standing in pretty much the same position, holding up the grapefruit.

I waggled a hand awkwardly around in a fast goodbye, and walked quickly away, out the door marked Entrance.

I found a history book at the library that had some photos of the winter of 1887. I found a travel book on Fort Lauderdale. I got a book on cancer. At home this afternoon I pored over the first 2 books, got slightly lost. Every once in a while I would remember my speech to Ned that afternoon and I would gasp a little in horror.

No matter what I did, I could not open the book on cancer, *Chemotherapy and Beyond*. Every once in a while I would look over at its cover art of a fuzzy near-smiling dandelion.

At the phone's ring, I jumped halfway out of my seat.

When I picked up, Mom was having an argument with a nurse. Her voice was loud and booming but muffled. She must've had the phone pressed against her chest, her voice echoing inside her.

No, boomed my mom's voice, No. I told you before. I have just one rule. Just one. You can do all your tests to me before 6. Anytime before 6. I am busy after that.

Mrs. Scullaley, said the nurse so distant and faint, I cannot arrange—

What word, asked my mom, Did you not understand?

Material rustled against the receiver. I heard my mom take a breath.

Look, boomed my mom, I tell you what. I feel sorry for you. I will let you take some blood after this phonecall. But right now I am busy.

In the distance I could hear something metal squeak in irritation. I could hear the power Mom had even there, even bald, even on her back.

Sorry dear, said my mom into the receiver more quietly, Now where were we?

In the hospital, Anna's dream of Canada faded a bit, as well as her memory of the noisy house named Brazil. She and the dream within her got lulled by the quiet doctor with his cool damp fingers. She got misled by the hospital's newfangled central air conditioner pumping out its icy breeze. Her dream got muffled by the fuzzy heavy warmth of the 3 blankets she used each night to stay warm, under the power of the air conditioner's chill.

She became hypnotized by the humming silence, by the pure whiteness of the walls, sheets and pillows like snow heaped up in every direction. She got hypnotized by the white uniforms, white stockings and white rubbery shoes, hypnotized by the trails of dampness the quiet doctor's cool fingers left on her hands and face when he took her pulse and temperature. In the hospital, everyone but him moved briskly and impersonally, quietly efficient. There were no yipping animals, no bellowing brothers, no noise at all except for the muted clicking of metal and glass instruments and the loudspeakers crackling on in a secretive undertone with messages for people Anna did not know.

Yes, Anna tried hard to convince herself that this Atlanta hospital room was Canada. She allowed herself to sink into the whiteness of her sheets and her anonymous paper uniform. She allowed her entire body to relax, each muscle deliciously letting go for the first time in her short life, as she was pushed and prodded and pricked by the doctor, whose pasty face and pale eyes had only the tiniest bit of color in them. He never gave out any order unless it was couched in the most extensive conditional clauses. Many were the widely divergent thoughts believed about him, for he was a man upon whom you could project almost anything and it would not be contradicted.

So the dream of Canada was pushed back in Anna's mind as she fell into a healing swoon, as she reverted to the child she had never been able to be in the house she had been born in. In that hospital there in Atlanta she let her life be taken over completely by these impersonal white-clad strangers who fed her and cleaned her and walked her to the bathroom.

And at the end of her hospital stay, she let herself be taken home by this quiet doctor man who had gotten all the appropriate clearances and papers from a person of the law. The doctor, her new guardian, held the farthest edge of her fingers all the way home in the taxi, telling her again and again that he would be keeping her only until she would admit where she really belonged, admit her family name or what state she was from.

This was when she told him her secret, told it for the first time, for she had always known she could not talk about without it losing some of its reality. She told him she needed to get to Canada, she told him she needed to live in the snow. He looked at her and said she would be free to do whatever she wished when she was a legal adult at 18. His hand squeezed tighter down upon the ends of her fingers in a gesture perhaps of support, perhaps of imprisonment, and she responded to his honesty by lying about her age, telling him she was 15 instead of the 13 she really was.

They both saw the 3 years ahead of them with a solidity that could be kept in the pocket.

. . .

His house, as she knew it would be, was clean and tiled like the hospital. As a surprise for her, the doctor had managed to have a central air unit installed in his house. This unit had been intended for the hospital and enough power to flap small papers away from its vents; it filled the house with the moist closed air of a fridge.

That first day she was not quite sure what she should take as her sign to leave for Canada. All night and the next day the house hummed quietly back at her without an answer. She had realized by now how much she had been in pain on her trip running away from home, to what extent she had been tired and hungry and lonely, even for her brothers.

That whole first week in the doctor's house she considered when to start walking again to Canada as she lay comfortably in her bed with the air conditioner on so high that the vents dripped half-frozen water. Each night she closed her eyes and imagined herself striding all alone against a blizzard. She did this to lull herself to sleep.

Sometime during the first month of her stay with the doctor, the realization bloomed inside her that she would wait out those 3 years in his house.

And her heart became the smaller for it.

The days of those years passed like rain, with nothing to distinguish them or to slow them down. During this time, the simplest events took her a moment to apprehend, as if they were muffled, heard underwater. The maids in the house were quiet and innocuous, and the noise of the school she attended simply reminded her of the barbarity she had once known. She retreated willingly each afternoon back to the doctor's house.

So his home became her home and one day she awoke to the knowledge that the man had installed himself in her life in ways that made her happy. She liked the quiet classical music he played in the mornings and the jello salad he made for dessert on the weekends.

Each jello cube was exactly alike in size, shape and bright color. Each melted in her mouth as if they had never been, leaving only the slightest aftertaste of sugar and chemical fruit. He got her an aquarium filled with fish, pets that were simply pretty and never to be touched, encased in their own glass world. Anna had become as dependent upon her doctor man as she was upon the health of her willowy body, whose tender skin seemed melted from some finer substance than what we know of as flesh, and whose insides throbbed away at their own speed, pink and intelligent, without her help or permission.

The man also seemed to be content there inside the house, with no desire for outside contact. When he talked to the neighbors, his voice was reserved and succinct, never chatting more than was precisely necessary. With the maids he was polite and detailed. With both he retired from any interaction as soon as it was socially acceptable. Only with her was he comfortable enough to be still, silent, sucking in each cube of jello salad, the click of a spoon against the plate, watching the fish, both of them quiet, waiting out the time left to them.

During the whole of those 3 years, there was not a single loud noise or real emotion to wake her up. At the end of it she looked down at her body of a woman with shifting awe, heard her woman's voice with a subtle fear, as though in lying about her age by 2 years, she had jumped herself forward 10.

When Anna turned 16, the doctor and she celebrated her 18th birthday at a small party of just the 2 of them, with the maids standing up against the wall like patient brooms. When the cake was eaten, the 2 of them put their bags in the car so he could drive her up to the border himself. For 4 days in the car he drove and she sat. The conversation was sparse and dealt mostly with the subjects of food, bathrooms and gas stations. He stared conscientiously at the curves of the road ahead, and she blinked intermittently at her hands, find-

ing herself filled with an irrational craving for sleep, a craving that deepened no matter how much she actually slept. She would lean over, half-dozing, and fall time and time again down upon his shoulder, his shoulder thin and angled and with the slightest hint of cologne.

Each time she awoke, she wondered for a split second where on earth they were driving to. Then the answer would come, that single ringing word: Canada. It seemed so far away and unlikely, so unattainable. A dream on which she had based her whole life.

During the drive they spent 3 nights in almost identical motels. Here, time moved strangely for Anna. The red flash of the MOTEL VACANCY sign outside clicked on to flood the room at what she could only suppose were even intervals, although time seemed to be moving in halts and jerks. The red flash almost had the consistency of blood, pooling up the sides of the twin beds and lapping over the tender curve of the doctor's shoulder that he turned decorously away from her. The red spilling into her nostrils and through her skin as though she were about to drown in the light, until the sign went off with a deliberate click.

The final night they spent in Niagara, their last stop before the Canadian border. Champagne bottles and wadded-up cocktail napkins with dirty jokes printed on them were littered across the streets as evenly as if they had snowed from the sky. Everywhere couples walked arm in arm, and Anna and the doctor were no exception. They walked over to the falls, arms linked, moving slowly into the onrushing sound, moving in such a careful rhythm, as if they were carrying something heavy between them.

The doctor and Anna stepped around the final corner and suddenly the falls were there. More vast than she could imagine, even while looking at them. They went so far up. They were wide and grey as a city block moving and shaking and being pulverized down to its base again and again. The falls seemed angry. The falls seemed furi-

ous. They shook the ground throughout the town. Made everyone and everything nearby tremble in fear. That tremendous chaos rushing headlong since its inception in only one direction, with only one possibility in its mind, only one purpose. That one purpose which led it to rush straight over the edge of the last rock to hurl out into complete emptiness. Anna knew that on the other side of that impossible cliff of water, on the other shore, was Canada. Canada. The word was the echo of things far away, the call of geese with grey bellies flying overhead through frozen air. Canada.

It was within her reach. She could drive there tomorrow.

She could see it, live it, step on it. Wake up every morning in it. Blow her nose and flush the john inside of it. Compare it with her dream.

She stepped closer and closer until her belly was stopped by the safety rail. That surprised her, that metal railing suddenly there against the warmth of her belly, and the cold wet of it woke her up deeply for the first time in 3 years, perhaps for the first time in her entire life, woke her up entirely. Her vision and hearing cleared. She was standing by the falls. The noise was terrific. It vibrated the wooden platform on which she and the doctor stood, and it made the far side of the river blur and run. The roar of the water rose up from the river and down from the falls to wrap her in its mindless fury, and it seemed to meet an answer in her very soul, an echo in her body, as though there had always been a roar within her. This power that had helped her walk 237 miles from Fort Lauderdale to Georgia, holding just a glass of milk.

She looked up into the center of that furious water and felt a terror within her soul, a terror so large at this first clear glimpse of her own personality she thought the fear would split her skin. With a gesture as ritualized and smooth as a nun crossing herself, she touched her heart and touched her ears and then turned and kissed her doctor full on the mouth.

His breath was decorated with mouthwash, and the surprise on his face was by far the strongest emotion she had ever seen there.

She married him that afternoon—in a chapel only a little bigger than a child's playhouse—where a wedding with rice and flowers cost just $17.95. There was a line of 8 or 9 couples outside the chapel, some of whom were still holding mixed drinks from the hotel bar nearby. When Anna and the doctor reached the front of the line to be married, they could not actually fit in the chapel, so they said I do into its open doors. Inside, the reverend and 2 witnesses crouched like an oversized living crèche.

And who knows what the doctor actually felt about all this? Perhaps he had been in love with her from the moment he saw her determined and terrified child-self sitting up so straight in that hospital bed. Or perhaps he had never had the slightest sexual interest in her, but he was so used to complying with others that he did not know how to stop now. Or perhaps he knew this was his only way of keeping her.

That night, in the farthest motel room she had been able to find from the falls, she came to the doctor's bed with desperation, to touch his soft wet skin. Together they were awkward, but she was determined. Never did their politeness fail them. Even from all the way across town, the sounds of the falls rumbled subtly in the walls and floors of the room, whispered distant but unstoppable warnings to her like the very breath of life.

She discovered a lightness in her touch she had never known. She found she was lighter of a lot of things. She found that for the first time in 3 years she was not thinking of her mother. At this point, that was a lightness she appreciated, but with time this lightness would turn to lack.

Within a few years her insides would lighten until they became hollow and dusty. She would become unreasonably terrified of losing her grasp on the ground at the push of people's breath. Her lightness would expand until it was a balloon blown tight and painful within her skull.

The day after the wedding, the doctor and she started back to Atlanta, where she would live out the rest of her life. She never got to Canada but instead turned all the formidable passion within her dream into a ferocious demand to have a son who would go to Canada for her.

What? I said. She never got to Canada?

No, said Mom.

But she wanted to. She wanted to so much.

Yes, said Mom.

But it was her dream, I said trailing off. Her dream.

Did you see your man today, asked Mom.

What, I asked, Who?

Oh, I said, Oh yes. Ned. I went over to where he worked.

Ahh, that's good, she said. That's nice.

We both thought for a little while.

You don't, she asked, You don't have a picture of him, do you?

No more packages arrived from my mom this day, nor would any in the days afterward. I assumed she was not able to ship them from her hospital room, could not get in contact with her truckers, could not make a peach pie. I imagined my mom packing for the hospital, not allowed to check in with more than one suitcase. It would take her 2 days to decide what to pack. She would pack Celia's sequin dress rather than her own nightgown. She would wrestle for an hour with whether to bring her own tooth-brush or Victor's Bible.

Once she was at the hospital, she would set out the 2 or 3 small objects she'd brought. They would look all wrong on the formica table. The table smelled of ammonia, the bed had rubber sheets. So many anonymous objects had lain here before, kleenex, glasses of water, dialysis bags. She'd move the family memorabilia around, rearranging it again and again, running her fingers over the pieces. Her breath slowing. This was the time she needed them most.

I knew I would not be getting any more packages in the mail from her, so after the phonecall I started to examine Celia's gun, the last gift. At first I was careful not to touch it except with the tips of my fingers, extended and cautious as insect legs. I picked it up that way, thumb and index finger like pinchers, a detective analyzing a clue. I had never really looked at a gun before, certainly never held one.

The gun's gleam was low and dark. Its weight was heavy and compact, much more solid than my hand itself, more purposeful and confident. In a way it was like holding a frying pan, so solid and metal. In a way it was like holding a typewriter, so many interlocking parts. It was large for a gun, proud. It lent reason and importance to my hand even when it was held awkwardly with 2 fingers up by my face or slackly down by my side. Walking into any restaurant with this gun would be like walking in from the ultimate stretch limo. I would get much better service; it made me someone worth listening to.

The metal was near black with the years. There was the handle—what do they call it? The stock? It was made of wood, worn down from a single person's grip. I could trace the imprint of each of Celia's iron fingers, could slip my hand round hers that way.

It seemed strange to me that my hand was bigger.

I pushed open the canister thing where the bullets were inserted. I had no idea what the word was for this part. The click and roll of the metal as it opened was satisfying. Inside, the compartments were dark and fitted, a bee's chambers, purposeful and designed. I knew already what satisfaction it must be to load, to slip the projectile into its home, to roll the opening shut. Knowing what has changed.

I fingered a bullet. It was aerodynamic, lean. A small ridge encircled its base. I wondered at its power. I wondered at its skill.

It slipped in as easily as I had assumed it would. There was a click as the gun was shut, a heavier click than before. More meaningful.

I stood up, the handle snug within my oversized grip.

Perhaps you won't be surprised to hear that this evening, after the phonecall, I took the gun and the box of bullets out to the back pasture, set cans up along the fence and stepped back 10 feet. I aimed carefully, gently eased back the trigger.

CRACK, the gun barked and jumped clear out of my hand. Fell with a dull whump into the grass at my feet.

I jumped back. My hands flew out from my sides as if the gun had been aimed at me.

For a moment I just breathed. Then I stepped forward and crouched down to look at the gun, inanimate again. It was as though, for a moment, it had come abruptly to life. Kicked back in irritation at my unprofessional handling.

I'd missed all the cans. I think I'd probably missed the fence by several yards. I picked the gun up tentatively, scared it would jerk again, this time without me pulling the trigger. I tried shooting again, kept my face averted but my hand firmer. After

3 shots I managed not to drop the gun. I shot for a full hour. I shot until my hand hardened into its grasp, until my hand barely jerked with each shot. Until it was too dark to see.

I practiced again the next afternoon after work. I had a lot of time.

The first time I hit a can, it pinged loud and shocked. It jumped right off the log, spun around and around. Little bits of it flew off into the air.

The next thing I managed to shoot was a bottle. It exploded into piecework sunshine, twinkling and twisting through the air.

It was beautiful. I was surprised how beautiful it was.

I shot more. My arm flattened into a straight line. The gun felt better in my hand, more natural. I sighted carefully, liked seeing the power of my aim. Each time I hit something I felt my insides loosen a bit more, calming down, deep into my very muscles and bowels, as if instead of shooting, I was easing myself down into a comfy chair after a long day, pouring myself some tea. I could see why little boys dreamed of guns, of their power. I could see how Celia had threatened her whole family with this gun for years, had enjoyed it. I could see how in times of trouble people might do some target practice to calm down.

Just holding the gun, I felt less helpless.

By the second afternoon, at least half the things I aimed at danced into the air.

Chapter 21

As a cook, Mom had always been known for her complex creations, her bouillabaisse, her shrimp *vatapá*, her green banana curry. For me, though, her best food was the simplest thing she made. Her 3-minute soft-boiled eggs. The yolk completely gooey, the white of the egg firm. She'd scoop the egg out onto strips of liberally-buttered toast, stir it all up, my favorite dish as a little kid. At 2 or 3 years old, the sense of taste is so pure. The pleasures of hunger and chewing are still so new, not taken for granted, not done mechanically. The body knows what it wants with great clarity, before years of dutifully choking down spoonfuls of liver and lima beans. I remember the sweetness of the butter, the richness of the yolk, the crinkling of the bib around my chubby neck. I remember looking up at my beautiful mom, who was staring out the window toward the driveway with her green startled eyes. I remember knowing from the taste of the egg that she loved me.

And, as always, at the end of 10 minutes she took the plate away, whether I was finished or not.

.　.　.

Mom, I asked, What exactly is the operation for? What drugs are
you on? Do you trust your doctor?

You're right, she said, Let's talk about my mother.

*It was only after not being able to conceive a child for 4 straight years
that the lightness within Anna began to incapacitate her. She became
so empty and desiccated inside that the ease of her sleep began to
leave her. Open windows bothered her. She imagined herself blown
crumpled and broken into a corner from a sudden gust of wind, and
the maids sweeping her up as they did the hollow skins of cicadas, her
papery eyes wide and hollow.*

*Anna took to breathing lightly and quickly in her fear, told no one
of her thoughts and dreamed of the first year of her marriage, when
she had been filled with the heavy happiness that comes from expecta-
tion. She had never felt her life to be a very certain thing—except in its
desires—but for the first 3 years of her marriage she had been certain
she would have a son. It had to be a son, for in the confusion of her life,
she had realized that her brothers had never been thwarted in what
they wished (though it didn't occur to her that they never wished for
anything much more elaborate than a big lunch and an occasional
scrimmage of soccer). She hypothesized now that the reason she had
never reached Canada—such a simple destination that even ducks get
there once a year—was that she was a woman. She thought she could
fix that with a son. A son of hers would be able to reach Canada. He
would want to go just as much as she. He would leave at an even
younger age than she had, perhaps only 7 or 8. In their simple goodbye she would give him only a fast hug and the address of the farm
where her grandmother's body still lay, attracting money, pilgrims
and the occasional bishop researching the claim to canonization.*

She could feel the completion of that parting like honey on her lips.

The only problem was that she did not conceive.

Neither Anna nor the doctor went through any of the tests that the doctor knew so well were available. Neither of them wanted the blame to be final. They were well-mannered to each other, still optimistic after the third year, or at least pretending to be. They kept trying. After the fourth year Anna thought of secretly going to some other man, but she knew of no one whom she could depend on, aside from the maids and her doctor. She schemed endlessly, and the constant coldness of her house finally began to enter her skin. When she touched the doctor unexpectedly, he thought of the purity of metal.

Finally a girl child was delivered. She was delivered at the age of 3 months with her own clothes and name, dropped off in a car by the woman from the adoption agency. The agency believed the couple to be a good risk, for the husband was a doctor and the wife seemed to want a child so strongly.

I cannot tell you why they were given a girl instead of a boy. I don't know if Anna was too shy to mention her preference, or if she thought it all so predestined that she need not even mention it. Or perhaps she and the doctor had fought over the gender; maybe it was the first time he had stated an opinion.

It's strange how family secrets are kept most carefully from those closest to them.

The marriage at this point was in its fifth year, and the whole house had recently been redecorated by Anna in varying shades of the silence of white, with thick fleecy carpets and pillows like drifts. I, named Gloria by my unknown birth mother, was delivered into the clinical hands of my new father, and did not see my new mother until early the next morning.

What? I said, What?

What what? asked my mom.

You were . . . I cleared my throat and looked around the kitchen, You were adopted?

Why honey, said my mom, I've told you that.

Oh no, I declared, Oh no you haven't.

Oh yes, I'm sure I must have, she said chuckling a little. You probably just forgot.

She inhaled and then continued.

The things I remember about my mother are conflicting.

But wait, I said.

I was looking around the kitchen as though I had been abruptly transposed here. As though up until a moment before I had been somewhere else, somewhere quite different, a small city apartment perhaps, or on a boat deep at sea. In the deepest tundra or jungle. I stared at the dirty dishes by the sink in bewilderment. I turned to the checked linoleum beneath my feet.

Honey, my mom said. It's no big deal. I've always been as much a part of my family as any blood relative.

Or more, she said.

The things I remember about my mother are conflicting. Anna complained frequently of her tiredness in a repetitive untiring way. By the time I arrived she had her hair cut short in what could be viewed either as a mannish or childish style. Her face was already as pale as the elderly and beginning to pouch out under the eyes, although she was only 21. As though, in the same way that her body had grown up faster than it should, it was now growing older faster than it should. She was quite busily transforming herself into an old woman, never having lived life as a young one. Her body was long and flat against each bone like a dancer, yet her hands were pale and swollen and covered with twisting veins like yarn.

In the first few years of my life, Anna carried me about on each of her errands like a lapdog with no life on its own. She carried me well into my fourth and fifth years, hardly ever letting me down to stand on my own feet. I remember her, at that time, as being very physical. Affectionate in a way.

Frequently she would jerk me to her, so hard it almost hurt, her face pushed down into my neck, her nose pressed into my child flesh, her eyes closed tightly against all outside facts. When this happened, I knew enough to make my body go slack, like a small animal in a cat's jaws, my face blank and my eyes motionless. I did not move until Anna was normal again.

During those times when her face was pressed into my neck, Anna would speak with complete honesty and in a monotone. The words she spoke were not meant for a child. In fact, I don't believe that much of the time she even remembered I was there. She was just speaking her thoughts. Because of these monologues, the first word I could speak was adopted. *And long before I knew that first word, I knew that Canada was where I should want to go, that it was the most beautiful place on earth, that snow fell there silent and deep. Yes, I also knew long before I was 2 that I was supposed to have been a boy, that men were preferable to women, that my mother was a female with a man's heart. Anna believed that was why she and the doctor could not have a child on their own, that she was better than just a woman, that she could not perform adequately as a woman alone.*

That phrase has always echoed within me during my life, "a woman alone."

When I was 5, during one of her monologues, Anna had gestured down toward her belly and then again harder. She hit her belly again and again, and each cough of pain seemed disengaged from her motions, delayed a moment or 2 too long, as though, in the pause, her belly were hitting her back. Pulled in tight against her, I kept my face pressed into her shoulder, stayed very still. Through her body, I felt each one of the hits like a blow against myself.

Sometimes Anna would get stomach aches, feel pain, tearing, something grindingly wrong. At these times all blood drained from her face until it went as white and flat as snow, and she would shuffle, totter her way back toward her room. Neither hand touching her belly now; they circled in brittle balancing motions at the ends of her arms. Inside her room, she closed the door. Not even the doctor—perhaps especially the doctor—was allowed through that door during these episodes.

But the thing that I remember above all else about my early childhood is the smell of my mother. It comes back to me easily even now. It seemed my childhood was flooded with this smell and it was truly important, for in spite of all my mother's other eccentricities, all her urges and cruelties, all her needs and spells, in spite of whatever else she might do or be, she always smelled like a mother should and I loved her unabashedly for that. She filled my childhood with the memory of a musky feminine scent, sweet and living as a rounded belly, kind and giving as fresh bread. It was not a strong and cloying smell like those that came from a bottle, not simply antiseptic and deodorized like the doctor's chin. Instead Anna's skin smelled like a combination of rich earth, cat's breath and Jergens lotion. She smelled like a happy loving mother, and as time passed, when her arms captured me and her pouchy swelling face pressed tight into my neck, I began to close my eyes like her. Keeping my body still, I sucked in great bowls of air like a starving child and brought it all straight to my heart.

When Anna got one of her belly aches, which sometimes lasted for days, she would abruptly tire of me. Before I was even a year old I was being sent regularly down to Fort Lauderdale to visit with my mom's family, to live for a while in the ragtag mansion there on the swamp. The first time the doctor delivered me to the doorstep in Florida, he simply handed me over with a few words that included my given name, whose daughter I was, and the fact that he would be back in a week to pick me up. He left then, before the shock could first appear on the face of the recipient.

When I was older, I began to believe that the bluntness of the doctor's statements, in such a situation, could only mean his personality and actions were powered by a crippling shyness.

But of course my impression was never contradicted. I never understood more of him than that he made good jello salads and loved my mom with a quiet and utterly-accepting intensity that came from having nothing else.

Even then, 23 years after it was started, the house in Fort Lauderdale was still being worked on. Hammers lay where they'd been dropped 5 years before. There was no insulation anywhere, and long sections of hallway had been nailed together in such a careless rush that if you stood outside the house at night, the darkness was splintered by light radiating outward like quills from a living creature.

Yes, there were still whole rooms open to the jungle as though from an explosion, doors left piled drunkenly up on one another, a sink sitting unconnected halfway up the front stairs. But after a few years people had begun to use the sink as a goldfish bowl, the spare doors as makeshift tables, and the toilets left in people's bedrooms had been adopted as nightstands or sock drawers.

This house was also increasingly filled with the trappings of Anita's enormous wealth. I remember from my childhood that everything glimmered in that house, the shimmer of lopsided chandeliers, faceted crystal and women's bodies wrapped in taffeta and satin, the glitter of loose wiring and silver statues, wet swamp grass growing up through a hole in the floor, the sparkle of men's stickpins, sweat and white teeth. Everything shivering with money, health and heat except for an old woman dressed in dingy black, an old woman who

*whizzed busily about in her wheelchair, mumbling stories to herself.
Everything sparkling except for an obese man, round as a boulder
and grey with disuse, a man who never moved from his now steel-
reinforced throne-like chair as he muttered his obvious orders and
trite advice in a quietly continuous steam like a teakettle.*

*From the day I was dropped off there in that house, I was pulled
into that dynasty of humanity without a ripple, a place made for me in
a moment amid the long line of infants in their high chairs at the table.
Later on, I moved into the line of children and then the young adults. I
was just one of many, but from the first moment there, I can remember
also an assurance building within me, a certainty of my central position and power in that house. I sensed it with every breath I took. It
was in that house that I discovered for the first time that I was smart
and strong, that I could run faster than many my age, and that I could
pivot and fake out those who were much older. Sometimes in tag I
would get caught on purpose just so I could be* it, *chasing after the
rest, watching them flee from me as I knew they should. Even at 5 or 6
I was frequently chosen first for softball teams because for every base I
ran, I stole 2, and the pitcher wouldn't be able to concentrate with the
knowledge of me crabbing forward low and tense somewhere behind.
Sometimes this feeling of importance and health—and what I didn't
recognize at the time was the force of youth—would be so pure within
me that I would simply spin and spin about, filled with the upwelling
of my own power, my hair lifting like a cloud with my speed, the world
rocking on its axis at my strength. And there was not one person in the
house that thought twice about my actions, for it was a house built on
the principles of the endlessness of energy, people and money.*

*I never told my mother what I felt in that Florida house, yet there
was no doubt in my mind that Anna knew. I think she sensed that,
each time I came back to her, my interest in Canada was diminished.
That I was developing more of an interest in the South, in that house
in Fort Lauderdale, than in travelling north anytime soon. I think*

that was the reason that sometime in my fifth year she stopped pulling me into those ferocious hugs, stopped treating me to those mono-logues about the beauty of Canada, those monologues about her being better than a woman, about how I should have been a boy. Instead she began to get those belly aches more frequently.

I was shuttled back and forth between the 2 houses, becoming more and more disoriented. Finding myself expecting noise and movement and color, and getting instead silence and whiteness and her sweet scent that was filled with at least the promise of love.

About my adopted father, I don't remember all that much, in spite of him living for a long time after Anna's death, perhaps living even now. I know he brushed his teeth religiously after each meal, and cut the fat off his meat with the ease of a professional. He did not say much, or move around a lot, and his polite expression was easy to ignore. In moments of contention, he tended to shrug politely, defer-ring to the will of the other person. Not a dramatic South American shrug like Anita's, just a small shrug, the smallest kind, moving only his hands and the muscles of his shoulders.

After Anna died, he seemed to disappear even more, and people talked around him as though he were a coat rack. He began to go away, to travel for short periods of time, then longer, leaving me at the house in Fort Lauderdale. Sending cards and money orders, typed, impersonal, well-meaning, from Tucson and Galveston and Minneapolis, the cards trailing off but the money continuing, until at some point even the money stopped and no one noticed for at least a year. By the time it was discovered that he'd gone missing, there was no recent address to search from. And the mystery of his disap-pearance was so without clues that no one dwelled on it for very long.

. . .

But I am skipping ahead. Let me back up.

When I was 7 and Anna 28, Anna's stomach began to swell out, to fill. She remained thin everywhere else, but she lost the flat line of hip and navel that had always depressed her so. Her stomach began to balloon outward and she was able to carry her hands cupped under her belly like a monk.

She smiled irrepressibly at unsuitable times and denied that she was doing so. Her primary mission was to keep this a secret from the husband. She knew if he found out, he would make her go to an obstetrician to check that everything was ok. From the way her husband talked about his patients, she knew that any doctor who examined her, with his handling and tests and vocabulary, would take away from her, in some essential way, the sole possession of her baby.

And perhaps—she never said this next part to me, but I still wondered—perhaps she sensed, because of her stomach aches, that there was the danger the doctors would decide to take the baby away entirely.

She took to wearing wide clothing, layers, large shirts. Clothing that emphasized her long arms and legs, her neck. She said she was feeling fat and wanted to hide it. No one saw. No one knew except for me. I saw. I knew. The happiness, the excitement, the anticipation. I saw my mother stand each night naked in front of the bathroom mirror, cupping her new expanding belly, holding her future in her hands, one hand on each side, the belly in the middle. The belly filling with my mother's real child, her first child, while the other child, me, watched silently behind her, out of sight of the mirror, my hands hanging slack at my sides.

Then one day it happened.

The pain began. It was, I can remember, quite a bit of pain. A lot of pain. Pain well beyond what Anna considered to be morning sickness, beyond what until now she had imagined even birth to be.

And so she slid down the stairs on her rear while announcing the moment in a clenched voice, the imminent birth of her own child. Her own blood, her son. As she talked, sliding down the stairs on her rump, my 7-year-old self walked backwards down the stairs in front of her with my arms out to catch her if she slipped.

The doctor rushed her to the hospital and within 2 hours they knew the swelling to be cancer of the uterus. Cancer that had already spread to the liver and the lungs.

It happened quickly after that, not much more than 2 weeks. But those 2 weeks seemed longer than any year or decade I have lived through since. They seemed longer than the rest of my life in comparison. I can tell you what was served for every meal that she couldn't eat, the pink froth of the ice cream heated to the same temperature as the grey roast beef in the hospital warming ovens. I can repeat the sound the nurse made with her lips each time she missed Mom's vein with her needle, and I can draw the wear pattern of every tile on the floor of her room. I can describe the manner in which each of the 3 operations didn't work. I can imitate every moment my mother managed to really sleep, how her face worked even then. I can describe both times she allowed me close enough to smell her skin.

It was her hearing that went first.

Silence, she whispered in surprise, and her hoarse voice was filled with such knowledge that the doctors desperately arranging machines above her lowered their voices. I was small then, the one watching so closely that I had hit the alarm bell in the first place, making them all rush in. In the confusion and noise no one noticed me holding onto the end of her bed, standing so still, so small.

Then Anna began to feel very cold, but by this time she could no longer speak and only the motion of her lips touched my quick eyes. "Cold," her lips framed.

After that the dark center of her eyes pointed straight at me, as her lips still trembled slightly with what she wished to say, but her mouth formed no more words. Death was like slow water rising up *the long limbs of her body. Cold water, snow. Lethargy. It was, I could see, like white drifts building up heavy against her hips and shoulders, making movement slow and then impossible; falling into her mouth and ears, perfecting the silence that Anna had always wished for.*

Anna's lips began to turn up against the creases born of a lifetime of harsh feelings, and the air escaped from her mouth.

Jesus, said one of the doctors, Who let the kid in?

And me, at the age of 7, I was sent down to live with my mother's relatives permanently. As I have said, my adopted father, the doctor, lived with us at first, only starting to travel to other places as time passed. My grandmother, Anita, took me in as completely as though I were her own daughter, as though I was the daughter she wished she'd actually had, returned 17 years after the real one left.

And me, from the moment of my mother's death, I behaved as an adult woman, restrained and without games. Now I no longer spun with my own power, laughed or played softball. Now I had only one pose: hands tucked away in my pockets, my eyes staring straight out at each event without hiding, understanding the world irrevocably as the deadly serious matter from which my mother had rushed so young.

I rubbed the line of my jaw, the bridge of my nose. One of the cats saw me stirring and hummed a lilting question. I did not smile at the cat. I did not sit up.

My mother's voice sounded even worse tonight. Her words had the exaggerated sobriety of the very drunk; whatever emotion there was within her was stifled by the strain of speaking clearly. She sounded like someone listing stock returns. She sounded almost British.

She must be reading these stories, I thought. There's no way she could tell stories in this condition otherwise. She must have typed them up and brought them into the hospital.

Still, I never once heard paper rustle.

And the way I felt about all of this was tired, very very tired. I thought tonight, I might just sleep downstairs, sleep right here, on the kitchen table. For some reason I seemed to taste metal in the back of my throat.

Mom. I asked, What medication are you on?

The pills are the most beautiful color, she said. A lovely blue, exactly like a person's eye. There are also these thick pink drinks they give me sometimes during the day. A bit of a chalky taste.

The pills don't erase the pain, she said. They just make it seem beautiful and distant, like a blizzard seen from inside a warm house. And, on the pills, I no longer get the dreams.

Dreams? I asked but she continued as though she had not heard.

Today, they finished up all the pre-operation tests, she said. Tomorrow I can sleep in. I am tired of being wheeled around in those little white paper nighties in any case. I look horrible in them.

My skin, she mentioned so quietly, My skin seems to be turning a different color now.

What color? I asked, without wanting to know in the least.

She said more brusquely, We have 2 days left before the operation.

What is the operation supposed to do? I asked. How will you know it worked?

My mom said without a pause, I'm pretty sure I can finish the stories by then. I will do my best. Although these next stories are the most difficult.

Mom, I said, I have one request. Just one. I want you to be reasonable about this. I want a phone number I can call to find out how the operation went. It doesn't have to be the phone number of anyone in the same town as you, they don't even have to be in the same state. Just someone to call to find out if things went ok. I don't think this is unreasonable.

She was silent.

And lying there on the kitchen table, with the phone to my ear, waiting for her response, I remembered the last time I had hugged my mother, 4 and ½ years ago. It was on the final night she lived on the farm, less than 2 months after that last loud fight, the fight when she had looked away from me to the car in the driveway.

That last night we'd had together I did not know it was our last night. I knew only that over the previous few weeks she had been increasingly silent, no longer telling me family stories or listing the traits of her mother that I should emulate. This last night she no longer even picked at my bad habits like at a scab.

Instead she was just quiet. Even more quiet than before, a different quality of quiet, as though perhaps she had finally given up, accepted things. The sudden peace between us seemed as natural as the summer's night air, and my heart and mouth filled with a lightness I had never known.

When I stood up that night to go up to bed, she stood up also, her mouth half-open as though about to speak. Instead I pulled her abruptly into a fast embrace. She had not expected it. We were not a very physical family, the 2 of us, and the touch of me stopped her cold in the midst of whatever words she had been about to speak. Her arm half-raised in an incomplete gesture, a wave perhaps, or touch. I pulled her into my arms with her mouth still open. Her raised arm, from my tall hug, was pushed higher up above her head into some sort of salute and her lips were forced against my neck, not in a kiss, just her lips pushed slack from surprise against me. Her lips were wet. Her body was compact and hard, and the zipper of her dress got caught on a thread of my sweater, so there was a ripping sound as we parted.

I strode off upstairs, grinning like a bride.

And my mother, standing silently below, her arm still half-raised, never said a thing.

On the phone, from the hospital, my mother exhaled through her nose.

Good night, Frannie. And she hung up.

I went out to the barn to sit by my great great grandmother's body.

I sorely needed some company, and the body was the closest thing to that around. I had known about the body for as long as I could remember, but hadn't realized until I was 12 or 13 just what it was. Early on, I thought it was some type of old leather harness, darkened and twisted, wrapped up in ancient faded flowered cloth. The whole thing had cuddled inward over the years, reverting to its fetal beginnings. The bits of protective wax that still clung to its skin had created a sort of piebald effect. The shape of the human features was fairly subtle by this point. It looked more like the image of a face you see sometimes in driftwood or the arrangement of clouds.

In the barn attic, out the window, I could see the sun was half gone behind the blueberry field. The start of the night was a soft purple haze creeping across the grass. One of the peacocks had clambered awkwardly up the staircase after me. He rustled through the hay near the staircase, pecking in a way that seemed mostly wistful, his tail filling with straw. I was surprised he had come up at all; the birds were awfully old now and I had not seen one of them venture up here for at least a year. The straw crackled beneath him, his feathers rustled and the few beehives that were still occupied hummed in the fading light of day.

Her body lay by the window. I had taken the protective shades and shutters off the window last year; at this point they could not help her anymore. I had left the window open. I thought a little summer wind and rain might be nice for her. At least she looked more animate now. What was left of her hair sometimes waved at me through the window while I worked in the garden, the few remaining strands black and strong as a horse's tail hair.

I settled my body down beside hers in the window. Sighing, I started telling her my troubles, one by one. At first I was a bit self-conscious, kept my voice in a half mutter as though someone else might come up here to find me talking to a mummified body. Gradually, though, my voice got louder, more natural. I told her about my mom, the phonecalls, the stories. I told her how Celia had turned out. I told her about my mom's old fights with me, and the way she had run away.

I told her about the cancer and was silent for a long time afterward.

I told her about my mom being adopted and glanced down involuntarily to her.

Checking for her expression.

I giggled. Glanced sideways at her again, giggled harder. That's when the irony—the cosmic humor—of my mother's adoption really struck me. I guffawed. I snorted, I hacked. It was difficult to control. I bent over with it. My head bobbed. My sides and shoulders shaking, my face folding in. My eyes tearing.

I cried. I cried all out, chest sobbing, head bobbing, loud loud barking bellows. I beat the floor with my fists. Of course I tried to stop it. That only made things worse.

It took me a long time to quiet down. I had to pat her hand, breathe slowly, wipe my face, count to 3 between each breath. I rested my long back against the window frame. Every once in a while a hiccup would jerk me sideways.

The silence crept up more and more and, because I patted her hand, the faintest lilac scent swirled up into the air. Around us, the hives buzzed more loudly in answer. 3 bees flew out to investigate, their yellow fuzz bright against the increasing gloom. I breathed from deeper and deeper down in my lungs.

Gradually the hives settled back to normal, a throbbing sound quiet as a purr, comforting as a woman talking to herself.

Sitting there, looking out the window at the darkening land that had been my family's for almost 100 years, I waited until night had truly come.

Mourne Family Tree

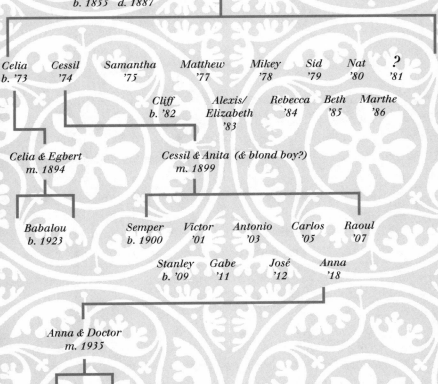

Great Great Grandmother & ?
b. 1855   d. 1887

Celia   Cessil   Samantha   Matthew   Mikey   Sid   Nat   ?
b. '73   '74   '75   '77   '78   '79   '80   '81

Cliff   Alexis/   Rebecca   Beth   Marthe
b. '82   Elizabeth   '84   '85   '86
                '83

Celia & Egbert   Cessil & Anita (& blond boy?)
m. 1894   m. 1899

Babalou   Semper   Victor   Antonio   Carlos   Raoul
b. 1923   b. 1900   '01   '03   '05   '07

                   Stanley   Gabe   José   Anna
                   b. '09   '11   '12   '18

Anna & Doctor
m. 1935

Gloria
b. 1940

Chapter 22

I will now admit something that might rather irritate you. I hope you take it in the right way.

I am editing these conversations. Not a lot, but some. Some things seem to me too private to share. Some moments between my mom and me, some particular information. Even more private than all I've already told you. I can let you know we yelled. There was a point we both cried. Yes, even my mom.

But I want you to know I am giving you the true flavor, enough detail so you don't really need to know the rest. I am telling you the whole arc of the story.

I think I've done well by you.

For some years now Cessil had been beginning to suspect, in the depths of his cavernous belly, that life simply wasn't as grand as it used to be. That men weren't as strong, that women weren't as lusty.

These days when he looked around at his remaining sons and their children, the product of his life and marriage, they all seemed like an awful waste of good food. His 6 youngest sons were nearing their fifties, and yet none of them had left home for more than a few hours at a time, or ever attempted to earn a living. Even when it came to the matter of marriage, they mostly had not wandered any further afield than Semper's suggestions, not far from home and the dining-room table, bringing back women who tended to have grown up within 5 miles and who did not require much courting. Women with atrocious accents, orange lipstick, and outfits whose colors and size were chosen by a community accustomed to spending a significant portion of the day in bathing suits. Women, Cessil knew, who were good for only one thing. The unmarred youth of their bodies quickly swelled out into brats, loud voices and curlers, the dimpled halves of their behinds still exposed in those obscenely tight pants women felt it was ok to wear now that it was 1950. The women always bending over or standing up, wiggling along in their walk down the hall away from him.

Cessil of the large appetites had not been with a woman in more than 25 years, because he had not been able to get out of his chair during that time except for brief moments. During those moments he would stand with his gigantic toad legs shivering like water under the immensity of the weight they supported, while his caretaker emptied the chair's porcelain basin of its contents, and then unceremoniously lifted the back of his robe to swab his backside clean. He made a steady huff-huff like the sound of heavy machinery. Even after he had sat down, falling back into the arms of the chair which had long ago become more comfortable than pillows to him, his breath roared in and out. He raised his 3-fingered hand gently to his neck and fanned it back and forth.

There was also a thin yellow tube that ran down the folds of his leg to add to what was already in the basin in the bottom of the chair. The person who had to empty this each day was the youngest wife of all the grandsons, a wife who exposed her small breasts to him each day in her indecent T-shirt as she leaned over to pull out the basin.

Cessil knew from those breasts that she wanted it. They had large brown nipples and were conical almost like teats. Unfortunately she was a lively woman who slapped him hard at the slightest provocation with the same easy swing she used on her innumerable brats.

Once a week she also dug down into the baby folds between his legs, unhooked the small plastic cup and swabbed brusquely all about, whistling all the while. During this time she paid no attention whatsoever to his breathless statements of love and lust, statements of how much he would pay for 5 minutes of her attentions or just for her to continue to swab. The only way he could get any reaction at all was if he used a dirty word. Then she would draw back her strong practical arm and crash it forward into his side, her dugs swinging back and forth under her shirt like wedding bells.

Cessil knew from her example that women were no longer what they used to be. He knew from his sons, who would no longer even answer him while Anita was in the room, that men were no longer what they used to be.

Yes, the world was falling apart, and Cessil could pinpoint exactly when the process had started for the country, as well as for his family. The days, the decisions. For the U.S., it was the day women got the vote—August 26, 1920. For his family, it was the morning that they had accepted Celia back into his house—September 12, 1923. They had all taken her in without a realistic thought of who she was or what she might want. His belly knew how wrong that was and how wrong it was that they had continued to keep her, kept even her son, the fighting twins adopting him for their own at town hall for all to see. That little child slouched more like a sack of jelly than any type of real male, that little nit who cried so very easily. When Celia's pup had still crawled around, Cessil had occasionally tried to slap his meaty hand down onto the soft doughy center of the kid's head, but the fighting twins had caught him calling the baby over like a dog one too many times. They had built a low crib around Cessil's life within the chair (whether to keep the child from crawling close or Cessil from stepping out, no one really knew).

And so Cessil, imprisoned like a common criminal in his own house, in his own chair, had been forced instead to watch the pup grow up unharmed, while Celia wheeled about free as a bird. Celia was allowed to do whatever she wanted: to carry a gun, to stay in the wheelchair when she was perfectly capable of walking, to spit each time she saw Cessil, to have ramps built about the house left and right for her to play on like a child in a go-cart, to shoot so many holes in the mailbox that when it rained no one even knew who the letters were from, much less what they said. Celia was free to leave her god-damn bank book lying about like the harlot she was, filled to the brim with money made THAT way, and yet to live here, for free, in his own house, the house that he had made with his own 2 hands for his family to live in, for his family, not for her. She was not his family, she was a goddamn SLUT.

And so he ranted on and on while his meaty white hands, fine and clean as marble, drove up and down in time with his words, slapping up against the flesh of his chest and then down against the tops of his thighs. The distance his hands had to travel each day lessened as the fat increased, his hands dancing around like he was just a toy, a simple wind-up toy that would play on and on, making its brittle ranting music, until the spring ran out and it fell over.

But Cessil did not wind down or fall over quite yet. He had one last spurt of energy left within his bones, a spurt of energy that would come out on the day of his seventy-fifth birthday, an amount of energy that no one had considered him capable of, that took even Cessil by surprise, that came about at the end of a 3-month diet imposed by the youngest wife with the breasts like teats who did not want to have to empty his basin anymore. So for 3 months she had been feeding him only grapefruits and oatmeal, and after 3 months the hunger and dis-gust within his body was raging at such a level that he was able to

stand, to lift his lightened bulk up over the low crib which still sur-
rounded him, even though Celia's pup had started walking more
than 20 years ago. From there Cessil was able to walk out across the
floor of the house that he had built with his once powerful hands, and
for one last night to know freedom.

Back before my mom died, back during my first visit to that house
named Brazil, I was a screamer. I have never felt conflicted about
making my wishes known. My first day there, I screamed without
pause from early in the morning until long after the moon came out
that night. I screamed because my diapers were folded in a rectangu-
lar manner rather than the triangular fashion my mother, Anna,
favored. I screamed in a voice not spoiled or out of control, but a voice
simply mechanically vindictive, willful and stubborn, patient and
strong-lunged.

It wasn't until that evening that Anita really noticed me, once she
realized that the same child had been screaming for more than 13
hours straight. Then she came over to investigate, more out of admi-
ration than concern. She appeared in front of me, still wearing her
floury apron, wiping her hands clean on a towel as she bent down to
examine this little hellion making all that noise. This was when she
was told whose child I was. I remember seeing her small wrinkled
face approach, a face so close to the size of my own. I remember
brown eyes bright as a squirrel's. A puff of cigar smoke hit me right in
the face. I sputtered and lost my screaming for a moment, then swelled
out again even louder into my rage. Meanwhile she just looked at me
and looked, while chewing thoughtfully on the end of her cigar. I did
all I could to keep crying while I stared back just as hard as I could.

Later she told me she gleaned all she ever needed to know about
my character from the fact that my eyes were not even damp with
tears. She nodded once decisively, pushed me over onto my back and

took off my diapers to re-fold them the way she had always folded diapers, the way she knew Anna would have folded them also.

Even before I stopped screaming, she was beginning to grin with a relief about as deep and primal as a person can experience. After having been married for almost 5 decades—the last decade with arthritis like the stubborn knots of death tightening about her joints each morning—after more than 4 decades slaving away in the kitchen all alone except for hired help, God had finally seen fit to bless Anita with a child with whom she could identify. A girl-child with a slow stubborn stare and a jaw shoved forward like a fist, a baby with enough gumption that Anita knew someday she could be trusted with a few pounds of cookie dough. Here was someone Anita could depend on enough, once I learned to walk, for her to be able to take a half day of rest, maybe even a full day.

Imagine a full day of vacation after almost half a century without even Christmas off. A single day for Anita's tired and aching bones to sink back into her bed and not get up for anything, not for nothing, while the swollen joints of her hands pulsed on in their rhythm of pain.

And so she hefted the no-longer-screaming me up onto her hip and took me on the first tour of what would become our kitchen.

From that day on, whenever I was in Fort Lauderdale, Anita kept me with her for at least half the day, teaching me to stir bowls by the time I was 2, to knead bread by 3 and roll out pie crusts at 4. Anita pulled me into work and spent hour after hour with me, poking her bulbous knuckled finger into my chest and the information into my ears. Even at almost 70, she was still shuffling around faster than anyone else, a thin upright skeleton with a stale cigar clasped between swollen fingers. Now she had 3 safes and a board of directors made up of young men who dressed too well, knew nothing about cooking and at whom she slung cookie dough whenever their pesky questions broke her concentration.

She was my first true mother. The one my biological mother had *chosen not to be. The one my adoptive mother, Anna, had not been able to be.*

Years later, soon after Anna's funeral, I was moved down to Fort Lauderdale permanently. There I demonstrated a sudden and fierce dislike of being alone, even for a moment. When I was left alone, my face clenched small and tight, and I would move quickly toward the nearest sound of people, even if they were people I did not really like. There I would talk loudly and authoritatively in front of them, my face still clenched, filled with fear, not enjoyment. Sometimes then, especially if the people I was talking to were kids, they would try to leave because they knew with the instinctive cruelty of children that this was what would bother me the most. So I would leap on them. I would hit them as hard as I could while screaming the worst insults I could think of, just so while they were hitting me back, they would be looking at me and know I existed, and I could be sure, in turn, that I was moving and alive.

My second true mother, at this point, turned out to be Celia. Even before Anna died, I had been the only one to listen to Celia's stories with interest and enjoyment. Afterward, I became obsessed. I needed her stories. I needed to know all I could about the family, to prove myself one of them, to hug the stories tight against my chest like a living person. When Celia told me her tales, I began to actively participate in them. I worked at learning them, my hands imitating the gestures of her bony hands, my child's serious face repeating every motion of her old woman's sagging face, my bright eyes never moving from those bewhiskered lips in front of me, my own lips following a fraction of a second later, memorizing the emphasis, the timing, the expressions, my mimicry becoming better and better so that by 8 years old I began to take on even the cavernous knowing hoarseness of a 75-year-old woman who had seen too much and was just about ready to die.

At 8 years old, I learned to talk to adults as if I were a cranky old woman waving a gun. The adults found themselves obeying me instinctively and with confusion.

I had only a few years of self-imposed tutelage to learn all I could from Celia, but I used the time well. I worked without respite. Whenever Anita let me out of the kitchen, I was at Celia's side. I listened to the stories hard, repeated them at night into my pillow, trying for perfect mimicry with each word choice and intonation, with each pause and breath.

Thus when my great aunt was murdered in her bed, just 3 years after Anna's death, I mourned deep and long. The only reason I was not completely devastated was that her cynical old breath still crouched within my throat to be reborn unharmed with each story.

And I could at least console myself with the knowledge that, for Celia's last 3 years, she had been happier than she had been since Egbert died. She told me this time and time again. She finally had someone to listen to her, someone who took the job seriously. A young girl-child who followed Celia around the house, watching each of her gestures with sharp eyes, her lips moving with each of the words Celia uttered. A girl-child whose face was puckered with the concentration of severe responsibilities.

But perhaps the gift of my attention had made Celia a little too happy, made her perhaps a shade too cocky, made her pranks get slightly out of hand. The gun began to get waved around with more energy than necessary. One day Celia shot up some holes in the mahogany sideboard when she was trying to hit an intruder who her old traitorous eyes could not find. The intruder turned out to be Anita's son Antonio, his voice made that of a stranger's by a bad case of laryngitis.

Antonio, although unharmed, was furious at Celia. He accepted her apology with grace, telling her not to even think about it, that it was no problem, but that night he led a revolt of his younger brothers against her power. Those 6 brothers—with the laughs of basking seals and souls as simple and airy as Wonder bread—snuck into her room to try to take the gun away from her permanently while she slept her senile old sleep.

They crept into her room when the moon was full and Celia was snoring. She slept sitting upright in bed, her eyes rolling white with the motion of her dreams. Her body had shrunk down through the years to just so much pride and wiry muscles, her nightshirt almost empty except where it filled out with the still impressive sag of her breasts. The gun lay slack on her lap, her right hand on it.

One long second after the sixth brother had crept on his belly into her room, Celia finally let herself open her eyes fully to fire the first shot. The Colt .45 bullet ripped a hole in the door the size of a baseball, the 6 brothers scrambling out after it like desperate lovers. Here the bullet and the brothers' paths separated, with the brothers taking a desperate diving left down the hall, while the bullet instead flew straight on, busting through the outer wall of the house to fly alone through the hot wet air above the swamp, the noise of the shot rustling through the feathers of dozing egrets and startling open the half-closed knotholes of alligators' eyes, the bullet flying lower now over the last of the knurled mangrove roots, spinning down over the muddy sand of the beach to plink forward finally into the ocean, the blue vastness of the sea rolling upward like a shoulder to accept it with a generosity as large as life.

All that long night there was sporadic shooting down the hallways of that large and rambling house, the bass bark of the .45 answered by the airy spit of appropriated children's BB guns and homemade slingshots.

With the slow dawn of the next day, an uncertain silence ensued and when breakfast was served at 7, the men slowly hobbled downstairs counting their injuries. Raoul came into the kitchen with one lens of his glasses broken in the dark confusion of the night. Stanley had to sit on an inflatable cushion for 3 weeks because of a bullet that had hit just behind him, spraying out wood splinters. And Antonio couldn't have breakfast at all because he was busy fixing the water main, which had exploded in a balloon of silver above them at 3 in the morning, a .45 slug in its heart.

When they arrived at the breakfast table, there was Celia already on her third cup of coffee, the gun at deceptive ease within her lap. She was grinning at their labored entrance with all the enjoyment of a toothless old hound of hell.

All that day and into part of the night, Cessil watched his sons' rage against his older sister grow. He heard them shift blame and give excuses, re-plan and re-structure. He heard them wonder why she was living here at all, that old biddy, and what right did she have to a wheelchair anyway. He heard them consider booby-trapping her wheelchair, or not allowing her food or trips to the bathroom, or ambushing her while she was in the bathtub. He heard them discuss each idea and discard them all until, once again, they settled on the fast frontal assault at midnight.

This was the day of Cessil's seventy-fifth birthday and he was about as happy as he could be.

That night, 10 minutes before 12, after the downstairs was deserted, Cessil stood up. His body had been diminished enough by the grapefruit-and-oatmeal diet for him to get to his feet, his breath huffing out from his still enormous weight. Cessil moved forward with ponderous grace, up to the ring of his confinement. He stepped over the low fence without a pause, gliding off as silently into the night as the near shadow of a very large ship, the thin yellow tube trailing after him like a slipped line.

That night Celia held the gun tight as a crucifix aimed along the tops of her knees, pointing it without hesitation at the crotch level of the door through which her 6 middle-aged nephews had crawled the night before. She was smiling to herself, thinking about the previous evening, her yodels of joy, the bright cracks of the gun in the dark, the lusty smell of gunpowder. She knew her nephews weren't any real threat and because of that she wouldn't aim too close. She simply wanted to watch them scramble.

Then a board squeaked and as Celia tried to place it, her night was eclipsed by the phenomenal bulk of Cessil's bloated face rising up by her side, grinning, his body looming wide as a commercial fridge.

Celia's gun was pointed all wrong. Her body started to twist around, to pull the gun up. Her mind already jumping to the unfinished closet, its back easily opened to the invader who had built it, providing access to him from the bedroom next door.

Cessil roared an inhuman scream of victory, withheld for 62 years, as he began his simple and graceful roll forward, arms raised.

Celia saw the speed of his descent and the molasses turn of the gun's barrel. As fast as that, her mind skipped backwards through the slow-moving drip of normal time. She knows again this morning's joy of having that little girl listen to her stories—she feels again that long-ago despair of her only child finally managing to slither from her loins—she stands once more in the bright mid-morning light on the doorstep of this Florida house 27 years ago with the gun in her hand and her hips spread wide by a stranger's baby—she lies down again as a prostitute dressed only in flimsy lace and fur for those 4 destructive years of her rage at Egbert's death—is hugging for the last time Egbert's bony brilliant body to her own in the dark of the stage with the thunderous applause like a breath against her cheek—in the night again with Egbert, his naked body and tender gripping hands, the emotions of laughter and desire roaring in her heart—him for the first time on the boat, his panicked skinny face, his eyes half-popping out as he tore down the deck knocking waiters and champagne aside—long-dead years of her adolescence waitressing in a Canadian town of men who wouldn't touch—walking alone away from her family home through the cold cold blizzard of her childhood—struggling beneath the mass of murderous siblings' fists and feet pounding down.

By this time Celia's eyes are large within her old and wrinkled face. They are not focused any longer on the trajectory of Cessil's body, or on the gun she is now pointing in the direction of his rapidly approaching heart. Her finger has lost interest in anger or in cutting a hole in his bulk, for by now she cannot stop his body from falling onto hers; it is much too late for that, 62 years too late, a lifetime of living too late.

So, that last moment before Cessil's still breathing body closes the gap between them, nudging her gun smoothly aside and her body into a hug made of warm heavy death, she is thinking only of her mother, of her mother's strong hands settling upon her narrow hips as she looks out at that cruel fall, out at a world preparing to die, her dark intelligent eyes filled with neither fear nor regret. Those eyes only blink twice at the beauty of the harshness of the world, and then she turns around to go back into the house, to get ready. The door closing as silently as a breath.

And Cessil crushed her.

The entire bed frame crashed down onto the floor. Front, then back. The gun misfired only once. It sounded like no more than a fart underneath all that weight. The jangling metal quieted, slowed; stunned silence came from beyond the room. A long and timeless moment passed before Cessil could lever himself up, looking down only once, no expression on his face. Then he turned and left by way of the closet again, just before the front door of her room began to bulge rhythmically in and out with the pounding of his sons' ineffectual bodies.

And at that point something within Cessil's overtired body and mind relaxed. He staggered down the stairs and out the front door of the house he had started building those 30 short years ago. A simple grin was upon his face as he stumbled out into the jungle around Fort Lauderdale, driven back to the time when he was 20 and strong, when he had strode through the jungles of Brazil.

They found him 100 yards into the forest, where he had tripped over a root that he either had not seen or perhaps had optimistically tried to jump with all his fading strength. In any case he had fallen forward onto his chest, from his full height, onto the hard-packed ground, driving fragments of bone through every major organ in his body.

Yet still he lived, for 2 long days, spending his last few conscious moments staring up at the corner of his hospital room where a TV advertised underarm deodorant, kitchen gadgets and Dr. Proxtor's all-fixing swamp honey.

3 days later the funerals took place, the twin funerals of the 2 oldest Mournes, held in the backyard of the house named Brazil, the bodies interred in 2 hastily erected and still drying mausoleums, built by Cessil's 6 youngest sons, the ones who had built most of the house named Brazil. One of the mausoleums was distinctly leaning to the left. Everyone within the house attended, all of Anita's employees, a significant portion of the town, people from all over the state. The relatives alone numbered over 300. Most estimates put the crowd at something like 2,000. There were infants and spinsters, cripples and young boys; there were fat men and skinny angry girls. Samantha was bowed so far over to the power of old age that no one could see her reaction to being left, finally and absolutely, in charge of her siblings.

Semper attended with his prison guard. He had aged quickly in prison, looked helpless now and old, but still his guard stood close to him, one hand at all times on his elbow in a gesture designed either to help or control. Semper had only one white camel-hair suit left. It *was a little dingy but he wore it well, with dignity and sorrow. He seemed surprisingly affected. He told anyone who would listen that this funeral of his aunt and his father was the first time he had cried since he had uncurled his finger from the trigger on those steps in Germany so many years ago, opening his eyes to see what he had wrought.*

There were Semper's 6 younger brothers all in a group, sobbing loudly, leaning on each other, throwing their hands around in the air, their wet faces tilted up, imploring. Even though they had discovered Celia's body in its original state, they were the only ones who never did connect the 2 deaths and thought only that it was cruel of fate to have struck down both siblings on the same day.

There was widowed Anita with her army of white uniformed helpers. The company directors and bank owners stood nearby, sneaking cautious glances at Anita to see what effect her husband's death would have on production. Her back was straight as a poplar, her hands clasped quietly in front of her, her dress as dark as her strong aggressive eyes. I could make out only the haziest of flour fingerprints on the hem of her dress as I caught her twice glancing back through the livingroom window to the clock, to make sure the next batch didn't burn.

And after the funeral was over, the loudspeakers crackled to announce that, as instructed by Celia, her lawyer would now read out her will in public. No one read Cessil's will, for not only had he nothing really to give, he had never made a will to say so.

Celia, her lawyer announced, had accrued more than $100,000 through judicious investments over the last 25 years. Also, over all these years she had legally owned the farmhouse in Ontario because it had been left by her mother to the eldest.

The loudspeaker sputtered for a moment in static, while the greed *rustled like a small animal through the tightly-packed crowd. $100,000 was a lot of money back then in 1950. A brand-new car with all the options cost around $2,000, a brand-new house cost $10,000. Looking around, I could see a few of my relatives trying to shift their features toward modesty and surprise, preparing themselves to hear their own names announced.*

The loudspeaker declared that all of Celia's worldly goods had been left to 10-year-old me, with Anita as trustee.

10-year-old Gloria, the loudspeaker declared, was the only relative, aside from Egbert and Celia's mother, who had ever treated Celia with any respect or love.

Every stunned face within that crowd of over 2,000 turned in the direction of my short child's body. There was a long moment while I was encircled by gaunt stares.

The moment was ended by the peevish stage whisper of a teenager behind me asking his mother, "So, who were the 2 geezers, anyway?"

Aww Celia, I said.

Huh? asked my mom.

She just let him crush her? I asked. Why'd she do it? Why didn't she shoot him?

I think, said Mom, She felt her time had come.

For a moment I didn't respond.

She should have, I said slowly and sneakily, She should have shot him. That way she could have told more stories over the next few years. You might know more of them now. You might know the stories of all her siblings.

My mother pointedly ignored me.

On the other end of the line I heard her fumbling with something and then water being poured.

I opened the screen door, stood there in the doorway at the

end of the phone cord, breathing in the warm spring night air. By this time it was early May, and the crocuses had pushed their way up through the lawn. My bangs trembled in the breeze. The phone was nestled in the hollow of my shoulder. I rubbed my fingers over the bones of my face.

Mom's voice, when she spoke again, was different. Weaker, more human.

The money, she said, then she had to clear her throat and try again.

Celia's money, she said, Has increased 700% over the years. I've never needed more than a little of the interest. Also, I still own the farmhouse.

Jesus, Mom, I said, You're rich.

Hun, she said, I want to give all of that to you so you can continue to live in that house, to live the life you've always wanted, to take care of the family keepsakes that have always been there, as well as the ones I've sent you. So you can continue to take care of your great great grandmother. To take care of yourself.

She breathed in.

On that condition, she said.

What? I asked. On what condition?

Understand, she said, I don't want my work on the stories, on you, to go to waste. I don't want either one at risk out in the world. I don't want you to leave.

Leave? I asked.

I realized so much had changed in 3 short weeks. Her voice was now hesitant. She was offering a bribe.

Somehow it seemed as if this moment was one I had achieved 1,000 times before. A moment that contained no surprise. I wiped my mouth with the back of my hand. I felt tired, dizzy. My height seemed somehow a new and unfamiliar pull on my bones.

I want that phone number to call for after the operation, I said.

No, she said.

A beat passed.

I asked, What do you mean by 'on that condition'?

You stay there.

Always?

Always. You have to promise. She added after a calculated pause, or perhaps on sudden inspiration, If not, I will give the farm away. Your home.

We were both silent then, absorbing that.

Mom, how can I promise to stay here always? I can't promise that. Why would you give away the farm? I want the phone number, I repeated.

No, she said.

A beat.

Aww Mom.

A beat.

Give me the phone number.

No.

Then no, I said, suddenly furious. No I won't. I won't stay here.

There was a silence, followed by her loud and righteous wrath. Yelling, cursing, insults. As always, once the argument started, I went utterly silent.

And maybe this next thing was just me being wistful, or maybe it was a hallucination caused by so many emotions swirling around together in the big storm of her fury.

But at one point I swear I heard her smiling as clear as a tired breath.

The board of Anita's company.

Family members my mom never got around to explaining.

Celia as an old woman.

Chapter 23

Mom was still angry the next day. I had spent the afternoon shooting down by the back pasture. I had had to make a trip down to the dump for more bottles to shoot at and then into town for more bullets. The grass was now littered with broken glass. The cats had gotten jumpy from all the noise and had begun to eye me sideways, even when we were inside the house. Even when I wasn't holding the gun.

But out by the fence, each time one of the bottles exploded, I felt something inside of me that was wound so tightly relax just a bit.

20 years later, I still do that now, target practice whenever I'm tense or upset. There's a range near where I work. I never understand why people want silence for thinking. Silence can be broken so easily, by a single dog barking far away, by the slightest creak upstairs. But the mayhem of a gun range—the sharp reports of guns, people yelling instructions, the surprised whumps of the target—nothing can break the stillness you get in such a place. In a way you are more alone there than you would be almost anywhere else.

And leaving such a place, heading back to my current home to where I won't be alone in any way at all, I find the creaks and crackles of my body seem smaller, less noteworthy. Yes, I still know that one of these creaks will one day foretell my death, but luckily I have no idea about which one. And, for a while, after the satisfying chaos of a gun range, I just don't care as much. I will wait for someone else, in telling my story afterwards, to pick and choose those details that show my whole life heading directly toward whatever my death turns out to be, to edit out all that is deemed extraneous. To make it seem as though there was no other possible way it could have been.

Mom said, Why didn't you pick up on the first ring?

I was down by the back pasture shooting, I said. You're calling a few minutes early. I had to run back.

The field with the old plow? she asked.

No, I answered, That's the lower 10. Don't you remember? The back pasture is the one next to the blueberry field.

Oh, she said, Oh yes. I remember.

What were you doing again? she asked.

Shooting, I said.

Celia's gun?

Yes.

Really? she asked. Really.

I have always had a good memory, back to my earliest childhood. I can remember several events from when I was wearing diapers: sucking on the edge of one of Anita's sweet peanut cookies for the first time; the hot confusion of fire ants in my diapers by the lake in Florida; a cousin's lips blowing a vibrating raspberry into my squirming belly;

my mother pulling a new shirt on over my head, with me wailing inside its tight folds. I've always thought most people could remember that far back if they really wanted to, if they spent some time on it and just plain concentrated.

I started keeping a diary when I was 7, once my mother died and I moved down to Fort Lauderdale. In my first diary I chronicled those years before I had learned to write.

So many of my memories, even before my mother died, took place in my mother's family house, the one in Fort Lauderdale. It was a memorable house. My earliest memories of it are that the walls tasted of sap and insects. Where the floor hadn't been sanded, there were splinters that jabbed me in my knees and palms as I crawled around. People were always yelling in that house, yelling happy, yelling angry. Their feet moving quickly by, thudding on the wood floor. The house was so large I got lost 3 times as a child, the last time when I was about 9. Each time I had to climb out a window and circle the outside of the house until I found the front door.

My parents, on the other hand, had lived in a modern 4-bedroom house outside Atlanta, in one of the clean-cut postwar developments. The house had 4 straight brick walls and a slate roof, no awkward additions anywhere. It had a chimney in the center directly above the door, like a child's drawing of a house, that drawing xeroxed for every third house down the street as far as you could see. The other 2 alternating styles of houses were a Swiss Alps chalet and a Southern plantation house complete with columns. The flower beds in between the houses were built up as carefully as battle lines.

Inside my parents' house there was one bathroom downstairs and one bathroom upstairs. You always knew where you were. Everything was painted white, a white so pure the walls and corners receded like the horizon. The walls tasted of vinyl and the slickness of new paint no matter where the toddler-that-was-me sampled them. Every room in that house was quiet, the walls and doors thick. There was always the hum of the air conditioner. My parents were polite and quiet, voices modulated. My mother's skin was as cold as the water faucet.

Most of my memories of the Fort Lauderdale house concerned my relatives. There were so many who lived in that house. I don't think anyone had bothered to count them, or to measure the house, to count the rooms. It seemed to me as a child the house continued forever, the wooden floors of the halls rolling up and down over the bumps of the jungle without the slightest attempt at maintaining a level. The boards squeaked like birds even under my child's weight. There were gaps in the walls so large I could stick the whole of my fist out into the wild, feeling quite courageous.

There are 3 particular relatives who make up most of my memories of that house. One of them, of course, was Anita. The smells of coconut, cloves and chocolate, the constant urgent movement, the orders bellowed, her bony finger jabbing and her ever present entourage made up of bakers, her hungry sons, and the obsequious members of her company's board with their well-made suits freckled lightly with icing where they'd brushed too close to a cake in their urgency to keep up.

In the midst of all these people and all this noise, Anita lost patience a few times a day. It could happen so quickly, just one too many questions. Fast as that, she would scoop a wad of dough out of a bowl, flick it across the room, tossing it with her wrist like a frisbee. Hard. The smack of dough against the offender's chest. The splatter. In the shocked silence afterwards, Anita would snort, not quite amused, and bend down close to me, to look me straight in the eye. With me she never lost patience. I remember us as always looking at each other, staring. I remember us facing into each other's eyes, mesmerized with recognition.

I remember noticing early on, at 3 or maybe 4 years old, that the adults tended to get a little quiet when Anita talked to me, when we looked at each other or when she gave me a bowl of dough to mix.

The bakers, the members of her board and especially her sons watched our interaction then, conversations trailing off. With each year that passed, the way they watched us became more intent.

I remember when the sons walked by me in the kitchen—with Anita nearby and watching—they'd look down at me, their lips pulled wide in a smile. They'd tell me what a cute dress I was wearing. But if they met me in another area of the house, with Anita not around, they'd stride right by me, regarding me with something quite different from a smile.

The second person my memories are full of was Great Aunt Celia. Celia tried to tell her stories to all those who would not or could not object. She tried to tell them to me even when I was still a baby. She would follow after my diapered rear in her wheelchair, tracking foot by foot, the stories spilling out like bread crumbs in my trail. They poured out in a low rumbling voice which never changed its volume or speed. Moments of excitement were punctuated by both fists slapping down against her withered thighs. Celia's body swelled out with humanity only at the breast, the sheer weight pulling at the shoulders, making her either lean far back into the cushions of her wheelchair to address the sky itself with her stories, or to rest forward upon her bent arms like a fold-up chair.

I remember sitting captive in her lap while she talked at me. I remember the knife-edged harshness of my great aunt's bones beneath the many layers she wore for warmth and padding. I remember the flat truth of the wasted forearms holding me tight against her breasts. I remember the scent and hair of horses on my great aunt (although I never found out where these traces of horses came from), and the smell of gunsmoke, grey and biting.

The smell of old age for me has never been the cloying stench of decomposition or leaked urine, or the overly sweet perfumes and air fresheners of the elderly. For me, old age is a cloud of gunpowder, metallic and burnt, dispersing raggedly through the air. Here in the hospital I just don't understand the patients shuffling outside on the grounds, the patients who wobble so cautiously at the edge of puddles.

I remember also the smooth chill of the gun barrel in Celia's lap. Sometimes it got wedged in the leg of my diaper and I cried at the straight-barrelled certainty of the thing.

As I got older, Celia grew in importance to me until a majority of my world's order and meaning came only from that raspy voice in that half-palsied face. Most images I saw or imagined came channeled first through the glistening black pebbles of her vision, through the grey and twisted matter of her brittle skull.

One night when I was 10 years old, I was awakened by a series of gunshots, each explosion so compressed with time and power that the only part I heard was the echo. The gunshots were answered by the light ping of BB guns and swears. I thought that the sounds must mean the world was cracking open along its hinges, and I stared at the walls of my room for the rest of the night, waiting for them to fly away. The next morning my Uncle Raoul came down to breakfast stumbling, with one lens of his glasses broken, and my Uncle Stanley carried around a special inflatable cushion that made farting noises when he sat on it. My uncles stayed on the far side of the breakfast table from Celia and seemed a little jumpy, while Celia herself seemed in a great mood. She rolled around the house all that last day of her life, telling me her stories with a triumphant voice and a wide wide grin.

And even now, almost 30 years after she died, I have never forgotten the stories she told. My great aunt leaning forward over the handle of her gun as she hissed those family secrets at me with such vehemence that they went straight in through my ears, straight in through my mouth and my eyes, straight in through my skin where her bony fingers grasped my shoulder. I sucked those stories in along with the horse-and-gunsmoke smell. The words imprinted forever on my child's soft brain.

As an adult when I think of those stories, when I think of the tales

Celia told me, I hear again her gravelly, ship captain's voice. It echoes still in my ears and mouth. My great aunt sits in my head even today, sits hard upon my brain with her stony shanks, looking out at the decisions of my life.

The third relative I remember from that house, back from when I was a baby, was my cousin—my cousin once removed—Babalou. He was 17 years older than me and loved to blow violent raspberries onto my belly, spittle flying everywhere. I remember watching his face lower so slowly into my world, the anticipation heavy in my skin for his touch. His face growing in size, his lips pulled back in a fierce grin. Contact. I would wrap my hands around his curls, wrap my fingers tight, as I felt the whistle of his inhale against my bare skin. Then my whole body shook with the delicious strength of his lips' fart.

And when he pulled away, his curls would slip through my fingers with a slight crisp sound, leaving no trace but the memory. Babalou would stand back up, his thin face above, laughing.

This was before the war, when he was only 18, and still laughed. I want you to know Babalou as he used to be back then. He was a sweet loner, a weirdo. The kind of guy who would play with a baby for an hour, never looking around to see if someone nearby might be impressed or about to make fun of him, playing just because the baby interested him. He was the kind of guy who in highschool had problems finishing sentences in class with everyone watching, the kind of guy who wore the same grungy raincoat all year round no matter what the weather, wore it just because he admired the large number of pockets it had. The kind of guy who looked permanently startled, especially around girls. The kind of strange boy who, if he'd been given the luxury of a normal adolescence and a few solid years of adulthood, would probably have adapted, gotten stronger, would have developed his own self-effacing humor to protect himself, would have found himself a small but loyal group of friends. Perhaps he might have become a computer programmer, librarian or writer, some career where introversion and a few key obsessions are useful.

He had a motorcycle that he'd found in the garage and repaired. It exhaled pure black gusts of smoke, gasped like someone permanently offended, and made loud explosions. As a baby I did not like that silvery machine. It vibrated with an evil too rich for any living creature. He would circle 3 times on it, round the driveway out back, spraying up dirt and twigs and noise, and then he went away. I didn't like the motorcycle for that reason also, because it took him away, over and over again.

From the way I cried each time he left, the family said I was in love. They gave my cousin the early morning watch, and my crib was moved to his room. As I said, he was a strange boy. He did not seem to mind. Perhaps he even enjoyed my company, because other than me he was pretty much all alone. Each morning when I awoke, he would feed me a bottle of warm milk and some oatmeal, and then carry me down in his arms to the playpen by the lake. After putting me down in the playpen, he would drop his pajamas to the ground and climb the old oak there to dive off the highest branch, slicing down through the morning air, arms extended toward the water as if offering something. The dark patch of hair in the middle of his body as curly as the hair on his head.

I would pull myself up by the sides of the crib to stand there watching him without breathing, watching the tension of flight.

Then one day he left. Not on his motorcycle, but in the truck with Uncle Gabe, the whole family calling goodbye over each other's backs, one at a time bending into the window of the truck with a single phrase and an awkward chuck to Babalou's chin, his fighting-twin mothers crying, unable to stop as they stood in the back of the crowd, their faces clenched bumpy as fists. Uncle Gabe started the truck and disengaged the brake. Everyone calling out to Babalou to remember their advice, their love. They all stepped back as the truck started bouncing away down the dirt driveway. All of them yelling things like he should write, keep his head down, send back some good French wine, kill a few Krauts, get those Japanese bastards, have fun. Calling lonely statements into the swirling dust of the driveway that gradually settled down till the air was clear and there was nothing left.

When he came back 4 years later, he looked the same, same thin adolescent build, still no beard. He was even wearing the same shirt as when he had left, although the pants were now Army pants.

At first everyone was overjoyed. It was at abut this time that the family was learning of the extent of Victor's crimes, and I guess the adults were relieved when it looked as if Babalou, at least, wasn't going to constantly remind them of the last few years. They hoped to forget the war and all that those years had meant, to them as a family as well as to the country.

But Babalou was different now. The way he acted, he made strangers nervous, made his family nervous. He did not talk much anymore. He had taken up smoking. His hands tended to shake. His hair was cut as short as if he had gotten gum in it and cut this short it didn't curl anymore. There was a small indentation round and smooth as a crater beneath his left eye. And now he needed to touch people, had to keep one hand on living flesh at every moment.

Ours was not a family that touched much. They did not hug. They did not hold hands or sit on each other's laps. They were the kind who poked each other in the chest at Christmas and slapped each other on the arm during an emotional crisis. The change in Babalou confused them, and they did all they could to ignore it. They sidled away from him, their eyes elsewhere. A slow-motion ballet was born, with the family jostling en pack ahead and Babalou following as counterpoint, one hand extended.

That summer the bond between my family and my cousin loosened, came close to being cut entirely by embarrassment and fear, by his continual reminder of what they wished so much to forget. Uncles, aunts and cousins would hear his gentle shuffle from a room or 2 away, and they would exit out another door, just ahead of him.

On the other hand, the bond between me and my cousin grew much stronger. I let him touch me. I was 5. He was 22. I was an energetic friendly child. I had dark hair and a skin so translucent that the beating of the veins in my temples and on the insides of my wrists was visible. My mother was still alive, so I still had the fierce belief that I was someone special. This knowledge made me generous.

I knew so many things back then, at the age of 5. I knew them deeply, without a doubt in the world. I knew that God existed as clearly as I knew my mother existed, as ice cream did and the color white. I knew I was the most powerful person in the world, that God was secretly listening to just me. I knew I was strong and determined, that I could do something closer to a cartwheel than anyone else in kindergarten. I knew I breathed the wind. I knew if the Pope ever met me he would recognize me at first sight and make me his special adviser. I was raised Protestant, but still I had no doubts about the Pope.

I did the talking with my cousin Babalou, in a loud child's voice. I liked having an adult listening to me, being needy. It was a new experience. He was silent, his hand on the crown of my head, his face turned away. I had to teach him to swim all over again, to not fear or fight the water, my confident voice talking the whole time. I led him into the lake with my body, gradually moving in deeper, just slightly ahead, him stepping forward, reaching after me, the water rolling unnoticed up past our legs.

Later, once he was more used to the lake, I got him to jump from the oak tree again, both our white bodies windmilling through the air, into the water. Summers were so hot in Fort Lauderdale that there was no transition between the air and the water. We simply became abruptly weightless, soundless, airless. All that was left was the other's pale face floating surprised through all the bubbles in between.

I liked to hold the first 2 fingers of his hand, to shake them back and forth for attention. I knew he needed me, my touch. I liked the feeling. We played my games together.

This was all when I was still young, before my mother thought she was pregnant, before she died. Before.

Afterwards I was moved to Fort Lauderdale permanently.

Things had changed. Some simple thoughts had entered my mind. I now recognized the limits of my power. I feared being alone. God died that year, in 1947. I understood then that the Pope would look right over my head, I would be just another little child in a sea of humanity, another child, and not even of his religion. If I had seen Waiting for Godot *performed that year I would have grasped the concept with my very bones.*

I was 7 years old.

It was at this time that cripples became attractive to me, their crutches, spasms, their twisted metronome walks. Such pity I felt within my heart. I sought them out to help, to make them grateful to me, to hold some power over them. I knew, whether or not God existed, at least I had greater luck in the world than these people. I began to use bigger words, to wear skirts and carry a purse. I wanted to be an adult as soon as possible, to have power in this world. I wanted to be proper and accepted, have a checking account, a job, underlings. I had dreams in which Christ slid away from me down the stairs in my parents' old house and from his skin came blood. I don't like talking about this time.

I never wanted to be alone again. I began to depend on Babalou as he already depended on me. Both of us with our fears. He helped me through a lot. He needed me. That was exactly what I wanted.

As I grew older, it became obvious to all the relatives that there was a special bond between me and Babalou. And that was fine when I was a baby and he was baby-sitting. And it was still ok when I was a child and he was a man, for after all I was only a child and no one else wanted to deal with him or even particularly with me.

(Part of the problem was that I had no real parent for anyone to complain to in that entire house. There was no one responsible for my actions aside from the powerful Anita, who would do no more than poke a warning into the chest of any who bothered her favorite grandchild. Then she would back away from the life that she assumed I was so capable of choosing.)

So, Babalou and I continued to nap together well past my childhood. No one ever took it upon themselves to tell us no. The guilt passed back and forth in a cloud that everyone in the family learned not to look at straight on. Babalou and I napped together in one of our beds when I was 8 and 10 and 13, buck naked sometimes, back from a swim. We had slept in the same room since I was a baby. And Babalou and I understood each other like no one else. Sometimes when he started to dream those dreams again, I would already be out of bed and walking across our room, from my bed to his, even before his breathing began to change, so I would be there to hold him close when he awoke, and he—even as he screamed, his face red as raw meat—he would be wrapping his arms around me.

We grew even closer after he helped me, saved me, from the Butler kids by Old Marquez Road, then walked me back home with my nose dripping blood. I was 12 and can still remember the speed with which he stopped them—not in the slow conventional way, using only the front of his tightly wrapped fists. He used his arms, his legs, his head. They were on me and then they were off me, and he was holding the last boy up by the head beside me. He was twisting the head so the boy was not even getting a chance to yelp, not even to squeak in surprise, his eyes bulging.

And then Babalou stopped, before there was that noise we all expected, the noise that was already there in the air ready to be heard, a muffled wet crack. Babalou stopped instead, put him down and patted the crown of his head gently like a dog's.

The boy stood in the road where we left him, a streak of liquid trickling down between his legs. Babalou held my hand very tightly. We walked away.

That week the boys' parents came by, along with some of the other parents from the neighborhood. They locked themselves up in the livingroom with Babalou's mothers, the fighting twins. The voices were serious, low, there was no laughter. Babalou's mothers had made cucumber sandwiches and pink lemonade, and through a knothole in the wall I could see them turning earnestly from one speaker to the next offering out their sandwiches. The twins had recently dyed their hair a rather hopeful color a little too close to that of the pink lemonade, and they smiled in genuine confusion at the group in front of them.

When the visiting parents had filed out, the food was untouched and the lemonade had gone watery from all the melted ice. From that day on, 29-year-old Babalou was forbidden to go off the property unless an adult accompanied him. From that day on, from my bed, I watched his face sometimes when he was asleep, waiting for him to need me.

Even though I was adopted, I grew up to look like him, perhaps from spending so much time around him. Sometimes, however, I fantasized that with his unknown father and my unknown biological parents, it was possible we were actually related. Maybe siblings. It could have been true. We both had dark curly hair, green eyes with an orange ring round the pupil, thin noses that tended to bleed strings of blood on lazy Sunday afternoons for no particular reason. The only difference was in our builds, for I was strong and thick, compact as a little motor, while in comparison he was tall and thin, spread out, just *waiting for disaster to happen. Each afternoon we spent hours at the lake, diving down through the heat, the same motion, the same position, heads tucked in, arms extended, falling into the area where there was no air.*

We were together in a way I cannot explain. Perhaps it came from growing up together, from sharing family, from both needing something only the other had offered to fulfill. We were together in a way that made every other contact I have had and ever will have simply a pale memory in comparison.

So when I climbed on top of him naked that first time, he helped me. I found that as it was happening I was thinking of my great aunt. I was 15. He was 33.

That summer passed the quickest of all the summers. We did it all the time. We did it like seals, like otters. We did it in the afternoon and the morning and at night. We did it in the lake while we swam and in the boathouse and the bathroom. We did it in each of our relatives' rooms while the relatives were downstairs having breakfast, the clink of the silverware echoing clear through the knotholes in the wood, the smell of eggs and maple syrup, the talk about Aunt Rita's cow, all of it driving our silent frenzy.

Large sections of the house and barn and lake began to smell of the wetness of our love, and the other adults in the house talked to each other about wormrot and mildews. They brought home various sundry packages from the hardware store, unguents and powders, paints and pastes, which they sprayed about at the walls or slopped upon the corners of the house. They worked noisily at solving the problem of the infestation of the house and kept their eyes turned toward the walls and ceiling, away from the way I held Babalou's hand. It seemed to me all the adults talked louder that summer so they wouldn't actually hear the words or tone of our conversation.

The adults on the porch sat firmly in the chairs on the adults' side of the porch, referring to the love which was glowing there in front of them as either Babalou's baby-sitting duty or as termites in the joists. They told each other that whatever else was wrong with Babalou, he was a patient cousin, he was being good family to me.

And once Babalou and I were making love in the hay in the barn, and the hay was shivering and rustling and the boards beneath us were groaning, and even as my hands began to clench in upon themselves and even as I started to suck at the air as though it were water, Uncle Gabe walked in. He had his back to us, leaned over to pull a can of creosote from under the workbench. Pulling one side and then the other out of its tight squeeze between the cans, he levered the bottom of it up over a board which was uneven. He straightened slowly, stood for a moment so that the hay finally settled and lay still, so our corner of the barn was as quiet as his, so all 3 of us could listen to the breathing of 3 people in a quiet place.

And Uncle Gabe leaned over his right hip a little to balance the weight of the can, and he lumbered out the back door, without ever looking at us directly.

I have to say, if I can be truthful, that I wish I had died that summer. I wish I had simply fallen over mysteriously dead of love with a wide smile upon my lips. I wish I had never heard the end of this story.

As the summers went by after that, Babalou began to get the dreams more often. Whenever I left his side at night, he would wake gasping, his eyes rolling white as marbles. Sometimes he would start shaking in the midst of loving me, shaking until he would try to get off of me, sweat beading up on his face and across his chest, and I would hold him, still inside me, and promise him again and again that I would care for him, I would protect him, I would not let him go.

And through it all he did not age. He remained 18. From summer to summer, since that first year when he went off to war, he had gotten no older. Thin build, large feet, listening to the old records that were hits when he had left. He never managed to grow a real beard or to hold any job aside from those 4 years in the Army.

As the summers passed when I was 16 and 17 and 18, I found myself sometimes telling him what to do. I found myself scared of him using electrical appliances on his own, of him wandering off the farm one day, forgetful. I told him to grow up. I told him when to go to bed. I held him tight. I was needed. I loved him even more.

And so that time when Anita, his aunt, my grandmother, walked into the livingroom at 4:30 one morning, heading for her pie crusts while Babalou and I were busy making love upon the couch, we did not even bother to pull apart or to stop, for it had always seemed as though we would be found out, as though we had already been found out. Anita had never been the type to keep her back to the uncomfortable. She walked right on up to us without a pause. She jabbed her long bumpy finger into my back, poking my spine because she could not reach my front, and she said with infinite sadness and determination, "Marry him."

The whole family was so scandalized that they could barely manage to stay through that short 20-minute-long wedding out on the front lawn of the house, and afterwards, as a wedding present, they gave Babalou and me the same truck in which they had sent him off to war. Perhaps at that point the whole drama of it would have died down if it had been 2 people other than me and Babalou. Perhaps if it had been anyone else they would have gradually gotten used to it, at least after a few years. If it had been someone other than Babalou who always wanted to touch them, who could not get over that horrible war, who could not stop reminding them about it with the way he shuffled through life all beaten. Perhaps if it had been someone other than me, a stubborn fierce stranger from up north, this fight-picking order-giving child without any parents. Perhaps if it had been someone other than me, who had already inherited all of Celia's money, as well as the Canadian farm, who now always had Anita's attention. If it had been anyone else than me, who seemed likely to inherit every last stitch of money the family had ever had.

Perhaps if it had been anyone else than us 2, they might have just let us settle back into the family.

But I am guessing. I can only tell you how they did react.

After the wedding out on the front lawn, our hair still sprinkled with rice, the rings round our fingers new and uncomfortable, they told us we were not welcome back into the house named Brazil, not ever. The 6 youngest sons of Anita were the ones to tell us, all the others standing farther back. Antonio (the eldest of Anita's still-living-and-not-imprisoned sons, the son who had hoped on and off before my arrival in the family to inherit the majority of his mother's corporation) spoke for the whole family when he said, Congratulations and get off the property or we'll call the police.

I remember clearly the way Antonio had watched me when I was a child, when he passed me in the kitchen, while his mother held out her newest kind of cookie for me to give a verdict on it. He had always watched these interactions carefully, his face so flat and focused. I was not an insensitive child. I thought I knew back then what he felt. But it was only at this moment, after the wedding out on the front lawn, that I realized how severely I had underestimated the strength of his feeling, underestimated my effect on him. This was the first time he looked at me with his full emotion, with none of it leashed. I took 2 steps back from the strength.

In this case, not even Anita could stop them, or would stop them. Perhaps it was the pain of being so disappointed in me. She was an old woman, a religious woman, a Catholic woman, a tired woman. She had placed all her hopes in me, then caught me having sex in a public room, having sex outside marriage, sex with a relative, a relative twice my age, the one with the least gumption of them all. Perhaps she just doubted me for the first time.

Still, Anita must have been the one to pack my bags. That's the only way I can figure it. For later on I found her last offering to me, her gift, folded in under my shirts and shoes. It was a package con-

taining Celia's dress and gun, Cessil's diaries and binoculars, Victor's Bible, a lot of family photos and an extra large cookie tin of beijinhos.

But I discovered those gifts later, when we unpacked. For now I only knew that while the 6 brothers threw our bags into the truck, Anita stood there on the front steps looking down at her arthritic hands. This was the only time I ever saw her unable to look at a situation straight on. This was the only time I ever saw her hands empty, holding nothing, not a spoon, not dough, not even an unlit cigar. She didn't look up once, not even as Uncle Raoul and Uncle Stanley helped us up into the truck. That tiny 79-year-old woman had shrunk so much over the last few years, she wasn't much taller by now than the back of a chair.

Uncle Stanley handed Babalou the key to the truck, closed the door and stepped away. Babalou and I sat there so baffled in our seats. I guess Babalou couldn't think of much else to do, so he started the car, shifted slowly into first, drove away down the driveway. I looked back. This was the last time I saw Anita. Her frame erased completely by the first medium-sized shrub along the way.

And I must say it's funny how it all worked out. I can appreciate that, really, the humor in it, the horror. That my work to become part of the family had succeeded so well that not one person remembered I was adopted. They all took the incest so dreadfully seriously.

And I haven't seen one of them since we drove off that morning in that rattling old truck.

Not one of them. Not once.

Well, my mother said, That's about it. You know the rest.

Her voice was tired, her consonants slurred even more than they had been over the last few days.

Immediately afterwards, the static on the line rose like a

roaring wave to smother all sound between us. I thought the line would go dead. I got to my feet in the center of the kitchen, staring across at the blank wall.

Then the static fell off until I could hear again even the subtle clicks in her harsh breath.

Yes, I said, Yes I do.

You will remember this? she asked. These stories? She was asking this with her voice all tight. Her voice wanting so.

Yes, I said honestly, not able to lie now, not able to push her. Yes, I said, I will.

I held the phone between my ear and shoulder and placed a palm on my flat belly. I listened to her breathing, to my mother's life, there within our silence. I listened to each breath as I had never listened to anything before.

Originally when she had told me about the cancer, I had thought, liver, what is a liver? How could something that small and hidden destroy my life?

Now I wondered, what wasn't a liver?

The whole world, my whole life, was there within the cycles of her breath, in those inhales and exhales; there and deeper, in the clenching of her heart and circulating blood; there and deeper, inside the slick skin of that blood-dark secret liver. The liver, I had learned from my reading, is what purifies the blood of toxins so it can continue to nourish the body. The Arabs, I had learned, used to consider the liver the seat of the soul, regarding it in the way we think of the heart. The liver is the organ inside our bodies that can best regenerate itself, no matter how many generations of mistakes we make. I rubbed my own gut.

Fran, Fran, said my mom, There were times when I missed you so much . . .

I held my breath waiting, thinking about all we could talk about, now that the stories were out of the way, now that we had broken the ice, were more comfortable with each other, could both really talk. I paused then, trying to pick out the first sentence of this new conversation. It seemed to me the first sentence had to be just right.

The change on the line was subtle. So slow and soft that I never knew exactly when it happened, comprehended it only in the past tense. Still I held on, disbelieving. Understanding in the grey empty space between our phones her hang-up as silent as the first slice of a scalpel.

Some things never change.

Mourne Family Tree

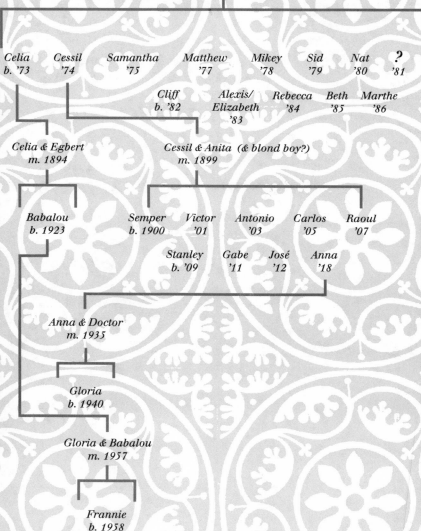

Great Great Grandmother & **?**
b. 1855 d. 1887

Celia   Cessil   Samantha   Matthew   Mikey   Sid   Nat   **?**
b. '73   '74   '75   '77   '78   '79   '80   '81

Cliff   Alexis/   Rebecca   Beth   Marthe
b. '82   Elizabeth   '84   '85   '86
                     '83

Celia & Egbert   Cessil & Anita   (& blond boy?)
m. 1894   m. 1899

Babalou   Semper   Victor   Antonio   Carlos   Raoul
b. 1923   b. 1900   '01   '03   '05   '07

Stanley   Gabe   José   Anna
b. '09   '11   '12   '18

Anna & Doctor
m. 1935

Gloria
b. 1940

Gloria & Babalou
m. 1957

Frannie
b. 1958

Chapter 24

I shot 200 bottles in the back pasture the first day after the end of her stories. My aim blew them up into the air, into glittering explosions, one after the other. Each one, abruptly, an ex.

I don't want to suggest that anything at this time made me feel good. That I was healing. No, I've got to admit even now, 20 years later, sometimes the memory of those phonecalls sweeps over me again in the early evenings, on spring nights. The sound of her voice, the smell of that farmhouse kitchen, the clutch of my chest. And every time, every time this happens, it is like the loss is happening again for the first time, right now.

No, I tell you, you don't get over things like that. You just get busy. You meet people. You become friends.

To each one of them you assign a tiny bit of your mom.

Let me tell you the end.

It is not half so exciting as my mother's stories, no year-long winters or vast sums of money, no muscle men or famous thieves, no canonization procedures. Instead it is much more of a

modern story, a story that could, perhaps, have been invented by
social services. The story of a family of illegal immigrants, a too-
young mother, a deadbeat dad. A latchkey kid. A medical abnor-
mality. The undeniable all-around need for Prozac.

I was born on the farm in Ontario. Because of course, my
mother and Babalou headed straight up to Canada, to the only
land she owned.

They drove up to the border without a pause, crossing late
the second night, rushing terrified and alone, right up to my
great great grandmother's farm. I'd like to make it clear that
they were both illegal in Canada, no permanent jobs, no long-
term residency visas. For the years that they were here, they
tried never to come to the attention of any official.

My parents had the vague plan of taking over the saint business from the small circus to whom Cessil's siblings had rented
their mother's shrine 4 decades before. My parents had no real
plan at all.

In the last 40 years not a penny of the circus's rent had ever
shown itself down in Fort Lauderdale, although no one had actually gotten around to complaining about it, for they were too
busy with all the ruckus and money that was already down
there. When Gloria and Babalou arrived, the old Canadian farmhouse was half-caved in with despair. The owner of the circus, its
sole human remnant, turned out to be a scrawny ancient man
who was bent over like a cripple as he hobbled down to the truck.
When my mother introduced herself, explaining the farm was
hers, he jerked up straight as a stick with surprise.

He disappeared that very first night, leaving behind a note
which suggested perhaps the rent checks had gone to the wrong
address. The note expressed his sorrow for this and explained he
was leaving behind as a consolation gift a menagerie of animals

consisting of 3 rare and valuable lizard cats, a hairless Chihuahua named Rita, and 14 male peacocks.

My mother cursed the man—not for the back rent, but instead about all the pets—and tried not feeding any of her new livestock in the hope that they would simply wander away. But she had not counted on the vocal powers of 14 fully-grown peacocks. Although their tails are what peacocks are famous for, their vocal powers are really just as impressive, somewhere between the yowl of a cat in heat and a belt sander on metal. At about 10 in the morning on the first day that the birds were not fed, they started shrieking. The 14 birds shrieked all that day and through the whole of the first and second nights, stretching their silky blue necks up toward the sky for the greatest possible volume, screaming out their hunger and their fury and their lust for a female, screaming into the quiet suburbia of tract houses and lawn ornaments which had grown up around the family farm during the last 40 years. The peacocks cried with the urgency of babies being throttled. Mom saw the neighbors peering across the road from their lawns. She thought the police might be called soon.

So she fed the peacocks. She fed all the new animals.

The scaly skin of the 3 lizard cats began to peel within the week as the glue wore off. The fur grew in slowly and in patches across their pale flesh, like a hazy spring in the desert. As the scales fell away, the cats jumped and played about like kittens, stretching their newly mobile bodies in the sun with a vibrant luxury.

Mom didn't even see Rita, the hairless Chihuahua, until a full 12 days after her arrival on the farm. It was a little after midnight in the unlit kitchen when Mom was drinking a glass of water at the sink. She saw Rita's tiny body, crouched down in a commando skulk, turning the corner heading for the cats' food bowl. Mom assumed Rita to be a rat and chased her, kicking out at her with her bedroom slippers. Just before Rita scampered away into her hiding place up the diningroom chimney, Mom realized her mistake from the length and delicacy of those thin dog legs clambering.

The very next morning Babalou set out to tame Rita. He settled himself down in the diningroom to quietly assemble a 5,000-piece puzzle of rolling waves out at sea. My mother told me he always liked puzzles, a game without competition or sudden movements. Perhaps I picked up my love of puzzles from him. As he spread out the pieces on the table, he sang softly to himself what words he could remember of *"La Cucaracha"* and *"La Bamba,"* for he thought that Rita would appreciate the language of her people. He made no loud noises, nor did he sit with the stealthy silence of a hunter. By the second morning, when he had assembled most of the outside frame of the puzzle, Rita had shown her long nose sniffing several times along the top corner of the fireplace. Within a week—by which point Babalou had filled in the bottom half of the puzzle—she had stuck her whole head down to blink at him like a bat, 2 big eyes and a face smeared with dust. And by the time he was clicking in the last piece of the puzzle, she was sitting within 5 feet of him, trembling with her eagerness to be able to brave the last few feet.

The circus owner must have hit her. It was the only way Mom could understand Rita's initial terror of humans. And, in a way, it is almost understandable. There is something about a hairless dog, all the bravado and bristle of the fur gone, the shrunken body displayed so vulnerable and soft, that diminished armature with its pouched-out belly; there is something about the almost powdery feel of that pigeon flesh under your fingers when you first touch it that makes you want to pull back and spank that bare skin like a baby's tender bum.

Babalou, though, never seemed to feel that urge, perhaps because he identified too strongly with Rita's fear of humans. Under his care Rita learned to follow him everywhere, big-eyed and tiny-toed, scuttering away only at the arrival of strangers.

Even the peacocks' discontent after a while seemed to lessen. They strutted and called only occasionally in a lackluster fashion about the farm and neighborhood, searching the Canadian suburbia for the females they were fated never to find. It soon became only during the spring that they would really call out their loneliness, perched on the top of the house, their long surreal shrills echoing like calls from the depths of a jungle hot and unseen.

None of this really interested my mother, Gloria, for she had no energy left to care for anything other than herself at this point. All her life people had been taken away from her, first her biological mother and father, then Anna and her adopted father, then Celia and Anita and her whole family of over 300, all the people she had worked so hard during her life to know and hold. Now she was left only with the helpless middle-aged adolescent Babalou (whom she loved beyond all meaning, but who she couldn't trust even to go to the store). She knew the only possible end to this story would be for her to die on the farm alone and without purpose, so she began to check her stools each morning with the complete certainty that somewhere in them was the news of her death. She was so lonely that she stopped stocking up on condoms and within a year I was born, her special guest invited solely to assuage her loneliness.

I was born into a farm grey with disuse, fields untilled for so long that they had turned into forests, bushes growing up even inside the barn. The ivy on the south side of the house was pulling the exterior wall gently apart, and the earth between the front door and the porch was caving in from a sinkhole created during some long-ago glacial millennium. Each day the hole sighed open into a slightly wider smile, ever-so-cautiously pulling the front of the house into a pit that exhaled the slow and watery breath of ice.

Inside the house the damage was just as widespread. The back staircase was quite unsafe. When it rained even the first floor was not without leaks, the insides of the house running with water like a woman crying. I was raised in a home with dust caked thick as mud into the corners of the closets and the bottoms of drawers.

It has always seemed to me that the main impact of time is to shrink everything until it can fit compactly into memory. My first toys were the tiny clothes and petite claw-footed furniture of ages gone by, pant legs the size of my sleeves and beds that my feet fell off the end of long before I reached the age of 15.

The disorder in the house was caused perhaps by Cessil's sisters and brothers leaving quite suddenly for Fort Lauderdale, in spite of their 9 months of warning. Or maybe they had thought moving out was a good excuse not to clean. Or maybe a fair amount of this might also have been the circus owner's contribution. Whatever the reason, there were dirty dishes still lying about, the withered half-eaten pie of an ancestor. Beds were left unmade. An open school math book had been placed facedown on a table decades before.

And then there was the barn. As I said, the body was still there. The circus owner had not cared for her, had not given her any new coats of wax. She had dried out, shrunken and gone piebald, losing definition in the face and hands, like a plastic figurine after handling and heat. She looked no more realistic as a dead body than a knotted shoelace left out in the rain. She was shrinking slowly into the size and shape of a baby. Perhaps in another hundred years she would become a fetus, then a zygote, then would simply disappear from existence. Her clothes had tattered so much I could not judge the original size of her. Still, the smell of lilacs in the area was unmistakable, and a streak of scent was left on anything that came near her. The bees had not given up. A few hives worked busily on, tirelessly filling the air with their patient hum.

I must admit I was not all that much of a help with my mother's loneliness, with her need for dependents. When I was born, my body was large already, unbabylike. When I moved, it was slow, contemplative and powerful. Taking after Babalou's infancy, my baby teeth appeared within 2 months. I was walking carefully, with measured breathing like an astronaut, before I was 9 months old.

For those first few years without her family, my mother strove to slow me down, to control me. She knew for the length of time I was a child I would be tied to her with a rope not even fury could break. She knew she was guaranteed company for as long as I was incapable of leaving. She did everything she could to keep me. Please remember she was a strong woman who had been broken by the repeated thievery of everything most important to her. All her strength had been turned to fear, a powerful fear. She waited for the next betrayal, yearned to lie down in front of it before it even arrived. Her hands were white and shook always with a fine vibration, like a needle graphing something unseen. She told me about all the scary things out there: poisons, bogey monsters, child nappers, embarrassing social situations, thieves and strangers. She gave me lessons in being young, slow and dependent. She gave me lessons in fear.

I was an apt student for her lessons. We both did what we could to play our assigned roles. I slouched around her, pitched my voice high and put my shoes on the wrong feet. As she wished, I also imitated her mother as much as I was able. And it was true, I did feel fear and uncertainty. I did pick that up from her. She happily scolded me about my childishness, her voice occasionally slipping out of an old crone's voice into the voice of what she was, a young and exhausted woman. Each time this happened, her eyes flickered slightly for a moment, then she cleared her throat and spoke again as an old woman, her eyes narrowing into her delusion. I looked at her. I wanted to touch her, but she would not let anyone fool her again that way, not with touching, not with closeness, familial or otherwise. She twisted away from me, arms all akimbo.

During this time Babalou and my mother drifted apart. She was too busy paying attention to her terror and to me, too busy palpating her breasts with clammy hands, examining her tongue in the mirror, yelling at me if I tried to make my own bed or dress myself. She slept, white and bumpy with tension, her hands clenched together for something to cling on to. Her hair darkening and sticking up with a child's sweet sweat, she was dreaming of her need to not be alone, to be connected. She no longer woke as easily for Babalou's nightmares; she had her own nightmares to wake her. She no longer held his hand as much, tugging the 2 fingers back and forth as she told him what she thought. She no longer allowed him to drive her over to the nearest lake at night, to swim into the center and make love like slow seals.

And he, in this homeland of his mother's frozen childhood, began to regress to ages younger than 18. He played with the tiny dolls and toy carriages of old. He played war games with the peacocks, strutting around them, holding his shirttail up as tail feathers until the birds roared and charged, Rita yipping nearby.

Sometimes I joined him in his peacock war. We would take

shelter behind the old horse trough, lobbing pine cone grenades over at the furious pecking on the other side. His laugh was short and wheezy. He had gained some weight, not like a middle-aged man's spread located all in the belly, but instead like a child's fat distributed equally all over. He did not recognize me anymore as his daughter, although he sometimes knew my name. His face got puffy and white as a baby's and his eyes wandered constantly, scared to look at a person straight on. He had a hard time controlling the finer motions of his hands and took to wearing a bib during meals. He called Gloria "Mom" in mimicry of me.

Sometimes Mom would let me feed him his lunch. He liked applesauce and I would roll it into his mouth one spoonful at a time. As my mother's fear and loneliness increased year by year, Babalou's eyes got worse. They wandered so far from what they did not wish to see that he sometimes walked into walls. He killed 2 of the peacocks by tripping over them. He no longer talked much. He held onto my hand all the time, rubbing and squeezing it, rolling my fingers between his own. His nose or cheek usually had a cut upon it, which made him look as if he still might be at war.

As worriedly as he worked at my hand, Gloria busily strove and ordered, roaring at both of us. And Babalou continued to get younger.

He walked out of the front door one spring morning when I was 7. I would say that, mentally, he was only a little bit older than me. My mother said it was a Tuesday. I was taking a nap on the couch. He walked right by me. I do not remember that day. I do not remember the time. My mother said I must remember. She was out getting the groceries. We had run out of milk. She was not there. She did not see. She told me he had to have walked right by me. Hoping to jog my memory, she told me the only pants missing were his beige Levi cords, and that the shirt he was wearing showed a picture of a Good Humor ice cream bar. She leaned forward, her face small and very tight. She told me to think. What was his expression? She told me to describe it to her. Don't I remember? Did he mean to do it? Did he know what he was doing? Did he look scared?

I am not like my mother. I do not remember all sorts of things. I do not remember my first bite of solid food, my first day of school, the smells of almost anything. In comparison to her, I feel like I have slept through my life. I cannot remember my father leaving because I was literally asleep on the couch. He walked right by me in what was undoubtedly those brown cords and that ice-cream-bar T-shirt, wandered out onto the driveway all alone, looking like a tall 10-year-old with some baby fat. His expression, whatever it was, was all his own, for I did not open my eyes, Rita snoring beside me.

He was going to get a carton of milk. He left a note. My mom saved it. It says, "*Mom, lhere is no milk.*" He forgot to cross the *t*. He did not return. He did not write us any postcards from wherever he went. I'm not sure he would have known the address of our home.

My mother was shaken from her self-absorption. Too late, she remembered their love. Too late, she remembered what family she still had. She visited morgues, hospitals, and mental wards for 7 years. She phoned the airlines, the bus stations, schools, the army, police, soup kitchens, his fighting-twin mothers. She put up xeroxed black-and-white pictures all across the province for 7 years. His picture next to children's pictures. His picture, as the others did, gradually fading and fuzzing from the frequent xeroxing until his was only the hazy grey outline of an unrecognizable head with the simple words penned in beneath,

"MISSING—APRIL 7TH, 1965" and some contact information. A declaration of loss, more than a hope of return.

My mother never forgave me for not remembering my father's departure. For leaving this hole in her story. After he left, her shoulders took on almost the same sort of slouch his used to have, her feet sometimes shuffled.

Within a year of Babalou leaving, the fights between her and me began to start, then to escalate. More than ever she needed me to somehow prove that I would never leave her, to promise with the very size of my body that I would always stay a child.

Of course that was impossible. With every year that passed I grew taller, bigger. Sometimes in the midst of all her yelling— in the midst of my standing there so cold and silenced, so stooped and furious—sometimes then, louder even than her words, I heard her fear, her terror, ringing its alarm clear as a bell over and over in the dark. I wanted to duck down and cover my ears.

7 years after Babalou left, she left also. She left one night while, again, I slept.

I believe my mother's leaving to have been a preemptive strike against me leaving her. That is what I believe. I believe she just couldn't stand the suspense.

When the 14-year-old me came downstairs that morning, the silence in the house was heavy as a rock. Before I even saw the note I knew. I had known all along.

Chapter 25

Thinking about it afterwards, I believe as my mom got closer to the operation, she lost concentration, was less involved in the stories she so loved. She sounded increasingly distant, as though she were thinking of something else, or listening to another person. She even breathed differently, like someone not so familiar anymore with the habit of breath. Although I know the last word I spoke to her, although I know the last word she said to me, I do not know which of my words was the last she really heard, what was the last dialogue we really had. She might have been physically there until the last conversation, on the other end of the line, but that is all I can verify.

The night after her operation she didn't call.

I told myself again and again that this was not necessarily a bad sign. I told myself she must be groggy still, perhaps nauseous from the anesthesia. Unable yet to hold a phone. Unable to speak clearly. She was a beautiful woman, proud, always hated to be at less than her best.

. . .

The night after that I woke up suddenly at 4:22 A.M. I was sleeping on the kitchen table, right beside the phone. I slept with the pillow and the blanket, my pizza puzzle all finished and laid out on the table beside my head.

Actually I did not wake. I just found myself awake, wide awake, my eyes open, looking at the kitchen clock while I listened to myself not breathe; listened to my heart not beat. It wasn't like I was choosing not to breathe; instead it was like when you fall hard onto your back from some height. You have no breath in you afterward, no heartbeat. You lie there for a moment and then, when that isn't doing anything to get you living again, you stand up and run around, wave your arms about in a desperate bid for breath, panicked because not only are you not breathing, not only is your heart not beating, but you also cannot remember how to breathe, when breath starts and where. You flap your mouth around like a fish, knowing something is terribly wrong.

I woke like that. I woke into that, only without the fall and without any fear at all.

The stillness was something I had never really heard before, never really listened to, the world without me breathing and without my heart thumping and without the blood rustling and scraping ever so noisily through my veins.

Instead I heard the world perfectly. Without all the background static of life. I turned my head slightly to look about at the night. I could hear the cats wheezing on the sideboard beside me and it seemed like such a labor. The ceiling was a vision above me, a luminescent stretch of purity I had never seen so clearly before. I stared up at it for what seemed like the longest time. Like a tourist poster, it seemed a distant and lovely place I'd like to visit someday.

I don't remember how this ended. I can just picture this sin-

gle extended moment regarding the ceiling. A moment as warm
and close as though I were cradled tight in another's arms.

It is possible I slid back into sleep before my body remembered how to breathe.

I have never received another call from my mom, not to this day.
I don't know where she is buried, or if she is buried. It would be
just like her to recover and lose interest in talking to me. Her
need gone. It would be just like her to have made the cancer up,
as motivation for me to learn the stories. I don't really believe
either of these thoughts, but they are possible. I try to believe
them. I look at the world map differently this way, the names of
the cities, the outlines of islands. I imagine any of them could be
my mother's new home. Any one of them might contain other
children of hers, relatives.

For the 2 days after that last phonecall, I spent every moment
within 25 feet of the phone. I didn't go into work, but called in
sick. I could hear in my boss's voice the lack of surprise. He had
always assumed me to be unreliable. The second day I called in
sick, he told me we should have a talk whenever I felt well
enough to come in. I could hear what the talk would be about.

On the fourth morning, 2 men drove to my home. I heard
their car from a long way away, driving up my street. It was mid-
morning. Not a lot of traffic around here during that hour, certainly not coming in from the main highway.

When I heard the car slow down to turn into my driveway, I
ducked behind the barn. I climbed to the attic and lay down by
the window, my great great grandmother's body curled up
beside me in the sweet dust of the hay, the bees working their
drowsy hum.

The car pulled to a halt in front of the house. It was blue

and dusty with dirt. The peacocks started their warning calls, arching their necks, shivering out their tails. The 2 men got out of the car in a way that said they were important and just moving slowly for now. Even from the barn I could hear the birds vibrate their display, their tails completely erect and spread, the feathers rustling audibly as the metallic blue shimmered in the sun. The men ignored the peacocks as though the peacocks were just plastic lawn ornaments, as if live peacocks could be seen on every other lawn in Ontario. The men wore sunglasses and carried many papers, clipboards and surveying equipment. Their faces were pale and their hair short. They kept the corners of their mouths down as they strode around the house and barn, taking measurements, gesturing at the land and shaking their heads.

There was some kind of official sign on the side of the car, but I was too far away to read it. They stayed for almost half an hour. When they finally drove away, the man in the passenger seat unrolled the window to stick his head out and look back at the house and the land. It was unmistakably the look of possession. I thought, Yes, my mother always was true to her word. She never did learn how to bluff, not even about giving away my home.

That afternoon I sliced open every bag of feed I had in the barn for the cats and peacocks. In the early morning of the next day, I opened all the doors and windows of the house. I spread the remaining oatmeal out on the back porch for the peacocks, added some Cheerios for good luck. I knew the neighbors would adopt them all. They had always loved the cats, vied for who could pat the peacocks. They would not be surprised at my action. They had long ago formed their opinion of me. They would figure that running away from home was a family trait.

Before I left, I cleaned every dish in the house, including those of my ancestors. I left nothing for those men to look at, to puzzle over. They would not understand its value. They would not get the meaning. I shook the dust off the welcome mat and lined it up carefully with the door.

And this next step, what can I say about it? I had made my choice days ago now, when I told my mother that I couldn't promise to stay on the farm always. Really, I had made my choice perhaps a week before that, maybe longer.

Perhaps my choice had been made before I was even born, it was in my very genes. It had just taken a while for me to recognize it.

So I left while the morning fog was still low on the ground. I left in the truck that my mother and Babalou had arrived in. I had taken good care of it, driven it into town for work each day, kept it oiled and gassed, garaged it in the barn. I had never thought of it as the vehicle of my escape. Before this, I had just thought of it as my mother's, something to protect.

Halfway down the hill of the driveway, the engine caught. Celia's gun was heavy and fierce in my jacket pocket, Cessil's binoculars lay beside me, and my great great grandmother was curled up on the passenger seat like a child.

At the bottom of the driveway I took the turn toward Route 16, heading south.